Josephine Plummer

August Island Rike

Paper Company

ISBN: 978-1-970083-14-9

To all the people who make our cities spin, large and small. The ones who work every shift and cover each base to ensure we are safe and taken care of whenever there is a need. To the ones starting out running around meeting deadlines, the ones retiring and everyone in between.

Then I realized something.

I was keeping

my old wounds fresh

and open, as evidence

for a trial

that would never come.

Mark Nepo

Chapter 1

September 2024
August

  The unforeseen turn of direction from Florida to Seattle is shocking. Learning the man, I knew as dad has passed. Others knew him as Garrett, Garrett Rike. Over two thousand miles is an endless journey to be with your thoughts when you know you will be faced with facts and planning you do not want to acknowledge but must attend to. Mom says it is all taken care of, but I am positive she will ask my input since I am an only child, even just to make me feel included. Now is when the guilt sets in of not visiting enough, leaving town directly after high school graduation, and leaving my parents alone to entertain themselves while working during portions of their vacations. They were always supportive of my activities and number one fans, acting as if it didn't bother them, but I could see it on their face when I would be gone a portion of the day for an emergency inspection. I could have passed the assignment off to another team member and now know I should have.

I arrived around 4:00 am, three days after the news. No one knew I was not at my comfortable house or even residing in Wisconsin when the call came through. My troubles are minute - old news to me anyway. The current issue, the top of the list, and worst possible reason to be here, one I had never imagined. The funeral is at noon today. I am barely used to being still after all the miles behind me, my body still in motion. I picture us at the funeral in the front row, who will be there, me, mom, other vacant seats? Mom wakes early, stands in the doorway between the kitchen and living room, I had let myself in and plopped into the recliner just an hour or so ago. I groggily see that time has not been something I have tracked in the past few days only miles. It is dark outside, with only minimal light. I see mom still has the same fuzzy white bathrobe, but she is different; her hair possibly, has she aged or lost weight? I feel I should have kept closer track of her, of dad, except I am too late on that. It has been a couple years since I have seen them in person. Now I regret not making more time to visit, why were my trips so far between each other. I hadn't even invited them to make the trip to me lately. I had been set in my schedule, day upon day went by and here I am now sleeping in the olive-green recliner that is older than me in my childhood home minus a parent. Not mom and dad but just mom. A regret arises from my knees inching its way to my head. Knowing I need to get up and talk, sit or just be silent with mom, my words are frozen I soon discover. I am not even capable of any coherent sentences; we look at each other knowing we need to sit at the kitchen table to change something even if it is just the location of our physical bodies.

Getting ready, looking at my breakfast, knowing where everything is located in my childhood home is comforting and full of despair simultaneously. I can feel dad's presence as much as I feel his absence. I picture him at the table drinking coffee laughing at the funnies in the paper, as he called them, occasionally reading one aloud. I offer to drive to the cemetery where the funeral will be held, this is still not current news to me, or mom it appears. We are in denial of our duties and walking through the actions as if out of body. She silently gets into my littered SUV and turns to ask why I didn't fly to be here sooner. She looks towards the back noticing it is full. I simply tell her that I was in Kentucky. Her mind is full at this moment, and asks no more, they had been married forty-two years with me coming into the picture unexpectedly about halfway through their marriage. I am sure by her expression of steel, concrete, or something else solid she is just holding it together for this service.

We ride through the ornate gates of City Square Cemetery; the grounds appear beautifully manicured, there does seem to be more people present than expected. The day is mild and sunny, perfect for the outdoor activity after the service. The rock sided building, giving a look of peacefulness with a fountain flowing off to the side, chosen for this somber occasion.

I help mom in the door, we are ushered to sit in front. The casket, one someone picked out, is in place already. We are forced to sit and stare at it, the unfaced crowd filing in behind. Me wondering when mom and dad came in to make arrangements for the funeral, so many steps to the process of living to dying.

My mind returns to all the years with dad. In reality, me being only eighteen before I left Seattle for college, just over half a lifetime for me. I cannot think about this with all the people milling about, I dare not turn around. I don't want to know who has come to this service for my father. I am positive from what I know of him that he has touched many lives. I wonder if the people here know me. No one has greeted us, for that I am thankful. We manage to get through the service. I am not sure what the preacher said. Others spoke and gave my father high praise, I had not prepared a speech nor seemed required – I kept my head down, staring at our names on the program. Dad at the top, Garrett Samuel Rike. Mom and I on the next two lines, Laura Rike with the title wife and me in succession August Rike, followed by son. Mom and I sat stoic as everyone filed out, me realizing this part was over. Now to move on as required to the next area. Mom wishes to walk and takes my arm after seeing the influx of cars in the parking lot and surrounding areas I do not think we could leave here if we wished to, walking was our only option. It wasn't far but felt like an eternity to the cover of the green velvet chairs and canopy on wheels. How many other tears had been shed under this rented canopy? There were more people at the graveside than I could imagine here, some facing the way of my dad's casket which had been delivered so casually we didn't see with our view blocked until arrival. The other crowd was larger than the one facing our area, there were at least two thousand people. I was confused that two funerals would be held at the same time with people back-to-back, the irreverence of this was the first feeling I had experienced in quite some time. Someone from the cemetery came to apologize, the other funeral was scheduled to be over an hour ago, but no one was leaving. They were all just standing without an expression, the service was over, they were not willing to leave. It was a sudden death of some sort of an official. I had noticed the overwhelming presence of police, people in all colors of uniforms, a distraction for sure but not why we were here today. We get through this part of the service facing the casket, mom and I do not leave until dad is in the ground. A couple people I did not know stopped to pay their respects to us. Mom and dad had a well woven marriage but ran in different circles so most of the attendees did not personally know mom or me. I feel it is still wrong to go, everyone else from both services has left for the designated restaurant or wherever you go after a funeral. I do not know where that is for dad, nor do I wish to attend but if mom is going, I will take her, food being the last thing on my mind. She simply says yes when I ask. She hands me the paper she had placed in her coat pocket as a reminder of the steps required for today in case she couldn't speak, being frozen with grief. On the way in we kindly accept all the words from the people I do not know filing them as if for a later date, I don't ask mom if she knows them. We sit with some iced water, the cold-water providing sensation from my numbness of spirit, unable to eat. My next feeling was one of relief from our departure back to the parking lot. On the way home mom asks if I would like to order a pizza, get a burger or something else. She is hungry and glad to be away from all the well-meaning people that she hardly knew, people she had briefly been introduced to at company events but not friends of hers. Dad was well liked as the owner of the paper company, but mom is a librarian and keeps her circle of friends apart from these.

We opt for a burger and eat at a table outside, it being a nice day, possibly one of the only ones we will have until June. I can't stop myself from looking at my phone to see whose funeral that was today, who had taken over the grounds of the cemetery. At the top headline I see it is Officer Dufort, part of the traffic / ticketing division. The article says he was highly liked by the community in spite of his occupation that he had held with the department for a dozen years. One quote was "He was the fairest man around." It goes on to say he passed away suddenly while on duty in the middle of writing a ticket, the person volunteered to pay the ticket even though it wasn't issued saying, "I was at fault."

August Island Rike Paper Company

Chapter 2

October 2024
August

    Being at the helm of a vessel transporting ore across Lake Michigan, wearing my usual attire of the well-worn brown leather coat and midwestern-style boots has always been my go to escape to envision piloting the ships as they pass through. I have only seen one ship captain in person while visiting Duluth and this is what he had worn. I envisioned him being from there, having local roots and memories. Until my move from Seattle in 2008 I had not seen many people wearing white soled boots. The majority of my time has been spent on the waterfront building sites since becoming employed in Milwaukee as an apprentice at Green Mechanical Engineering right out of college. These buildings were aggressively becoming more popular and elite as the population grew. Of course, that is many miles behind me, my past life as I call it now, I may be in denial of my location and situation. Alice, my beautiful, and what I thought was my ever-steady, wife announced she wished to move to the waterfront into one of the towers I designed. Elevated living is her current desire she announced one day; we have sold our home by sort of mutual consent. The one we loved on North Hawley Road, the house we adored and vowed never to sell with the radiator heat forever ticking away in the bitter winters. The wind gusting right off the lake, and the first days of autumn as the great maple tree outside the kitchen window slowly turns its leaves in an extravagant array of color for a show before shedding that beauty for our bitter cold winters, snow swirling as we watch outside. The thought of remodeling we agreed was not needed, the refrigerator was only a single wide and in an inconvenient location, but we loved the pantry with the beautiful, scrolled woodwork and the tulip stained-glass windows in our library where we spent the majority of our time often reading aloud to each other both holding onto the same novel to follow along. Now Alice is Alli, she has transferred half of our assets to her own financial institution and dropped our shared last name of Rike. Alli Baxter is no longer my wife, and I no longer reside in Milwaukee; I am not piloting a ship but sitting at the top corner office of a building in Seattle on 6th Avenue South that could resemble a ship. Being a mechanical engineer by trade and investigating this building's structural integrity I am not reasonably sure why it has stood erect this long. As the winds whip across the industrial streets off of the Puget Sound the rusted tin siding rattles, rattles to the bone especially out in the warehouse where coats or fans are needed depending on the season. Don't get me wrong I belong here, this is where I grew up, graduated, and took a twenty-year vacation from but my roots are here, now to get the rest of myself to line up with my current reality.

Somehow, I knew deep in my being this would be my place of employment, not just where I work but my business. I grew up in this company being employed during vacations from school with my grandpa Otto as did my dad and every other person listed on our family tree. By the time dad took over I was nearly 2000 miles to the east and focused on my studies. I am focusing on my future journey rather than reflecting on the one established over a century and a half ago by a man I have never met.

There is one difference though I may not be a junior as I am five generations separated from the start of this business and my four times great grandfather August Island Rike but that is my name too. There have only been two of us deemed to carry the same name, the rest who have graciously passed this trade of paper on were named from other generations.

I shall carry August Island Rike Paper Company with the same utmost respect and reverence as from the beginning in 1870. Seattle was just starting to be known as a bustling town with the shipping, fishing and ship building industries. Rumor through our family has it that my great, great, great, great Grandpa started this business after being fired from his position at the lumber mill for partaking a bit much from the local distillery one too many times. He was an intelligent man just preferring his drink and freedom more than showing up when he was required to. The town was not large enough to outrun his reputation so as he was in the saloon he started thinking about the woes of his bosses while in his various positions. He purchased some board clips as they were referred to back then, found an old straight piece of metal, ink, a glass pen and patented an accounting system for each industry he knew about and calling this service August Island Rike Paper Company. The company grew from its accounts needing envelopes and other office supplies.

I am probably the first person to own this company who has located the original records sealed in a decades old metal container with rusted wheels resembling a steamer trunk in the attic on the second floor adjoining my office. After dragging it to the opening, I knew it was too large to pass through the current door and pictured Augusts' office was most likely on the upper level in the back corner. He possibly only rented that room and later expanded to the entire building. The first thing I notice are the accounts, a few of them are still the same clients who we currently supply to but then there are files labeled with the months of the year in Augusts' precise penmanship that is eerily so similar to mine I cannot tell the difference between them. Is penmanship passed down in genetic codes? I take some time to research this on my phone as the current model of this company appears to run itself. I have walked the floor in each department, jotted down names and job titles but then retreated to my corner loft that overlooks a minute slice of Seattle where I feel the rumble of trains as they enter and exit the city, but can't quite see them unless I stand up tall, peering between the building across the way, imagining some are carrying passengers. I have heard on one occasion the roar of the stadium as the Seahawks played, smell the mix of it all, food, exhaust, the Puget Sound and just city life. The city I grew up in but not one of my current memories. I mentally come back to my office from this perpetual autopilot mode and see the day is almost over, I close the door, lock up my rustic office. After cutting through the city, I head north taking Elliot Avenue W. over the Ballard Bridge in my Volkswagen Atlas to the one-bedroom apartment I rented to be close to mom since Dad's passing. Mom seems as if she has a life and doesn't need me around, but this is where I will be for the one-year commitment of my lease in a basic box of walls. Thinking back, I already know there is more to the crate of files I found today and will return tomorrow to investigate. It feels as if no matter what location I am physically in my mind is in another, bringing them together will be my goal.

The weather in Seattle is mild compared to what I have endured the past two decades. I am grateful for the roads clear of snow, just traffic at a standstill everyone with no mind on the next person as if they are the only car on the road. This city appears to run at a faster pace than Milwaukee. I was never on a strict schedule there either, working in the field and clients waited for me to arrive. Mostly my occupation required I stop in during the day to update the plans or see what stage the building was in. Truthfully, I was growing weary with my job. It paid well, I had freedom, but it was the same thing over and over and now that Alice has moved to one of the buildings where I would consistently pass, I do not feel I could stay feeling her presence there but not having anything to do with my life as it had been for nearly two decades. Now I am an 8:00am to 4:00pm person on the other side of the country. I only gave a confidential notice at work and didn't tell anyone of the divorce, one day I was just gone. What would I even do in this business during all those hours, what is my job description? I pull in greet a couple men who are out smoking in the rear parking lot with no recollection of their name no matter how hard I try to place them even in any department. Later after lunch I will go to the floor and help, I do know how the business runs, at least I did twenty years ago.

The January through December files are each quite thick as if they had been added to consistently. Noticing the writing on each tab is not the same as the first files I found so I am not the only person to have located these. I start with January; there are eight people in this file all with different positions in the company. These files must have been known to everyone who has run this company over the years and not just Augusts' knowledge. I see additions to the February file and recognize the handwriting as my dad's. Why didn't I know about this odd filing system prior to this? These must be the inner workings of the company, how it was run from the beginning. I know I should keep the door secure on the attic access and purchase a new lock in case someone else has a key. These files mean something and that will be my new occupation to figure this out. I own this company and can make my position do anything I want. Ever since I drove away from Milwaukee, I have felt lost, wandering, without a sense of purpose. Before I always had a plan for each day handed to me. I didn't have to work anymore, so I left the firm. No one was more surprised at that decision than I. I didn't have a plan, I thought maybe I would just drive or settle somewhere else. Milwaukee had been home but now Alice was gone, my house, work history and I felt uprooted in my own city living temporarily at an upscale extended stay hotel. As I departed all I could see was the life I had built and was now left behind. But what exactly was I abandoning? A couple slow days into the trip I thought was to Florida or somewhere along the way mom called with news of dad's sudden passing. She needed me, and the paper company needed a leader. She was talking about me needing to make decisions about the paper company, saying I was established in Milwaukee and wondering how this would work as there were stipulations not to sell the business. I knew the moment she called and delivered the news I would go there and stay, run the paper company with my name on it but I couldn't tell her then and let her ramble on since I was not prepared to speak of my misfortunes that apparently happened just when they were needed to. I didn't need to pile on my news as it would be new and overwhelming to her. I headed west on I-74 inching my way north by GPS direction to I-90 and eventually Washington, crossing into the thick trees and surroundings bringing memories of family vacations. The familiar aroma of the Pacific Northwest brings me back where I belong. Thinking only of the emptiness of my life and now dad was not part of it either, at least he or mom didn't know of my recent life upheaval, he didn't pass with that on his mind. It was extremely new to me or so it seemed, stuck in my throat, and not processed yet. Another calamity to process through and jump the hurdle back to normalcy, if that is possible with all of my life changes. I hate this feeling of the loss of control of my mind, how it keeps wandering to what if or how come. I am on track and not unstable, it is just my focus that is off. I keep starting a task and get sidetracked with memories or whatever it is. Usually, I am focused on every detail in real time not letting a minute be wasted everything was on schedule. I return to Seattle, mentally, after my imagined trip back on the road and the February file still sits in my lap open. I hear people milling about and see it is lunch time. Shaking my head at behavior that is unlike anything I have experienced before; I open the mini fridge and pull out the roast beef sandwich I packed with the applesauce mom had sent home with me, grab the bag of Doritos from the coat closet, laying this out on my desk as if in grade school now I am not hungry. Only now it feels more of a survival measure. Eating is mechanical these days and only done because it is part of whom I have always been. I don't feel hungry, have a desire to eat or actually taste food anymore. The sandwich is dry without mayonnaise, ketchup or anything else on it, only meat cheese and bread. I should do a real grocery shop not just a minimal one, four items in the cart are not acceptable for an adult for a week. I locked the files away, not knowing anything else except there was what looked like a recipe in one subfile. Chocolate Angel Food Cake. Did a lady give it to dad or was it from one of my grandfathers?

I had a more productive afternoon; I am positive the staff was uncomfortable with me just showing up in their already made system and helping out. Maybe it was a hinderance, I wasn't any help to Clem in the print setting department, my thoughts were there are a lot of products in this confined space. It was entirely too noisy in the actual print room to have any conversation or gain knowledge with Lloyd who has been here since 1968. He was finishing up a rush order for one of our long-term customers, him knowing precisely what to do, what colors and font styles are needed. Who are the suppliers? Can we get our supplies consolidated? Office Management would know the answer to that question.

I spent most of the rest of the afternoon in the warehouse and shipping department where I see one of the men from the parking lot, Hector, who picks orders and Patrick, who oversees all outgoing orders. Today is the tenth of October 2024, I want to know each person here a bit more and listen to what works for them and what doesn't. Do they have requests, rituals, company parties, after hours hang outs? I would not feel comfortable crashing any after-hours activities. It appears everyone gets along. We are a small company compared to most only twenty-six of us including me. I will make sure everyone is cross trained, and, in the process, I will learn from their experience too. After three hours of being on the floor I finally feel like I belong here. These boots will not work out on the concrete all day, maybe I should have left them in Milwaukee too. I plan to stop at the North Face store downtown in the near future. I live in Seattle and need the disconnect from Wisconsin, if only I could lose the crazy accent. Today I feel much better about my choices even though some were harder to make than others. I could have sold the house and moved to the new condo on Lake Michigan with Alice Rike and / or Alli Baxter, but had we outgrown each other? I sure didn't see that happening. There wasn't a falling out or a line of before and after just one day she was there and here I am.

Wednesday at lunch I head north on 6th Avenue to Pike and locate paid parking a couple blocks away, find some lunch at Pike Place Chowder and the location of my new shoes. My first reaction upon entering the store, I am taken back by the styles, colors, shoes, and boots sold by the sport or activity they will be intended for. I picked up a pair of waterproof midrise boots and a pair of tennis shoes made for walking on hard surfaces. I throw in a rain jacket, lighter weight pullover than the one I brought with me and a zip up multi-layer jacket. I have spent equivalent to about a month's rent but feel better about residing here now, thinking I don't even own a hanger. I didn't return to my office today but headed to a bookstore close to home, The Secret Garden Book Shop, make a few purchases to start my library, go to Trader Joe's and fill my cart with basics and food I love to cook and return home with a carload being thankful today for my assigned parking spot and the community flatbed cart supplied by maintenance. I even feel a smile coming on. The first happy moment I can recall since I arrived.

Nothing better than being at home relaxing with a new book, plenty of food and a view when I am distracted by the thought of the recipe, I am sure I saw. I had forgotten about it with my mission to gain a somewhat normal life. Tomorrow I will know the answers and tonight I have my new book. Cheese, crackers, grapes and a new PNW brewed beer are dinner.

I arrive early to work or whatever they call this place. It's not a factory, possibly a warehouse / work sounds better. Taking the stairs two at a time, not bothering with the creaky freight elevator, I enter my office. I start

to lift the blinds on all windows and then realize I have
not closed them. Who else has a key? There isn't
anything of importance here except the crate in the
attic that may not be of importance in the future but is
to me now, maybe it is the janitorial staff. I investigated
the quick notes I took during my initial tour and see it is
Sven, the custodian who has been with the company
sixteen years, the only person in that position listed. His
shift must be later than everyone else so he can bring
this place back to order after each day's work. He must
miss my dad. If he stayed here for sixteen years, he has
probably been satisfied with his employment continuing
it here that long. I will make a point to meet with him
and see what his schedule is and mention my dad to see
his reaction. I feel Sven deserves a raise, possibly
everyone does. Another task is to locate the profit and
loss statements for the last couple of years. I do know
what it takes to run this company, I just have to think
like a CEO and not a mechanical engineer where other
people set my appointments, and I showed up. I am
sure dad had systems in place to make everything run
smoothly. Starting with Office Management I meet with
Patricia and Allison who share the job with varied days
off and both being here on either Thursday or Friday
each week. One has a child to tend too and the other a
relative she helps with the care of, so it is beneficial for
both of them. They state this has been the norm for
them for over 20 years. I learn how kind and flexible my
dad was to this group of employees, like he was at
home always letting the person be the best they could

be, so far each has had respect for him almost like he was a friend. I realize with his passing everyone here probably wonders what will happen to their position, paycheck, and lives as they have known them. I ask Patricia and Allison to schedule a meeting with lunch provided tomorrow if possible, realizing I need to put everyone at ease. Looking at my actions in my first week I see it may not look good from the other side if the boss stops in, closes his door, walks around taking notes and then doesn't show back up after lunch. Could he be meeting with someone for a sale of the company? Who will be in charge if he doesn't sell? It certainly doesn't appear he will be keeping it or be involved. I have even seen some mail on my desk about offers to purchase my company. That is not happening, I am maintaining ownership as the will directed, after all my name is on the sign out front.

As I enter the old cafeteria style lunchroom, I see everyone is present at this meeting looking a bit on edge, even Patricia with her little girl possibly a grand child who is eyeing the sandwiches, doing what a child should do at lunchtime. I ask if she would like to explore the options of lunch, she shyly shakes her head looking back and forth from the food to her mom/grandmother not keeping me as part of the equation. I have Patricia get her and her child's lunch before anyone else. Isn't that what happens at family dinners the children eat first? I see them go off to the food, look at the rest of the people in the room seeing a bit of the tension roll off but they are still leery of me and their future only being used to my dad's way of operating. My one natural gesture does not mean anything at the moment with so much uncertainty hanging over the room.

I decide to start the meeting with a brief discussion about my intentions, tell them I plan to stay and keep each one of them in place if they wish to continue on with me, my need to look at the books and meet with the accountant, ask each person to fill out the form I created for needs, wants, what works and what is not working and promise to address each issue in the order I draw the forms out the basket. Also state if there are any urgent matters at any time, please see me, my door is always open. Then we have lunch like a family that all know each other. I see the connections, the joking, the cohesiveness of this group of employees, me being the newest and unknown but being accepted into the clan either by need or want but I am here to help and understand how their system works. It has worked for 153 years so far; we will see how we can as a team continue and adjust with time and technology. At the end of lunch, I asked if there were any pressing orders that had to go out today. Everyone in unison said the orders had been picked up by the shipper and I gave them all the rest of Friday off, even Sven who had just arrived for his shift to the pleasant surprise of lunch. Another thing to figure out on my list, if shipping comes before noon who is in charge of getting an express order out later in the day?

Monday again, the weekend was spent charting my tasks as head of this company using my bullet points as a guideline. Somewhere there should be job descriptions, emailing Dustin in Human Resources with my list of questions will give answers. He promptly emails back the files by department, the first I see is Dads, Garrett Samuel Rike, CEO, September with my name next to it more than likely added recently if not today and October following my name. Each file has a department name, but the individual files have job title, name, and a month. Is that the month of hire? I go back and get the February file from the attic box and see these hard copies match the digital ones. The month listed on every file is the birth month of an employee. Feeling the need to go through the box in the attic and not just one file at a time, I pull an entire month's file out, line them all up on the floor. In the back is a rustic looking tablet bound together by twine possibly over 100 years old. This tablet has not been opened for many years, on the first page it has instructions on how to run the company and a simple request that will violate every hiring practice and discrimination law in the state of Washington, city of Seattle and county of King, United States of America. In order to run this company, I have to hire a person according to their birth month. There are twenty-six positions remaining unless it grows by twenty five percent or more. If someone passes, quits or resigns, a new person will need to be hired born in the same month as the previous person except the CEO. I see this has been revised up to 26 individuals since it started with one and more were hired through the years. Dad must have been the latest to make entry to this tablet with loose leaf sheets of lined paper. There was one more stipulation on the first Friday of each month there will be a birthday party with cake for the two individuals celebrating a birthday that month. I create a current spreadsheet of the dates of birthdays on my laptop. This is not what I had signed up for to break laws and interview until I find the qualified applicant born in the right month. Fortunately, all positions have been filled, and I do not need to think about that now or in the near future, I hope.

 I emailed Patricia and Allison to find out the system for ordering the cakes. Who is in charge of this and what are the particulars? Who picks them up? Who decides what flavor to order? How are they paid for? Suddenly this small task feels overwhelming, a task that doesn't have anything to do with running the company or so I think, and I wish I was back in Milwaukee looking at blueprints and imagining the height of a new building, not how to get a cake, how many, what kind and from where? This shouldn't be what breaks me down or trips me up, but it does. These small things are what bring my mind backwards instead of staying on task. Now I am reminiscing about all the cakes in Milwaukee. Alice or someone at work always oversaw the party details, now once every month it is on me. Do the people here know they were hired for their birth date? I will never mention that part of the hiring process to anyone. I sure hope everyone can perform the position as they say on their resumes. I am in October and dad was September, it is good I could take his place with this insane hiring practice. This is something I can't talk to anyone about except mom, maybe she knows. Surely, she didn't make the cakes. This explains why there was a recipe in the January file for Chocolate Angel Food Cake. Maybe that is when it all started with that cake. I will see if mom wants to make one with me this weekend.

To my relief Patricia informs me the cakes are ordered in January for the entire year from Bergett's Bakery on 4th Avenue and a list of favorites for each month is decided in November at the company meeting. If two people cannot decide on one cake flavor, we get two smaller ones or a variety of cupcakes. I see a note in the file that each person is valuable and deserves their month of celebration. They even get to pick the lunch menu from a list of vendors for the company meeting midway through the month. Patricia calls me to ask if I would like to have a special flavor of cake ordered for my birthday or just keep the two for Renee and Alana's birthdays. I declined to get a cake of my own thinking I have never picked one out, just have eaten what was provided in the past. I am not even sure I have a favorite, that is when I realize that my life has always been a show up and partake in other people's choices ordeal. Why has this not bothered me before? Do I not have preferences? Who would have guessed I was getting into this? I figured I would head up the financial accounts, dig in to see where costs could be cut or if we need to put more money into the company for growth. Then I'll meet with the heads of each department and learn about the supply chain. It appears each department has two individuals working in it and everyone knows the routine from start to finish. Watching from up here reminds me of a restaurant; taking a ticket from an order and distributing to the proper link in the chain and shipping out after Quality Control double checks the order. This has me thinking can I expand this company online? We are mostly local, and our advertising is word of mouth. Are we in the position to go global? The profit and loss sheets arriving on Friday will give answers. Perhaps we could make growth happen slowly and some of our local accounts may have branch offices out of town that could use our services. The weekend is full already, making my Chocolate Angel Food Cake and foreseeing the numbers for expansion is possible.

Some of our orders are picked up or delivered locally. One of our local accounts is the Seattle Police Department. They are one of our largest accounts, even though policing has gone online they still need incident cards for each officer to carry and hand out, stickers for evidence bags, business cards, letterhead, envelopes, and other office supplies. I volunteer to go on this delivery mainly to see the process and how the paperwork is handled for each order, and it is close by so I will not be committed for a full day. I wait in the alley while Carlton loads the delivery van with not just this order but three more. We head north cutting over to 4th Avenue turning onto Cherry and then again on 5th Avenue. There was no need for parking, we entered the building from the loading dock next to the admission for the jail. I see several police cars outside waiting their turn knowing the entrance next to us is busy. I realized for the first time that the streets never sleep. Carlton steers the cart knowing where his route is through the basement of this building. We get to the proper door labeled Records that Carlton has the code to, he steers his cart in as I hold the door and instantly from behind the counter a uniformed officer comes out and hugs Carlton like they are long lost friends. Carlton turns to introduce me to Officer Skylar who holds out her hand to shake and says, "please call me Hazel." We complete our route stopping two more times Carlton not seeming to mind that I am with him, he knows his work and will do it the right way whether I am here or not. I am just surprised how well-liked Carlton is at each stop, not that he is unlikable but is truly welcomed. I am realizing this company that I am leading is a family and an extension that supports other families in our community. Seattle feels more like home each day, I haven't even thought about calling Alice since I arrived. Last I spoke with her I was at the extended stay hotel in Milwaukee making decisions about my future as hers were already set in place, probably prior to her letting me in on the plan. She always said I was not as flexible in my ways as she was. Wouldn't she be surprised now?

Chapter 3

July 1948
Lucine Mrs. Peterson

In 1948, I first set foot in the United States of America from France. Marvin Peterson and I saw each other at my Papa's bakery a day or two after the war had ceased to exist physically but not mentally and both instantly knew we belonged together. After all the red tape of our individual countries we were married, and I was on my way to a new land, becoming Mrs. Peterson. The Navy stationed Marvin at Sand Point Naval Air Station in North Seattle but I would go downtown and walk each block looking at the shops so similar to home all in a row smooshed together. The crowds walking by with a dialect I was not accustomed to. I didn't know anyone but felt comforted in the city as it reminded me of home imagining there were other strangers strolling too, who were just as out of place as I in a land not their own.

I was strolling along during one of my various outings, knowing the housework was done, Marvin would be gone a couple days more, and I had half of a sandwich in the refrigerator for dinner I was content. It was the black and white scalloped awning that caught my eye as

I turned the corner to 4th Avenue. It drew me in as if I
had been transported back home instantly, I was not in
this foreign land but in France. That is the same awning
as Papa's bakery, the place I had grown up, just seeing it
I could smell the aroma that drew me in every day in
France. There were men trying to remove the diner
booths out through the front door which appeared too
narrow as they pushed and jostled the heavy vinyl
seating. I watched them turn this way and that, but
each piece was too large for the opening. Suddenly
before I realized what I was doing I ran to them asking
them to stop the move immediately. When I came back
to where I was, I said I was the new owner of Burgett's
Bakery and wished to keep the furniture. I am not sure
where that all came from as I had never seen this
location prior to this moment, but the men stopped all
movement relieved that their task was complete. The
owner of the building came from a room towards the
back, someone must have run back to verify my
existence, I suddenly had a plan as to how I would
create the small bakery right here in my new land. He
agreed to my terms to run it as a bakery and leave all
the equipment. I retired in 2014 selling the
establishment and building to Remy Morilli on an owner
contract with the stipulation that the business keep the
name of Bergett's Bakery on the sign.

Remy came to me about twenty years ago needing
employment, possibly 1994. I taught him every baking
trick I knew from back home. He was natural in the

kitchen and seemed to enjoy the space. He said he cooked for his siblings as his mother was always gone. I never asked him to elaborate on any part of his life as I felt this was business. All the accounts were mostly commercial, we did have a few booths and a counter with our daily croissants, cupcakes, and cakes but most items were delivered and ordered ahead of schedule. I eventually sold the business to him on an owner contract in 2014 as I was ready to retire.

Remy loved to create new flavors, is a talented artist and has always remained current on his contractual payments to me. He wasn't exactly a good fit working the front counter or on the phone but was precise in taking orders online and set that system up for me. He was quite knowledgeable in web design and kept up on it daily with our new flavors, any holiday coming up or his latest creations. His photography skills are surely up to date. He runs a blog about Lake Union for his HOA and the other houseboat owners. He told me he grew up on the houseboat, owned by his grandfather. "When his mother passed away, he bought out his siblings share of the houseboat, so he lived there his entire life, or at least the majority of it."

Since I have been gone from the bakery, I receive a delivery or two monthly of different flavors for various fundraising functions. The quality has never changed but the delivery person is always different. I have never asked about Remy's management system since the company is no longer mine and the reputation and payments are both consistent. I am overjoyed that the quality has stayed the same or improved with my resignation. Remy appears to have an advisor or someone who brings new flavors to his attention using natural products like lavender or rosewater. My original recipes were all from France direct from my Papa's linage. I can still order them and picture myself back under the striped scallop awning a continent, county, and ocean away. It is hard to believe I have been gone for as long as I have. Seven decades have passed by since I have set foot in my homeland. I would not have traded this journey for another but am happy I did not return to cloud my vision, otherwise my bakery may have suffered.

Chapter 4

October 2024
Remy

I have recently had some serious thoughts of liquidating everything. The bakery, houseboat, blog, car they all have to go. I will move and destroy any evidence of my actions prior to anyone discovering the truth. I am positive my ways will be viewed as devious, deceitful and cruel by my loyal customers and acquaintances. Even the individuals who stroll by on their way to work or on a lap around the block who have smelled the delicious aromas coming from my establishment will be forever changed. I will be seen differently, viewed as an outcast and not a member of this trusting community. My hands are in many areas—photography, the homeowner's association, numerous businesses, clubs and classes. I even have connections to the Seattle Police Department, and they trust me. This all shows how no one can know anyone else for sure. Last night I made the decision. I ordered Chicken Parmesan, salad and bread sticks just as I always do on my reminiscing nights. The meal Phillip used to bring us when he was trying to take over our household on the nights when mom was out. He actually wanted to take mom away, but she had many social circles, and we could see his intentions and her use of him. He would bring the same meal every week. Of course we accepted it, I didn't have to cook, and it was free. Then he was demanding, wanting to take us all individual places, never together. He had been on several dates with our mother and was obsessed. One night he called demanding to take Everett for a drive. I knew that wasn't happening on my watch. He said he was coming over anyway, I told him no we were already asleep. He called from the top of the stairs, in the gravel parking lot saying he was on his way. I knew he had already arrived; I could see his headlights reflecting on the lake, faintly make out his voice through the wind and hear the gravel as he located a place to park. He wasn't fooling me; I ran to the steep set of stairs that connected the pathway to the dock that reached our home and waited for him. I was the man of the house even though I was only seventeen, he wasn't taking over with his perverted conceptions of our lives. We had gotten this far and had the system down, no one paid attention to us because we kept our heads down, were all clean, dressed well and attended school as we were supposed to even if it was mainly me who saw to all the small details to keep us together and not in foster care.

I reached the bottom of the stairs, still seeing his headlights. I had warned him to leave, we didn't wish to see him. While still on the phone he became more belligerent saying, "you young punk after all I have done for you. You think you can tell me to go away. You will do as I say." I am not entirely positive how this story will end with Phillip, but it will end tonight. He will not be coming back. I slip into bushes along the metal piping used as a handrail as I hear his car door close. If it is not him, I will stay so still no one will know I am here. There are thirteen steep steps, resembling a ladder but with wooden planks for surer footing. Steps I know by heart from carrying groceries for many years and escorting mom home from her late shifts at work. I see from my vantage point it is Phillip, cocky as ever. I can smell his spicy cologne, like he splashed on the entire bottle before leaving home. Did he do this to impress a group of teenaged boys or was he hoping mom would be home? As he draws closer, I am at the fifth step. I can see his shiny hair gel and the comb lines bringing out the slim patches of scalp showing through. I become aware of the light reflecting off his keys which may or may not be his only weapon. I take one quiet step out of the vegetation and ask Phillip to return to his car. He laughs and says, "I am coming over to visit." Something in me snaps. He is not scared, nor does he act startled at my sudden presence. I grab his neck and steer him up the stairs as I am at least a head taller than him, with a larger build. I picture placing him back in the driver's seat and sending him on his way. That was not what he had in mind, grabbing my neck, talking about respecting elders and individuals with authority. Then he does a spin, like an outdated karate move, possibly one he

learned in a class when he was much younger. I
snapped when he came at me, talking about spanking. I
grabbed his keys, demanded he get in his vehicle and
leave. He was very adamant about not doing that. I
opened the trunk picking him up and placing him inside.
If he had just stayed in there, I could have driven him up
the road and he could have started on his way. That is
not what happened at all. As I tried to close the trunk
lid, he popped his head out and I was picturing Everett
and Logan safe at home. The curve of the lid hit Phillips'
neck, and he bled, it was squirting all over the parking
lot with pressure pumping out as if to a musical beat.
My thoughts were he had to go; his strength diminished
at a higher rate of speed than I could think. Being
thankful for the rain as if on cue it washed away his
blood from the gravel. I had never driven before and
was imagining backing over the cliff to the sidewalk
below. Trying to think fast I find a secluded spot up the
road behind an abandoned light blue restaurant. I
glanced up to see there are cameras on the roof and I
hope they are not connected. I roll Phillip to the ground
thinking this is not the way this should have gone, me
being faced with decisions forced upon me. He is a
small man and surprisingly with my adrenaline at full
speed I move him easily from the trunk to the asphalt
parking lot. Thankfully, I found some gloves on the
center console before taking off. I let the air out of his
rear driver's side tire, grab the tire gauge out of the
console and lay it on the ground. I find the jack and
spare in the trunk thinking I am glad he did not bleed

much in there. I jack the car up having no idea if I am doing this correctly, undo the wheel cover and lug bolts, lay the empty tire down, gather the carpeting from the trunk, position Phillip as if he had been changing a flat and had been attacked. Almost forgetting to leave his keys and retrieving his wallet.

I walk the mile or so home to my quiet community and brothers, knowing we will not have to fend off the advances of Phillip anymore. Rethinking my steps, knowing if they were wrong, I handled this in a way that could jeopardize everything but if I was right, it may have saved us from who knows what. Phillip could have just left instead of trying to manipulate an already vulnerable family. As I walk, I am not sure why I took the carpet full of blood, it would be something they would look for since it was a newer vehicle, not one that had anything missing. It's too late to return it now, I cannot go back, and risk being seen at that location. The carpet makes it further up the road over a mile from our houseboat. I ditch it in the vines on the opposite side of the street from the lake. As I am in the bushes, I leave the wallet thinking I should cut up every piece of it and throw it away around town but know I need a clean break now, not toting pieces of evidence around. There is $139.00 in the wallet, I do keep that and nothing else burying the bright credit cards with the silver strips on the back that reflect from the moonlight. I find myself studying them as I have never held a credit card. Wondering how these could help us but know I need to be as far from this story as I can be and as soon as possible. Now to head home. As I round the corner to go down the stairs, I can see blue police lights reflecting on the south end of the lake. Dipping into my designated space I return home without anyone knowing I had left. I try to finish my social studies homework but keep going to the window looking left. It is a quiet Tuesday night, eventually the faint noise of police radio chatter stops reverberating over the ripples on the lake, the lights disappear, and all is back to normal except my homework isn't complete and everything has changed in my life from that moment on. I fell asleep in the chair facing the water with the smell of Phillips cologne stuck in my olfactory and an image of his haughty smile etched in my brain. I do not think I will ever put up with a bully again, not feeling remorse but knowing I had to protect my brothers and myself. Thinking who he was to have put me in the position of laying everything on the line.

I became obsessive watching the news, at first police needed leads for the killing of Phillip Nikas, it appeared to be a robbery while he was changing his tire off of Eastlake. I think I should have punctured the tire and not just let the air out, wondering if I put the cap back on, fingerprints would be impossible to trace from the ridged cap I hoped. I am not sleeping, nor am I cut out for this type of crime. Nikas was head of the Greek restaurant chain that held locations in most states, that is why he brought us food not from his establishment but a neighboring one. Did anyone know of us, had he talked about who he was taking the food to each week? Were there other boys he was after? As we didn't have much money, we would never have eaten at Nikas, so I had never heard of it before. I saw a few newspaper headlines through the window on the corner boxes and at the selling cart downtown. I stopped and pretended to look at mints but was in actuality reading the story on the front page as he was a well-known and an upstanding citizen or so everyone thought. They were asking for leads on the location of his wallet, a fancy name brand. I laughed when I read that part and purchased some fruity jellybeans so as not to draw attention to myself. After a few days more crimes happened, and the story died down. I did buy one paper; it had Phillip's obituary in it. I will keep that forever as a sign of my heroism, if anyone sees it and asks why I have it in my possession it will be reasonable because of how nice he has been to us and mom.

When I started working at the bakery, since it was part of the food circuit in Seattle, I would hear four years since Phillip has passed and still not a break in his case. Every year it was the same story, the people told them, the newspaper and television broadcast it as if it had become a cold case, showing no new photos of the evidence each year. No more clues, no one knew he wasn't killed there probably since it was so close to the actual murder scene for that to be determined. I would go over it each year with the same meal, Chicken

Parmesan, salad, and bread sticks. It wasn't the same meal since I had no idea where he purchased it, but it was close enough to celebrate his exit from earth, my own personal celebration. I knew I would never let anyone bully me again, these human resource people that call demanding cupcakes "today" they say, deliver now. I tell them they will need to come in and pick from what is in the case, that way I can take notes on what they like and even get more future orders. It all helps with my system for the good and tragic.

Chapter 5

October 2024
August

On Monday, I suggested that everyone attending the October cake party have something to say about dad if they wished or felt able. A simple request that could break the awkward moments. I also needed to get a hold of Hector since he was on vacation the week of the party to see if he wishes to make an appearance and give him time to make a statement about dad. Tuesday mom and I had to go to the courthouse for the will to be filed. We met at a small deli at 11:30am, hoping to get through before the lunch rush. Neither of us eat, we just stare at the turkey sandwich on our plates, being thankful we split one, neither opening the bag of chips, just occasionally taking sips from the sodas we ordered, me thankful for some flavor but too unsettled to eat. We each have the paperwork that is needed for the court, neither one of us has ever done anything like this before, I am not sure if I have been in a courthouse. All of our planning documents for my previous life were purchased or submitted online by the contractor, like building permits. Here I am again there and need to be here, present with mom who is staring off into space as

I must have been too. I wrap the food up, return the sandwich and chips to the red and white checkered bag, buy a to go soda and cookie, get napkins and mom says for me to take the food. I nod; I will pass this food onto someone on the street prior to reaching our destination. As we turn onto 4th Avenue, I see a man leaning against the wall of the building. Knowing he is who I will give the bag of food to, I excuse myself from mom who watches me approach the man, hand him the bag and drink and return to my previous route next to mom as the man stands thanking me at a high volume. I nod, then he yells, "I know everything that goes on in that building." Mom may be embarrassed and acts as if we do not know the yelling man, but I know she is proud of me for my gesture, and she is thankful for all the people on the street, so no one knows he is yelling at us and glad the food will not go to waste.

After our filing at the long wooden counter with the industrial black and white clock hanging on the wall we waited. Seeing a few other court cases and our brief time with the judge, we turned to leave. I ask mom to wait, through the small window on a courtroom door I see who I think is Hector on the bench in the back. I do not intrude on his privacy but now know for sure it is him. We leave, mom asking if I am okay and if everything is fine, her knowing I am acting differently. I assure her all is well with me, walk her to her car wanting to go back in to see what is going on in that courtroom and if Hector is listed on the roster, as we were, I saw hanging outside each court room. This is Superior Court, so it is not a traffic issues. What could Hector be involved in? I say goodbye to mom, reassured that she has locked her doors and is on her way. Suddenly I realized I had no idea where to. I should have asked but was mentally in the courthouse. Will I ever be where I physically am?

Entering again through the metal detectors, not taking note of this on my previous trip through, I am impatient this time wishing to read the paperwork. I can see down the marbled hallway the line of benches like church pews waiting patiently for people to come out or arrive at their new fate. This is a scene that happens daily, hourly, but is new to me. As I watch the benches and go through the scanner, I see Hector leave at a high rate of speed checking my watch right at 1:10 pm. I am not sure why I need to know this, but it has become obsessive in my mind in the past thirty minutes. Hector does not see me as he exits through the lanes leading outside to my right just past the entry scanners.

I get to the courtroom I am almost sure he was in, now they all look the same, all the cases are posted in the order of hearing them not alphabetically at all as I would have assumed. I check the schedule of cases outside of all six courtrooms on the left side of the hallway. I know he was in one of them, his name not appearing in any documents nor was anyone with his last name Martinez being seen in any of the court rooms today. I leave feeling defeated and am not entirely sure why, just that I was positive I was onto something not knowing what, if anything at all. This mystery is not solved.

I drive the few blocks back to work, park in the rear parking lot in my designated Rike CEO parking slot. I see all the cars and do not have a clue which one Hector drives or anyone else for that matter but at this moment Hector is the only person who I am thinking about. I hope this goes smoother than the last mission I attempted, all the files with the months on them I have not returned to. I have been sidetracked by the meetings, cake, reinventing myself, the will and now Hector and his mystery courthouse appearance.

After returning to the warehouse, I go upstairs to my office with the intention of revamping the website but cannot concentrate on any task here by myself. The shipping department is where I need to be. Patrick may have some clues about Hector. Patrick is home sick today and it is Hector who skillfully reloads the labels into the printer for the next orders to go out. I offer my assistance; Hector gladly accepts and leaves. This makes me feel as if he knows I saw him today. Did he see me? When he returns to the shipping dock, I mention my morning at the courthouse doing some estate planning. Hector has no reaction to this information, it doesn't have anything to do with him, he is not acting guilty. He doesn't bat an eye or miss a beat with his orders, of course I wouldn't know the real process so maybe he does but no unusual behavior stands out to me.

The next day Patrick returns, and I do some inventory in the warehouse so I can monitor Hector's lunchtime activity. I may learn what he drives, which direction he heads and the rest of the story, if there is one. I see Hector through the tall metal racks on the next aisle over, he looks at his watch, grabs his dark gray sweat jacket, doesn't go to the parking lot as I had imagined, this threw me off. He leaves out the small, rusted metal front door that no one uses and steps onto the sidewalk. By the time I get to the door and go outside Hector is close to two blocks up 6th Avenue, running like he robbed a bank. The next day I park four blocks up the road in a small lot and watch as Hector runs by at full speed. I am almost positive he is going to the courthouse again. Later today, after Hector returns, I will go to the courthouse to set up a surveillance position for tomorrow because I will be there to figure out this unusual behavior.

Hector arrives right on schedule at 12:05 am, slips into a side stairwell I wasn't even aware of and disappears like he owns the place. I waited downstairs at my vantage point not realizing the second floor is laid out the same having not even thought he would go to another floor. I see Hector leave at 12:50 pm looking like he doesn't have a care in the world. He exits the building and breaks out immediately into a high-speed run. I go upstairs repeating my actions from yesterday, reading all the case names and knowing no more than I did when I came, baffled to say the least. Why would someone choose to spend their lunch hour this way?

I approached Hector that afternoon about a discrepancy in inventory and mentioned I had seen him a few blocks up the road on a corner. He is a man in short supply of words, smiles and says yes, then explains the inventory miscalculation and tells me it is best to do inventory in the morning before any movement of product or at the end of the day. Then states we have a company that performs all the inventory once a year, which is good to know since I do not wish to be part of the count. I still don't have one clue of what Hector is up to. Tomorrow I will make progress on this and find out when the inventory is done, something I should know, I guess. It seems this place runs itself or at least the employees do. Maybe after the next cake party I will have an idea what dad's purpose was in this company. I feel I come here and learn what others do but have no clue what my function is.

I will miss a day at the courthouse due to a supply chain order which made our orders later than we had hoped. We always tell the client two weeks and wish to deliver in one week, but this will bring it to possible overtime for our staff unless we produce a late order.

Friday I am in place at the end of the hallway just before 12:00 pm, I almost missed Hector entering the building with a large group of people. If he hadn't split off from the group, I would have missed him, he slips into the first courtroom as if he belongs. I am concentrating on Hectors movement so hard I almost don't hear my name, August, being called out. It is a lady, and I cannot see her due to the vast amount of people walking up the corridor. Maybe I imagined someone calling out to me, or someone was speaking of the month, no one would recognize me here or I hope not. The crowd parts, revealing an officer. Her face is similar, but I cannot recall her name. She has given me her first name, which I also do not remember, and Carlton had referred to her as officer something. I smile in recognition, and she sees my confusion saying it is her job to never forget a face or name, giving up hers again to me, Hazel Skylar, a name I can never forget now. I am relieved she has introduced herself again. In awkward situations the details of life become magnified. She asks how I am settling in Seattle and says she has seen me here a few days in a row as she delivers records to the clerk's office every day. Hoping she is not being too forward but asks if I am ok. I explain about dad, the will and probate. Hazel looks at me in a peculiar way then she tells me a short story of her mother, Vera. Somehow, I have the feeling she knows I am lying; I change the subject and ask what goes on in each courtroom. She has a great knowledge of the court proceedings, evictions and civil matters on this floor, criminal traffic over there, on the other floors are more complex cases and criminal trials. Hazel seems to know everyone here. Four or five people have stopped to talk with her as we have been visiting. Hazel genuinely is in whatever conversation she is having. She has a way about herself that makes everyone feel special. I tell her it is good to see her and start to leave but she hears her name and turns with a belly laugh while motioning for me to stay, me thinking this was my out and now I am roped in further. This man looks important in his tactical shoes like the similar ones I saw on my shopping trip recently, open olive-green wind breaker revealing a holster and bullet proof vest with FBI clearly displayed now that I am looking. I think he looks like a detective, but she introduces him as Special Agent Frederick Ford. I stand awkwardly listening to them feeling guilty as I am up to no good but haven't committed any crimes and that is the only reason they both have a job. I excuse myself after the proper amount of time to be polite saying "good to see you again Hazel and a pleasure to meet you, Agent." I am thinking as I leave Ford, Agent, Frederick, which one should I have called him, I have never met an FBI agent before. I am a man who owns a paper company, have never been in any trouble or dealt with legal cases. I know by this time I have missed Hector and should not return to this place daily with the knowledge I am invading Hector's privacy and not even gaining the information I am looking for. What would I do if I discovered something about Hector? He completes his tasks at work, is always punctual and gets along with everyone, there must not be any harm in his actions.

I walk back at a slow pace thinking I am wasting time and turning into a stalker, behavior out of the ordinary for me. When I return my office has been cleaned again by Sven in the time I was gone. I can smell the products, the windows are clearer, the trash dumped, and the carpet has been vacuumed. He came in earlier than usual. I don't spend forty hours a week here and when I am behind the closed steel door I may only physically be here. I wish I had seen Sven to ask him what he knows about dad's position in the company. The website is gaining orders from around the country, some are from the offices of our current clients with other locations in various states.

Chapter 6

October 2024
August

Production, orders, and shipping have been at an all-time high since I have returned, this has nothing to do with my presence though. It is the time of year when businesses use their yearly budget to replenish their stock for the following year. This means the economy is picking up if all these orders are coming in.

My time has been focused equally between past and present yearly budgets, learning each position precisely, getting to know the employees, and rebuilding our website. Sales have risen yearly, costs have risen at almost an equal rate, shipping and delivery are at an all-time high with the price of packaging, labor, and fuel. We have automated some of the system to keep up with orders and make a more efficient inventory of the printed products.

Friday is finally here, and I can see the entire picture coming into place. Just over 3 weeks in Seattle and one week as the leader of August Island Rike Paper Company. Still no word from anyone in Milwaukee, I wonder if they know I am no longer a resident of

Wisconsin. It feels as if I was never there but know I left a vast part of myself at that location. Alice has not made any contact with me, not even a text. I know the divorce is happening since paperwork arrived in my email for my e-signature. The world has become impersonal. I suppose this system would be best for couples who fought but Alice and I just stopped talking as soon as she moved to her new high rise. I am sure she knows I left my position at Green Mechanical Engineering, at least by word of mouth. Since we have a commonality of friends. Thinking back on the chain of events, we sold the house, she had moved prior to this, I moved before closing, quit my job soon after and left town the next day. I just knew I didn't want any part of my life the same if the two main pieces were different. I am grateful there were no other lives involved such as in children or pets. Sometimes through the years I would imagine life being different with them but when Alice and I got together we agreed on having no other attachments. I just didn't think her attachment to me would snap suddenly and be nonexistent, me out of her picture as soon as she moved. We were together twenty years, had recently celebrated our 20-year China anniversary. All our friends attended the detailed party on Lake Michigan. She acted normal then, there wasn't a clue shown to anyone of her plans. We were happy, I thought. Nothing had changed in our routines; work, eat at home six days a week and out to eat for one good meal on Saturday to touch base, cover all the topics of the week and just relax with each other. Two weeks after our anniversary we came home from our Saturday out, listening to smooth jazz on the car stereo, relaxed and as we were ready to watch a movie, she turned to me and said, "I bought a condo, overlooking the lake. You can stay here or come with me, doesn't matter to me either way, it is what I have decided." I knew at that moment I wasn't going, not if it didn't matter to Alice if I was there. Maybe she worded that wrong, but it was her proposal to me as how life would be. She had a lot of time to present this offer to me, ask even if I wished to move but didn't. She subtracted me from the equation with the words of not caring. Here I go again, being here and feeling as if I am there. This happens frequently to me and takes hours of my week. Fifteen minutes here and there, like small bites of my time wasted. Maybe I am processing or grieving at the sudden loss of my life as I knew it, I may be concerned I have missed a clue that things would become different. I really wish to be here since I am here, I just do not know how to stop being there.

My goal at the end of this productive week is to find the recipe for Chocolate Angel Food Cake, buy the ingredients and pan to make it. Mom laughed when I asked her about wanting to bake a cake and said she didn't have an angel food cake pan or smidgen of baker in her. I'm not sure if I would have found it so fast in the February file if it wasn't handwritten on a pink piece of paper. I make a copy and replace the original. Seeing I don't have any of the ingredients I thank everyone for an excellent week, get in my SUV and head north on I-5 at a snail's pace, thanks to Friday night rush hour. I begin thinking I should have routed myself differently but then relax, knowing I have nowhere to go except a grocery store and home. I get off on Northgate Way and merge onto Lake City Way remembering Fred Meyer is north somewhere also knowing there is one by my apartment, hoping I don't regret my decision to drive and forget my former thoughts. Suddenly hungry and looking for food I bypass Wendy's wishing I had stopped and see a Dick's Drive in sign on the southbound lanes, I turn in, get out of my car, order, and find a parking spot perfect for watching people on this fine windy Friday night in Seattle. I know the cake will turn out well tomorrow and am pleased I went out somewhere this evening, even if it was for a burger and groceries. I am actually here and not mentally in Milwaukee, merging my entire being on this sidewalk almost as far north as I can go and still be in Seattle.

Saturday, I didn't choose to bake with mom having all the necessary cooking apparatus and ingredients at my place. It is starting to look like I live here, now to make it smell as if I do. Baking a cake or anything else has never been on my list of things to do in life. I possibly should have paid attention earlier but do not even know where the cakes came from that Alice, and I had for our celebrations. I would believe they were from a bakery or the grocery store. I am seeing how the important but trivial small steps in life were overlooked for years by me. How many people just get through each day doing their share of work and no more.

The eggs are whipped according to the recipe, after reading about angel food cakes they are one of the most temperamental batters to bring into true form. I double checked that all the ingredients were in the batter, they should be, before starting they were all on the counter, so I didn't miss anything, and each was put away in my nearly empty cabinets as I used them. With the oven preheated to 375°, I put the cake in and set the timer. While waiting for it to finish, I text mom to see if she wishes to have dinner. I will have it delivered and bring the cake as a surprise, if it turns out, she has not asked about it, me knowing she was not interested in any baking antics, she probably figures I have forgotten about my baking whim too. She texts back that she gets off work at 4:00pm so could meet me at my place if that works for me. I have not invited her over previously, she probably just wants to know what it looks like here, make sure I have a proper roof and food, towels, and furniture. This makes me glad I have made some purchases like dishes, silverware, furniture, and a couple throw pillows.

Mom shows up precisely at 4:20 pm, she has a six pack of soda and some napkins, me knowing they were both clearly purchased at a convenience store since they were unloaded from a black plastic bag. I know the invitation was a last-minute thing but feel I should check on her next week. She appears okay, of course she has just left work and would be presentable to the public but how is she at home now that dad is gone? Is there food there, how is she making it through the days when she is off work? Walking through a family member passing is not something I have experienced before.

I placed the cake in an empty cabinet as a surprise after the meal of delivered lasagna, salad, and garlic bread. Mom eats like she hasn't eaten in weeks, perhaps she hasn't. We have both been getting through each day as we know how. I was gone for multiple years and my parents were always there for me and eager to talk when I called or accepted me with our infrequent visits to each other but with me living thousands of miles away I think the bond of reliability on my part was severed. I could count on them, but they never asked anything of me, even when they would come to visit it would be when I wished, and they would plan around that.

Losing dad is much harder on mom and now that I think of it also the people at the warehouse. No one mentions him, if they start to, they will stop at the beginning of the sentence saying, "Garrett did it, Garrett kept it, Garrett would have…." It should not be like this; I feel the need to discuss my dad and hear his strengths and weaknesses. Something to address at the next company meeting.

Mom and I have dinner, I try to knit him into our conversation on a few occasions, but I think this is too hard for her to talk about. After giving up and going for a walk around the block, mom says she is tired and needs to get home. I coaxed her back in telling her I had a surprise waiting. She sees me bring the cake out and has to sit since she is laughing so hard and crying at the same time. I cannot understand what she is saying then I get it. That is the cake dad used to bake from a recipe given to him by a lady named Nancy. It was always his favorite. I slice us both a sliver with her instruction of gently using the serrated knife. We ate a slice in honor of dad and Nancy. I think the cake broke the ice in our conversation, mom took some home and left with a smile not looking as weary as when she arrived.

Chapter 7

October 2024

~~Hector~~

    Between work, school, my newly found exercise, and my self-induced studies play out in my head day and night I am exhausted. Days turn into nights and nights into days, it is fortunate for me that work and court are only accessible in the daytime hours and my classes are at night mostly online. I live in Pioneer Square where crime has become increasingly terrifying at times - bullets flying outside my window sometimes, carefully stepping around people lying on the sidewalk on my way to the bus in the mornings wondering if they are alive or possibly reach out to grab my ankle or not. I love to be here and have lived here most of my life since I moved in to help take care of grandpa shortly before he passed on. He wished to remain in his home. I kept the brick apartment and most of his belongings on the second floor overlooking Occidental Avenue. The tree lined street brings me comfort. There is always activity of people and cars, but the trees are my favorite to watch. I leave the ugly brown upholstered recliner by the window that grandpa would holler out "autumn is upon us, or spring is coming" and we watch the seasons spin by. His days were undoubtedly slow compared to his fast-paced life prior to his injury, maybe he withered away from boredom. His entire life becoming the view from his second-floor window instead of physically being on the streets, working the neighborhoods and people for answers. Nearly forty years on the job as a detective, one severe unplanned twist of his ankle, coming down off the curb on a wet dark night leaving that parking lot with obtaining answers on his mind and it was over. They said a desk job was in order but that would never have worked for him. He scoured the street, and knew people that would not feel comfortable coming into the station. He met them in private places like under bridges or behind buildings for resolution of cases, more scared for his informant than himself. Knowing many cases would not be solved if it weren't for his CI's. He didn't want paperwork to push around, file or read. He was a crime solver, it was in his blood, and I do believe mine. I will not join the police force, but no one knows of this decision, all of grandpa's friends still believe I am going to apply for the academy someday to be like Detective Martinez.

Grandpa insisted I either work for the police department or become a private investigator with my inheritance. I do believe he envisioned me quitting my warehouse job, going to school, and hiring into an agency immediately. Thanks to him I am all signed up with a couple prestigious firms, but I am not ready to be anything except what I am. I don't want to be told what to investigate. I cannot even legally look into anything without my license but there are no laws saying I cannot watch court cases and study human behavior and probability. My schooling is approximately halfway completed. I will take the last courses one at a time since I have added other activities to my itinerary and have no intentions at this time of leaving the warehouse position. With my time full job that I love, every moment of each day, there aren't many spots to relax but I can still hear grandpa and feel his presence to keep me moving forward on his wishes on some nights when I watch the activity below from his recliner.

Garrett never paid much attention to the warehouse area. He was a paper man, a man who wanted status and data given on all orders. His method of working was to make a printout of the orders for the week and check them against what had shipped. He would walk around with his clip board and highlighted lines. Don't get me wrong Garrett, being the owner of the company, was more than fair to every employee, actually he treated us all like family. This is why I feel unable to leave this position. I cherish working at August Island Rike Paper Company. My life is here. These people are my family, I don't have anyone on this earth who I am related to, grandpa was the last. The police check on me only because I am Detective Martinez' grandson, now much more infrequently but they are not the people I see daily. My coworkers and I have a silent agreement, possibly deeper on my end, that we will be there for each other at all times. During the daily tasks, the company picnics, if someone needs a ride, a day off, has a family crisis we are there. I may feel this considerably deeper than most. I have more time on my hands without my family, so I volunteer to round up supplies, drive the van and set up or just fill in whenever needed.

Now that August is here, I am not as comfortable as I have been with Garret since I do not know him, and he is forever present. Their mannerisms are extremely comparable, their voices are similar but their strategy of running the company are absolutely opposite. Garrett never learned all the positions, maybe he already knew since he says he worked with his grandfather before running the show and just never cared to use his skills. August was not here back then, nor had I personally seen him before he took over. My nerves were on high alert but now I feel he knows we are all family and need operations to flow as they are if not to expand. My only problem with him is he followed me to the courthouse during lunch breaks. Why would he do that? Does he think I am in some kind of trouble or am a threat to business? My answer for now is I am learning a trade and have no intention of leaving my position here. My actions are purely investigation. I am not completely sure of his actions so do not plan on telling him my story. "Along with watching the court cases during my break, I have another case I am interested in. I found the private files in grandpa's closet- they must have been brought home before his retirement." Now to

August Island Rike Paper Company

study the case notes and follow his leads. So far there isn't any proof, only speculation but 33 people are dead, and I suspect two more recently. No one has ever caught onto this case except grandpa and with his direction now me. How could a case of this magnitude be left uncovered for so many years?

Chapter 8

November 2024
August

These past few months have rolled by at a speed I didn't anticipate, by November the strong winds threatening to topple this monster of a building. I picture it rolling over the train tracks and into the Puget Sound. With a background in mechanical engineering, I perform some inspections and hire crews to replace the tin roofing, siding and check for leaks and exterior damage. Surprisingly the building and foundation are solid, it will stand for many years to come. As this knowledge overtakes me, that is exactly what it does, my future is undecided. I know I will remain here to manage my company, but I wonder what else the future holds for me. Do I just go to work, go home, bake a cake now and then and drive across town for supplies? I don't even know anyone here. My high school friends have most likely moved on. If they were here, would I even want to see them? I need something to do different with my life, something new that I have never tried before.

The holidays are upon us, and I picture the various trees Alice, and I have picked out and hauled home in our two decades together. So many of our belongings, like the ornaments that had no sentimental value to me, are gone. I have no idea where all of our earthly goods ended up. Alice said she was moving and when I left all I grabbed was my gym bag and a couple boxes. I never returned; she may have our mutually held stuff, but I doubt it. I reminisce about the window I loved so much in the living room where the small Japanese Maple tree grew, just to the right side, blocking the view of the porch. I always wanted to move it to the left and Alice insisted it stay where it was.

  This year I am getting a Christmas tree—a full - sized real one. I need the fragrance and ceremony of decoration. Memories of the lights, ornaments, wrestling the stand with the screws to center the tree, all items on my shopping list and a vacuum cleaner. The Fred Meyer up north is a comfortable location to shop. I will look at condos in that neighborhood also. It has only been three months since my return but feels like an eternity looking back on it. The days seem much longer when you spend them alone. The people at work are filler for some of the hours but I know nothing of their lives except snippets of information I hear in passing. I need to join a club or take up an activity; I am not into sports except to watch an occasional game on television. I used to enjoy photography. After I acquire the necessary festive items for the tree, actually get one and decorate it, I will have all day Saturday and Sunday to sketch out a plan to fill my time. I cannot continue to just read, work, bake and drive.

Traffic is much heavier heading north on a Friday night, making me reconsider living so far north since changing my profession is not an option. I have nine months to decide where to live before my lease is up, if I choose to move at all. After my newly inserted quarterly dinner at Dick's I head to Fred Meyer, the lines are long with Christmas shopping in full swing. I selected a blue, green, and silver theme for the tree at least for this year. It matches my mood. I am not able to see where I am going with life, hence the muted colors. Remembering our family tradition of cocoa and donuts at Christmas time while growing up, I head to the garden department and pick up a five-foot Noble Fir. I check out with my newly acquired vacuum cleaner, tie the tree down to the roof rack I have never used prior to this and hope the needles will still be attached by the time I arrive home and head south. While shopping suddenly, I experienced a bittersweet moment as I reflected on my father's absence. Although I did not spend every Christmas or most holidays with him, his presence on this earth was always a source of comfort. In all our years together Alice and I spent every holiday planning, making it special, choosing a theme or color combo, now what is she doing? This is our first holiday season apart in over twenty years. Is she alone? How can I, we, us be discarded and not considered overnight. I turn around and look in the back seat as I hear a noise, the cocoa falls to the floor, I realize I forgot marshmallows. That is a deal breaker for me. Nearly home after stop and go traffic in the rainstorm, I pull into the store by my house, run in for my forgotten item, race through the rain, get in the car and the string has come undone from the tree. Getting out I see the tree is no longer attached to the vehicle. I honestly have no idea if it was stolen while I was in the store or flew off while I was deep in thought. The tree decorating is happening tonight despite hurdles, theft or thoughts. I stop at the Fred Meyer on NW 45th Street, needing only a tree now and rum. I check out and ask for an associate to help tie on the tree not sharing the story of the last tree.

It is nearly 9:00pm when I return home, glad I have chosen an apartment with a carport right in front of my entry. I unloaded the tree first to make sure it gets inside. After going back out for the rest of the bags, and thankfully making it in one trip, I sit down looking at my pile of goods. I hear a noise upstairs and become aware that I am sleeping. It is 1:50 am. I hadn't been aware of dozing off taking in half a night's sleep sitting on the sofa. I remember all my bags that I had fully intended to retrieve are just inside the door. The tree is laying on its side as if it has given up the fight being second choice. I start laughing as I have not laughed since arriving here or possibly months before leaving Milwaukee. I cannot stop. All that is on my mind is the first tree—where it went, imagining, hoping it didn't cause harm and if stolen I truly hope the people who have it enjoy the tree. My tears flow. I am genuinely happy at the moment as I set up the stand, center the tree on my window and add water. The hot chocolate and rum are just the things to top off my night as I decorate the tree with white lights and ornaments. I didn't get a star for the top but may leave that open for discussion later.

It is almost time to get up if it were a workday. I have a piece of toast, get my pajamas on, and read. Knowing I am onto something called peace. I have no idea where it will take me, but I am content for now. I turn off the music, leave the lights on the tree, open the laptop, and see an advertisement for camera packages for Christmas. Knowing tomorrow or Sunday I will be stopping in to purchase myself a present. Nikon has always been my favorite brand. Since I have done any photography, technology has advanced beyond my comprehension so I may need to take some instruction to get up to speed with my new hobby. While looking at the ads I there are mirrorless, DSLR, package with tripods, memory card and cases. I suddenly wish to be serious about photography this time around. I can afford it and possibly make money with my prints of the city. No one has been in my thoughts except me since leaving both Fred Meyers. Suddenly I remember to ask mom what is on her wish list for Christmas. I don't even know what her hobbies are these days.

Chapter 9

~~*~~

November 2024
Remy

    Another shift has ended just like the other 5980 times I have locked the door. Monday through Friday, the monotony of it. It's four o'clock in the morning and I unlock the steel alley door that has considerably more rust on it than a decade ago, two decades. When do I buy a new door? I make the decision to sell the bakery with this door, it is the one I unlocked all this time. I can feel my exit happening before the actual pieces are in place. I know there is a buyer. I can sell the houseboat, destroy my evidence and be out of Seattle before anyone discovers my actions. Each year the guilt lays heavier. I am slowly putting my plans in place. The months go by. On the first Tuesday of each month I celebrate at home, the waves slowly rocking my houseboat, the meal the same, dessert, whatever was served for that particular case. No one comes to see me, and I prefer it that way. I store my secrets in the cedar chest at the foot of my bed, where I sit twice daily to put on and take off my shoes. This helps me keep everything in order while avoiding the temptation to dwell on my accomplishments and tackling societal bullies. I know this isn't true because I cannot control what happens once it leaves my hands but knowing the bully will have pain of some sort is a comfort to me. I don't think right, I know that I have acquaintances but not friends, I have never wanted them nor craved any intimate relationships with anyone. If I had crossed the line ever my secret of Phillip, then the rest would have spilled. My actions have caused my solo life, everyone I know is always happy to see me. I have never acted out of line in business, galas I have attended, homeowners' association meetings, the photo club, or any other activities I could join and still be anonymous or the hero for bringing dessert. This train of thought has brought on some OCD in me. I check to see if my windows and doors are locked three times before leaving, arriving home and sleeping. Sometimes I must complete the task before sitting down to read. I do not want any trouble here, ones that could bring attention to my home. I am an upstanding citizen with nothing to hide as long as no one looks too hard.

I used to have nightmares about killing Phillip and his shiny hair, the expensive car he drove, being all cool he thought until he made the fatal mistake of sticking out his neck. I stop and laugh hysterically at that train of thought, such a mundane cliche. We should all mind our own business and not disturb others. I blame Phillip for the start of my files and the need to create them. They are part of the OCD I did not have prior to that event, I must complete each one with the same paperwork, bullies must be documented. Truthfully the cedar chest is getting a little cramped with so many cases of bad behavior, some are not perfectly in place. My estimated guess is around forty but am not entirely sure of the exact count. This weekend I shall have to take inventory as there will be time to go through them, item by item to make sure they are in chronological order and perfect. They are artifacts on my mission. This is why I am on edge; the files are not precise they must be perfect to be destroyed before my departure. Today is only Wednesday. I have a few days to prepare for my weekend at home, on the lake with the rain falling, wind blowing and the turmoil inside of me as I set the system straight. I know how my mind works. By Friday at 4:00 am I will want to close the bakery for the day and start my weekend, but I need to stay until at least noon, my normal time to end a daily shift. In twenty-three years, no matter what the circumstances, I have not taken a day off or had a vacation. This week will be no different, my discipline is what holds my secrets.

I was correct. On Friday I fought with myself to open the door, standing in the alley, with my key willing myself to enter and dump flour into the mixer. Friday, Lively Lemon, Chunky Chocolate and Sweet Strawberry. Every day had its own flavors, I have never mixed up a day but have had the urge to get back in my ratty little car and drive home or somewhere other than here. I put my keys back in my pocket, turn towards my car in the two stalled parking spaces between the brick buildings in the alley knowing I will go back because this part is almost over. The last payment will be handed over to Mrs. Peterson and the bakery will be mine to sell. I am positive she will not want the outcome to be like that, but it has to be. I cannot stop this roller coaster and forget about it all without selling everything and leaving town immediately after my final payment. I can see myself on the beach somewhere hot. I could bake or not, maybe that would start my obsessive behavior again. My biggest fear of leaving this all behind are the files. Can I live without them after twenty-three years of meticulous work and countless hours spent creating them? With each passing day I have become exceedingly inflexible with both sides, trying to balance each other as they have in the past. Keep going or stop, just stop. The weight of it all is overwhelming. I have such pride in my work, it is perfect or will be by Sunday but cannot continue. I do have a conscience that seems to activate now and then just not when it should. My value of justice is the most prominent trait in me, and I fulfill that role not as often as I wish but if I did, I would not be a free man. They would deem me as insane; I could not live knowing all the people who have valued me over the years would think any less of my being. My reputation will remain intact with the plan I have to cease my mission, thinking of myself with a one-person military assignment. This reminds me of the witness protection program; when I leave it will not bother me to be away from anyone except Everett and Logan, but I do not see them often as it is. I envision spending the holidays in Seattle with my family for Christmas. However, I also consider the less pleasant aspect where neither Logan nor Everett extends an invitation to holiday dinners or to their homes. A couple of times they brought a leftover meal. Me not wanting it and them not wishing to be on the houseboat ever again has caused them to not visit. Truthfully, me being a bit older than them may have caused the two of them to be distant from me since I was their authority figure, enforcing homework, meals, laundry, curfews, keeping our heads down. When they see me, I am sure they are immediately faced with mom leaving, grandpa passing and whatever other issues arose as a child from not having stable parents. All of which are things they wish not to think about anymore and just live in their houses mounted to the ground with perfect pictures of their lives that they created. Thinking back, this all started with me protecting them and then the OCD started at a young age for me. I had to make sure all their needs were met so we didn't end up in foster care since there truthfully were not any parents, just a lady who called herself mom that delivered groceries once a week if she remembered or for whatever reason she chose to appear. I wonder how she kept on with her life. She must not have had a conscience either, or could turn it off and on, thinking her only duty to us was a few meals a week. She never asked anything when she came over. She even knocked and waited for one of us to open the door as if she did not reside here any longer. I wonder now what would have happened if we hadn't answered.

Would she have felt relief and left the food outside or taken it for herself? I don't think she was a drug addict, possibly she had a love addiction, always chasing the ultimate dream. We were not part of that, just a piece from another scene in her life that lasted too long in her opinion. She would buy a cake with the week's groceries when it was one of our birthdays but there was no mention of the actual celebration. I bet she got food stamps for all of us. I don't even know if she worked, where she resided or how I could have gotten a hold of her in an emergency. I bet the police would know how, they know almost everything except my activities. I've been stuck in my thoughts for so long that my weekend has almost begun. Elora brings me back to the present time, understanding myself more in depth after that trip down memory lane, I smile at her knowing she loves this place, the customers, the seasons and change of scenery out of our floor to ceiling windows that she insists on keeping spotless. Maybe she will purchase the bakery from me. She has not shown any interest in baking, but we can find another baker. Truthfully, I don't care what the baked products taste like once I am gone. I will be happy to escape unseen and undetected.

Chapter 10

~~⚘~~

November 2024
Remy

  Everything felt right on schedule upon waking this morning. The houseboat was slowly swaying in the water, the smell was right for this time of year. With the pleasure boats not in season the water was calm, gently lapping against the pontoon that keeps me afloat. I prepared for work just like any other day but knew something was off, I started the car vividly remembering Phillip's expression when I placed him in the trunk. He was not expecting me to thwart his nasty plans. He had been used to bullying us around for a meal he had probably gotten for free. Maybe that is what is wrong with my day. Thoughts of Phillip, maybe even a dream of him but none that I can remember. My intuition tells me something else is off.

  When I pull into the alley a wave of caution falls over me. I tell myself I am being paranoid this is just like any other crisp morning with no one around. As I exit my vehicle and open the door the cold, which has never bothered me all these years, suddenly feels as if it is bouncing off my skin and chilling to my bones at the same time. I need to get into the bakery where the ovens are, and the wind is not part of the morning anymore. I am stiff with adrenaline racing through me. My senses have never steered me wrong; I am exceedingly aware of every possible movement or noise that I think is happening between my car and the door to the bakery. I know something is not right today.

I lock the alley door behind me and check the bakery. Every window, both doors, the till, safe and storage closet; it all appears to be in order. This makes me more antsy to not know the source of my anxiety.

I go to the kitchen and check the back door again. It is for sure locked. I look out the front windows to the street seeing as far as I can up and down the sidewalk from different angles. No one is out at this time of day, just a few birds and an occasional car or someone waking from ally sleeping as the city comes to life. I return to the kitchen feeling more on edge than I ever have, look at the clock and realize I am almost thirty minutes late starting the cupcakes. Not that we don't have enough for the morning crowd, but I have a system, and everything should be in the mixer and on speed two by now. I quickly gather flour and sugar from the back room, placing a wedge under the door in case someone tries to lock me inside doing the same when I get the eggs and butter out of the cooler. This has gone too far, no one is around, today is the same as every other day except I know it is not. It is the day I give Mrs. Peterson the final check for this place that I have worked at, owned and acted like I am a normal member of society, but I am not. Maybe it is that my plan for escape and a new life have become reality. As my thoughts race and take me to warmer climates and out of here, away from my secrets the front door open with a gust of wind blowing leaves all the way into the kitchen. This brings me back with a charge. It is too early for Elora to be here. I move behind the wall next to the doorway leading to the lobby for a better vantage point as I hear a laugh. It is Elora. She is half an hour early and with me being half an hour late after all my shenanigans, I am extremely off, and it isn't even 7:00 am. She says there is a special order of sixty cupcakes for an unexpected going away party at Wright's Printing Press on 7th. She thought she had told me, but I am sure that is not the case. I get out the boxes for this delivery and load them myself with a variety of cupcakes from yesterday. I will even deliver them just to get out of here for a few minutes and regroup. Elora helps me load them. I'm watching the alley like never before when, Elora says "Hey Remy, are you okay?" I look at her like she is missing marbles and respond by pointing at the boxes of already loaded cupcakes with a nod then another bigger one, so she understands everything is fine acting as if the surprise order has thrown me off. I am glad the back door locks upon closing so Elora will be safe from that direction anyway.

Once I drive away, I circle the block three times, scouring the alley, sitting in different vantage points to watch. Upon my third pass I see Elora open the front door and stare at me as I drive, acting as if I am not there. She knows something is up, but I can't tell her what since I do not even know.

I deliver the cupcakes to the front desk and Hector is there dropping off an order of company business cards. I hadn't seen him since the last photo shoot at the beginning of November. We have never spoken much. I just know his name from eavesdropping on conversations he has been in. He eyes me with recognition but doesn't speak to me. We nod at each other; I know he is connected to the police department somehow but also am sure he works for August Island Rike Paper Company. On our next encounter I should get to know more about him. It couldn't be a coincidence I see him on this day when I am out of sorts. I leave the cupcakes with the receptionist who hands me a check which is unusual since most of our business is prepaid, then I leave, thanking her. Hector walked out and said, "hi I see you every month at the Arboretum" and introduced himself. We chatted a bit his hair coming up off the top of his head like a paper plate blowing in the wind. I wasn't sure what to say, being shocked by his forwardness after months, if not longer, of us being acquainted in the same group. I turned to my vehicle so distracted I realized I hadn't said anything, turning back I gave him my name and explained I was in a hurry for the next delivery. Which I know wasn't true, but Hector didn't, or did he sense my edginess? Hector turned towards 6th Avenue and broke out in a full speed run away from me as if he could feel what I did and wanted to be as far away from me and this mixed-up morning.

Chapter 11

November 2024
Elora and Remy

I arrive back at the bakery a few minutes later wishing I had somewhere else to go so I won't be analyzed by Elora who knows something is up. I drive by once and head into the alley as usual so as not to raise any more suspicions. When I enter there is a police officer sitting a table next to the window. I wonder why I hadn't seen him when I drove by just moments ago. Elora looks guilty, like she has told them something about me. Something I wasn't even aware she had caught on to. All I know for sure is that this day is off everywhere I turn.

I'm unsure whether to stay in the kitchen and pretend I don't know about the officer in my bakery. Since he hasn't seen me and isn't acting like he knows I'm here, even though he likely heard me enter, I'll stay in the kitchen to avoid drawing attention to myself. He is taking notes at a high rate of speed as Elora answers his questions. I look around the corner again, I hear the bell on the door ring and the officer waves at me, not acknowledging Elora at all.

Elora turns to me with dread in her eyes. She says she has to tell me something and should have long ago before the police arrived at work. She apologizes and sits with her back to me. I knew this day was not right and hoped the police were not here for me and the crime relating to Phillip. I can't think of any other reason they would be here. Elora turns back, looks me in the eye and says she has always been a reliable employee and needs help.

Elora says, "Niko has gone off the wagon for the twentieth time. I have been taking care of him, probably enabling him for years. It has only been the two of us for the past ten years since mom passed away. Dad was in the picture here and there more there than here. This time Niko has gone too far. The neighbors have had enough, we have moved twenty or more times in the past twelve years. Not long after mom passed the first time, we just couldn't afford the place with only my income. Mom's gone with her and Niko has not been able to hold a job since he was younger with so much potential. He went to the University of Washington graduated with honors in 2011 holding a Bachelor of Science degree, then he just turned off not long after that. He worked for a short while and enjoyed his freedom after graduating and one day he decided to not be part of society. Like it was all too much to get up and go to work, he thought his boss didn't know what he was doing, other employees were not on the right track or doing what they were hired for. Niko just quit thinking he was too smart for this entry level position; he started hanging out under the Viaduct not mentioning to me that he was no longer working. Somewhere downtown with his final paycheck he purchased Krokodil a drug I had never heard of and has not returned to his usual loving self in a decade or more."

  This time he couldn't find his drug of choice after being released from rehab for the fifth time, his dealer had moved on, been busted or died. He had resorted to Corn whiskey that he acquired on the street his usual mode of purchase. He couldn't just buy beer or other alcohol from a store. He had to get something homemade with who knows what type of dangerous chemicals in it. Whatever he had ingested this time had not set well with him or the neighbors who have put up with a lot from him. Making excuses for him when he passed out in the entry way either stepping over him or helping him home, me surprised each time at the memory being intact enough to arrive at the correct location since we have relocated frequently. Me finding him in a chair that will need to be replaced immediately with his bodily fluids leaking out of him in such a comatose state. This time he was laying barely behind the azalea bush with the pink smelly flowers naked, his clothing in a pile soiled and folded by the front steps. No one was sure if Niko was alive and unwilling to help him up the stairs being naked.

I am listening to Elora but realize I am relieved that this mess is not my ordeal and that my anxiety is over like a reset but there is still a small doubt in the back of my mind. I return mentally to our conversation hearing her say she doesn't know what to do this time. She can't continue working and paying for his roof and food but is divided about putting him in rehab and moving while he is gone so he can't come back. I know now why I don't have attachments and live a solo life. These types of decisions are not something I wish to make or be involved in at all. I let Elora talk for a while longer then against my better judgement ask what can I do to help? Elora says she knows she will just go home, find a new place to live and take Niko with her. That has been the decision she has always made. She is unable to have the real life of someone her age; she missed her twenties and now the thirties are starting the same way. Niko has to get better, as she states. We both know that is not how this story will end. I am grateful she did not ask for assistance and regret I know anything about Elora and now her brother Niko. He will either go on or not, but I hope I do not hear more. He better not show up here naked. With that thought I turned and asked Elora if Niko knew where she worked. She shakes her head from side to side indicating no but I know that is not true. This is another sure sign that my plan to sell and move on should happen sooner rather than later. Returning to the kitchen I see this morning has not been the usual day, the mixer has dried up batter sticking to the large silver bowl, cupcakes are on the sideboard well past cooled off, the pink frosting has set in the large newly purchased glass bowl. I have never in all my year been this inefficient with my time but am thankful the police were not here for me, and all is well with my plan to sell the bakery and escape town for my sanity. The chances of being caught now for Phillip's murder are slim.

Once Elora had left for the evening, I sat a long time knowing I had built a small empire and needed it to protect my investment. She had to go; she couldn't work here with Niko getting worse. Now the police were showing up. I do not want any dealings with them. Worse yet what if Niko shows up naked or passes out during business hours. Customers would soon realize that Elora knew him. I couldn't have that here. I would have to fire her or sell sooner and leave the tragic story she had just relayed to me out of the sale. No one would need to know I knew this. I am good at keeping secrets. What if it didn't sell quickly enough or Niko came here tomorrow or even at this moment? Now I am back to the mental state I was in this morning. It was not how I have acted before today, maybe the crime of my past is just weighing on me. It is odd to wake up this way one morning, a day so close to my departure from this life.

Now to figure out what to do with Elora, should I be supportive but actually not. Give her a bonus and send her on her way? She has been loyal to me all these years but that was before I knew the truth. This is why

80

people should keep their business to themselves, but she had to tell me something since the police were here. Looking back, I wish she had lied to me and said it was about an incident on the street that she had witnessed. There is no turning back from the new roles we are playing now. To be honest I feel extremely bad for her, but she is choosing to put up with Niko out of love for him. Apparently, this has gone on a long time. Probably the entire time she has worked here and there hasn't been trouble brought to my door before today. I will watch a week or two before deciding if I should let her go or act like the situation didn't bother me. I leave out the back door just like any other night but with more on my mind than usual even staying later on this shift. Now I am aware of carrying the burden of Elora and Niko which I have always carried but the situation has just been made known to me. I back out and there is a crunch behind my driver's side rear tire, it is an empty bottle in a brown paper bag that is now disintegrated by my tire marks and the rain that has been falling all day. Kicking what I can between the rear wheels I get back in and proceed home not bothering to throw it away.

As I take my usual route home turning on Denny Way towards I-5 and turning north on Eastlake Avenue a patrol officer heading southbound turns on his lights and flips around. I become so paranoid this is new to me. Yesterday and every other day of my life I have held a quiet confidence, had the stature larger than most and didn't have a care in the world. Today I saw the police and pull over for no reason, he is in the inside lane probably enroute to a call not related to me or Niko who is involved in my thoughts. If this continues Elora will have to be out of my picture. I just need to get out of town without any speed bumps blocking my exit.

Pulling into my parking area I noticed a gray van in my designated parking space. This entire day is off, it worries me that someone could be at my house looking in my files that are not exactly as I want them to be. That is another thing I need to take care of. Being on edge I proceed down the stairs, turning to the left and seeing a stranger leaving the boat next to mine with a heavy cardboard box and struggling with the key. Being as on edge as I am today worrying about being seen here then coming back to reality and knowing I belong right here like I have my entire life. I need to get a grip on this feeling especially since I have no idea why I feel this way.

For dinner I called in a delivery order of Phillips' famous dinner of chicken Parmesan, salad and bread sticks. Maybe this will clear my mind. I waited not wanting to encounter anyone and requested it be left at the door. Getting out my own plate, bowl and silverware is a ritual for me. It has to be just right. Already normalcy is returning until I get the food and cannot eat with the smell reminding me of Phillip and his sneer. I scrape it off my plate, climb the stairs and dump the food in the community dumpster. Then I get in my car and drive to the restaurant where I left Phillips' body, which is now a club of some sort that has pounding music exiting the back door and a couple patrons smoking in the outdoor covered tent. Playing out this scene from my past and the beat of the music covering it has broken my anxious feeling, I think. I drive back, enter my parking lot, suddenly get tired, take the stairs past the ones I need and walk the docks a bit before retiring for the night, skipping dinner altogether. A good night's sleep ahead just like normal.

Chapter 12

November & December 2024
~~August~~

  Saturday is dreary and quiet, with my late-night decorating and spiced hot chocolate. I had every intention of going out and creating a life, but I stay in my pajamas and enjoy the tree, the smell and lights are comforting. I don't believe I have completely relaxed since moving here. All the events that are behind have overcome me this weekend as if leaving work on Friday was a door opener of emotion. I need rest, but my mind would not stop until last night. There was something about the synchronization of decorating the tree by myself. An act I have never done. It was always about someone else and their ideas. The tree brought order to my compartmentalized life.

  About 4:30 pm there is a knock on my door, I have only had one visitor since moving here and that was mom. No one has even asked where I live and come to think of it there would be no one to ask about anything in my life, I don't know anyone here. I suddenly start to feel small in a city this large with no connections. I do need to get a hobby and meet some people. The knock happens again, see I am always somewhere else when I need to be here. I open the door, and it is mom, she is as surprised about the tree as discovering me in my pajamas on a Saturday evening at home alone. She said she sent a text without reply so decided to stop with dinner. If I wasn't home, she would have food for a couple of days.

She wants to talk, wants to know where Alice is, what about my job, do I plan to stay here and work, is this apartment temporary? She says she will feel better when she knows if it is not invading my privacy. She realizes we have lived apart for more years than we were together. I unravel the story backwards. Starting with the call from her and long drive here unwinding the spool all the way back to Alice moving, the house sale and my decided departure from Green Mechanical. We look at our food as I talk but don't eat, boxing it up for later. We have hot chocolate with a splash of rum; Mom only wants a capful as she is driving. She looks at me and says, "welcome home son."

Sunday is equally dreary outside, me realizing I have missed this weather. I set my GPS for Kenmore Camera, wishing for a drive further than just up the road. I head out and take Bothell Way looping around the north end of Lake Washington, memories automatically flood me with Ron Sanborn and his ski boat, the summers spent at the lake. It has been more than two decades since those events, wild long hot summers. He was also an avid snow skier, but I never went to his family's chalet at Crystal Mountain. Before I know it the soothing voice of GPS says take the next left and your destination is on the left. After pulling into the parking lot, feeling good about my progress of getting out of my house, I enter the store with my newly found confidence and see I am out of my league again with this event similar to buying shoes recently. I have entered a serious camera store that sells various styles with all different letters, looking about with each camera brand and model numbers it reminds me of types of airplane models.

After an incredible amount of patience on Willow's part with me having no knowledge of cameras I now know how to load the SD card, set up my tripod, own a backpack for all the other accessories and a Nikon D 7500 to experiment with. I will enjoy photographing the city. I am being true to my nature and mentally downtown at an outlook viewing point when I should be here in the camera store in Kenmore. Willow hands me my receipt, tells me to feel free to call with any questions, included in the paperwork is a handwritten note about The Seattle Photographic Society and a map of the Washington Park Arboretum. Under the map is a note that says maybe I will see you on December 16th at the entrance to the park 2300 Arboretum Drive E, Seattle. There will be a group of us taking photos of ornaments in the trees, bring one if you wish, Merry Christmas.

I get back in my car feeling like a new person with plans. I will for sure be there arriving with my dusty green ornament, newly purchased two days ago. I didn't know at the time of purchase that it would be involved in my new outdoor adventures. I look back at the store and cannot see in due to the last sun of the day reflecting on the glass doorway but know Willow is in there watching my departure. I roll down my window and wave as I exit the parking lot. I am exceedingly happy with my decision of photography.

 Heading east until Bothell Way turns, I remember eating at Spud's Fish and Chips as long ago as I water skied. I head south on NE Juanita Drive into Kirkland, seeing snippets of the lake and places to visit with my newly acquired camera. I know this is the right decision to come here and fully plan on attending the ornament party.

 Two weeks have flown by. We had the December birthday party for Erin and Hector on the first Friday of the month and then the company Christmas party. The Olde Spaghetti Factory on Pier 70 where they had held our annual Christmas party is gone. The employees were not happy with wherever they had chosen last year so they voted on a lunch at The Victor Tavern on South Lake Union on the afternoon of the 15th. They all decided there are too many obligations during this time for an evening event and ask my input on making this a company lunch instead. The food was great, I ordered The Victory Burger as I sat with this knitted group, I had a connection to. These people who relied on me to keep the roof over their head, food on their table and to supply their other needs in exchange for their loyalty to their job well done. December being here I have not sat and thought about all the changes of my life yet. Just looking at the newly inherited workforce of people and knowing they need me or someone in my place brings a sense of belonging. Taking over for my dad is a large investment of my time. I am still not entirely sure what my purpose at this company is but am slowly learning to be the leader, getting better acquainted with the staff while staying out of their space and assigning myself tasks like a boss would give me. The city is festive and buzzing with holiday excitement but not as full as I am with tomorrow being my ornament party. The past couple of weeks I have studied every aspect of the camera so as not to be a novice in front of this group and especially Willow. Purchasing this machine may have been a mistake, the basics like shutter speed, aperture, iso all are subjects to be studied separately and integrated together.

I am not fully at the Christmas party due to my outing tomorrow. I have the area mapped out, have driven there twice just to be certain of my destination. Sleeping will not be happening tonight, before my life flowed with work, home life and various outings but this is the first on my own since relocating to Seattle.

I leave at 9:45am almost forgetting my ornament, leaving ample time to travel and find an appropriate spot to park. I pulled in at the south entrance not knowing what to expect and find out who belongs to a photography club. Bus 11 stops across the street blocking my view of whatever I was mindlessly staring at. As it pulls away, I see a man looking similar to Hector inching around the rear of the bus trying to cross the street and ensure he will not get hit. He has a fancy camera hanging from his neck and a backpack identical to mine slung over his left shoulder, his gait is familiar as Hector. I feel uneasy suddenly barging in on his club, especially since I had been following him. I calmly get out of the car as he approaches the entrance to the park and retrieve my gear as if I had not noticed him prior to this. I am greeted with "hey, boss man." There is an air about him that shows a definite awareness of his surroundings and he appears comfortable with me being here. As we nod and part ways Hector talks with a few other participants in the group, and I can see he clearly knows these people. There is one other man I have seen before but cannot place him, hopefully he does not recognize me from the courthouse, or did I see him at the police station? In truth I need to wholeheartedly pay attention to faces and where they are from.

Seeing Hector has made me forget all about meeting Willow today. She is not in attendance as we proceed down the path heading north through the park, the trees bare, limbs sticking up as if stuck in dancing poses in the sky. I picture them with leaves but think I prefer the bare soul of the trees; it fits my life in this phase. Muriel, who is possibly the leader or someone with the idea of the single ornament photos stops and takes the first picture. Her camera is already set up on the tripod she has been carrying along in her right hand like she is an old pro. I realize I am not with this game; my camera is still in the bag. As I unzip it, I see the price tag dangling from the zipper pull, showing me off as an amateur. I slip over to a stump and quickly pull my camera from the bag, not feeling confident enough with the tripod to mount my camera on it with professionals watching. Hurried footsteps are behind me on the dirt path, it is Willow. She arrives with a simple smile, a silver snowflake ornament and a small camera, not what I was expecting. I pictured her with long lenses and a monster camera. We walked in the cold, being a few short days from winters' onset taking photos, thirty or so of us. They all know each other, me knowing two, possibly three if I could place the other man. It was over almost as soon as it began. We had looped around some way, I wasn't paying attention, there was Willow to watch with her precise movements. The other experienced members and Hector, who was quite agile, knew his way around a camera and this park. We went to Cloud City Coffee on Roosevelt Way NE after our outdoor event, me not realizing how cold I was until my return to the Atlas. I suddenly decided I needed another vehicle. I love this one, but Alice picked it out for us, and she is not here. It is time for me to get what I wish to drive. I followed the car ahead of me that had a person from the club, I cannot remember her name. I just know that Willow is somewhere behind me. Hector is at the coffee shop. I did not see who he rode with, nor did I think to offer him a ride.

It has been an exciting day so far, more activity than I have had in three months since I have arrived. The man I do not know is here too, he is in a corner having a serious discussion with the lady who appeared to have an immense amount of knowledge of plants and gardening. I see out of the corner of my eye she hands him a trifold brochure with a large red flower on the front. Willow and I talk about pickleball or at least she does, I know nothing about it, but she plays at a court across from here that we agree to meet at for a walk next Saturday. Maple Leaf Park, I wonder how many of this group will be there but don't ask. I am just grateful for this opportunity to meet others and slide into easy friendships with the mutual bond of the camera. Willow leaves, I ask Hector if he would need a ride home which he declines, me knowing I will look up his home address on Monday. I left heading west a different person that when I arrived, now part of a group and home to study pickleball.

Chapter 13

December 2024
~~Remy~~

  Baking has always been my outlet to any obstacle in life even as a child. When I met Mrs. Peterson, Lucine, and she invited me to an interview at Burgett's Bakery I am positive she was flabbergasted that a person of my age, seventeen to be exact, could possibly outperform her in the kitchen. After careful consideration I had decided on Italian Cream Cupcakes. My wellbeing, house, meals, and dignity were resting on this interview. She sat at a table in the dining area with her back to the kitchen, occasionally hollering out an ingredient, vanilla bean paste, buttermilk, coconut, as the smell of the batter traveled to her and the aroma of the finished product. I pulled the cupcakes out of the marvelous oven; one I would cherish forever and placed them on a wire rack to cool. Then I am not sure if this was forward or not, but I brought Mrs. Peterson a cup of tea and a cookie from the glass display case, ringing it up and paying out of my pocket before serving her. I knew she was watching me when she heard the till open but didn't say a word, just looked out the window with a smile on her face I could not see but know she was pleased by the remainder of her expression as she turned back. She probably did not have many chances to sit and watch people stroll by since working here as she was the sole baker. To my delight no one entered during my interview. I was able to have her full attention while making calculated precise steps to ensure a future for my brothers and me. Not asking if she would like some tea but placing the mismatched rose patterned saucer and delicate cup, a single cookie, and napkin in front of her I returned to the kitchen to make my frosting. We went through the same motions with this, as she sounded out with butter, almonds, cherries, and pecans. I plated two cupcakes, one for her and one for me, sat at the tables, me at the one next to her both covered with the black and white checkered table clothes. We ate in silence, her all the while taking a bite, carefully tasting and inspecting the cake's spring, density, sweetness, moistness and crumb. She turned to me and started talking business. "The delivery of sugar will be here later today, Wednesday butter, milk, cream cheese and flour will be arriving. I go to the whole sale market downtown for nuts, Selzer, spices and shortening. There is a file in the office with lists of specialty product and seasonal suppliers." Asking if I drove and would be able to handle the schedule of this and bake daily. Explaining most business is on a schedule of orders done on a monthly or yearly basis. She never said I was hired or commented on my cupcakes; she just asked me to be in at 6:00 am tomorrow. This is where it all started and ended.

Looking back at that moment I do believe Mrs. Peterson wished to be gone as much as I do right now, but it took her thirteen more years to let go.

I have had the pleasure of supplying the majority of the downtown corridor with cakes, cupcakes, croissants, dinner rolls, and other seasonal items. I do not make bagels; they were a suggestion but there is an unspoken agreement between Fenton's Bagel House and us. They remain making only bagels and we take care of the rest. They are kitty corner from us on 4th Avenue. On Fridays we exchange products, never telling each other what the exchange consists of just a box with four items inside.

In 2013 Mrs. Peterson wanted to take me to dinner. We met at the base of the Space Needle, the wind was blowing, rain plastering our clothing to our frozen bodies. I was wondering why she didn't even look cold when I was freezing, we both lived next to an oven most of our waking hours. We ate in the Seattle Center food court. This surprised me as I would not have pictured her here and had never toured the city much even though I grew up here, not ever thinking of eating here before. We had a simple dinner of turkey sandwiches, chips and soda. This evening felt off to me as I had never been asked to accompany her anywhere, even though we worked together almost daily. Our lives existed in the kitchen almost silently for the past thirteen years. I don't recall her ever revealing any of her activities to me, never seeing her leave with anyone but everyone knew her. She pulled a legal folder out of her puffer jacket and started explaining she would be selling the bakery and asked if the terms on the paperwork would be suitable for me never outright asking if I wished to purchase. I didn't have any other offers, nor had I thought about owning anything except my houseboat but quickly scanned the legal document, signed it and she said, "payments are due by the tenth of each month, I will not be back in to work." That was ten years ago, and it was the best decision I could have made. It was a ten-year contract and today Mrs. Peterson phoned to say she would be by to pick up the final payment at 4:00 pm so as not to disturb the flow of customers.

Mrs. Peterson was five minutes early, always punctual. She used her key at this time of the day as I locked the door while cleaning so unwanted guests didn't surprise me. A few months prior I thought I was a goner when an unfortunate wild eyed, bushy haired man who stunk up the place walked in through the alley door demanded money and food saying he knew who worked here. He was lost and needed directions from the lady out front. I had already emptied the till for the day except for the change and smaller bills that would be needed for the next business day. He didn't know that as he stared at me through the greasy dark ringlets that had fallen over his face. Somehow, he looked familiar to me, but I could not place his face in any situation. Was it the eyes, the expression? He was very familiar to me but a stranger for sure. I thought of my work here for nearly ten years to the point of owning this business and now I could be erased, that would in reality be justice served but no one knew. After my refusal of money, he grabbed a box of cupcakes and fled. I was relieved he was gone but the thought kept surfacing of where I knew him from.

As Mrs. Peterson entered, I could feel her agitation, something that had not ever emanated from her prior to now. Possibly she was upset due to my final payment being made today and the contract fulfilled on my part and her final separation from this business that she had poured her entire life into. My check was ready, along with a pen sitting on the long wooden shelf that held the baking pans. I was honestly relieved to be through with this end of our business. Every month I had to meet with Mrs. Peterson at the location of her choosing to pay. She wouldn't allow direct deposit or for me to mail a check, it had to be her way. With all the payments complete I could replace the booths and tables with any color I want, she would no longer have any say. The contract stated in paragraph 16 as she reminded me upon almost every meeting that I would keep the colors and name of the bakery. She walked past me saying something under her breath. I figured she was trying to locate one last item to take as a memento of her service to this city. She turned sharply with fury emanating from her entire being, violently pointing her finger at me, if I hadn't taken two steps in reverse, she would have poked me in the chest. I attempted to let her know I had the check, hadn't made any violations to our fully executed contract, and tried to make sense of her fast-paced speech. As her volume increased, I retreated to the dining area forgetting the check. She followed saying, "I am on to you and your horrific antics, I know, I know." I had no recollection of her accusations; she didn't tell me what she was there for. Suddenly I thought I had never seen her upset let alone raging mad prior to this moment. She didn't have the contract and wouldn't accept my check. Then in the kitchen she said she was going to the authorities, and she would own the bakery again. I am not entirely sure what happened in my mind at that moment except I knew what she knew, and she could not go to the police. She had known them longer than I, but I know them also and supply their functions, they frequent this place on their beat, stop in for cakes for family birthdays and other celebrations.

Grabbing Mrs. Peterson's arm was the last memory I had before I had to dispose of her body. First, I needed to get my last payment to her house, find the contract and forge her signature. I am not good with this, have never faced death like this, used my hands for any violent acts or for sure not killed anyone in the kitchen of my bakery or anywhere else. It was difficult for me to search her purse for her keys knowing she would have to stay here next to the floor drain with her head cocked to the side until after dark and I had supplies to move her. There was a noise in the lobby like a chair scuffing on the floor before someone stood up. After my brief investigation I was mistaken and my mind paranoid realizing the noise was from the alley. I suddenly was glad, an unusual feeling at this point, but glad nonetheless that she had taken the bus, and her vehicle was not here but in her garage at home or so I hoped, eliminating less proof of her arriving here.

 I changed into my dark green, insulated parka, took one last look at Mrs. Peterson, feeling terrible for my act of hostility but justifying it with all I had to lose. As I exited the bakery from the front, slowly walking by each window peering through to ensure no one could see from any vantage point what I know is in the kitchen, Mrs. Peterson. Not a piece of her body or clothing showing not knowing how she got there, that piece of my memory gone. I take the bus to her residence after looking up the schedule on the map right outside the bakery and one block west, not risking an online trail of my activity. Before boarding the 358 accordion style bus I check one more time for Mrs. Petersons keys and my check, which I placed back in the checkbook to ensure it would be flat, they are both in my zipped jacket pocket. I am not used to these gloves and am uncomfortable but don't want to leave my fingerprints on anything except the check where they would naturally be. I arrive in north Seattle, as I walk the block to Mrs. Peterson's a person waves at me. I think a man but with darkness falling on the city and a glare forming on my sedan from the streetlights reflect off the window my mind is not entirely here. I wonder who would think they know me here; must have been a mistaken identity. I enter her alley off North 46th St and Aurora Avenue North, look to be sure no one is at any of the neighboring windows or driving by, I am not doing well with my acts of deception of this plan but am sure no one sees me here, I desperately need the contract. Of course, it wouldn't be unusual for me to stop by especially this time of the month for the payment to be made. I should have started at the front door, knocked, and then used the key. This terrible mistake that I cannot pay for has led me to be careless as I am not used to committing crimes. I cannot concentrate or stop shaking and know I can't hold a conversation if contact with a neighbor should arise.

I walk by the side window and enter through the front which seems more logical at the time. I hear something inside, so I ring the bell, a small dog barks. Now there is a larger problem. I cannot leave it here since I know its owner will not return. I also cannot come by several times a day to walk and feed it. It must go with me after I find the contract, now dog food and any accessories. The contract is on Mrs. Peterson's desk. I suddenly realized I have never, on all the occasions of visiting, been anywhere except the front entry. I didn't even realize she had a dog. The dog is a small, wiry haired brown and gray friendly creature. It doesn't mind if I am here, even seems to be enjoying my nervous company. After signing the contract, being glad I brought my own pen so as not to use one from here, I took one copy and left my check on top of her copy. I retrieved dog food, a leash, dog toys and bowls all from the back linoleumed porch. As I hook the leash up to the turquoise collar, I see a tag. Remi is the dog's name. This day couldn't get any odder. Now I wonder if Mrs. Peterson named the dog after me or did it have its name when she acquired it.

I exit through the front door after looking out several times, the dog keeping his eye on me with each move. I walk several blocks knowing I do not wish to be seen with the dog or the bag but do not want to order an Uber anywhere near this residence. After about a mile, carrying the large lawn bag of dog paraphernalia and the dog who is obviously not used to walking, I sit at a bus stop and order a Lyft, not to the bakery but a few blocks north on 3rd Avenue.

We arrive at the bakery, me and Remi, the dog who immediately runs to its owner. With the sidetrack of the dog, I had completely forgotten about supplies to dispose of the body, placed her keys back in the coat pocket I retrieved them from, placed my copy of the contract in the file with the original purchase agreement, returned the company checkbook to the locking desk drawer on the right and took the two steps back into the kitchen seeing the accusing eyes of Remi staring at me knowing I had caused this mess. In my paranoid state I imagine the dog talking to everyone about this. I transfer the dog stuff from its original bag, put Mrs. Peterson in the bag, wrap the sheeting from the flour delivery around her, tie the dog with his leash to the cold leg of the stainless-steel table and go to the dumpster several businesses down to dump my bag. After walking a few steps back, I realized I need to retrieve the outer wrapping of the bag, it could possibly be linked to my business. I have to climb into the dumpster and grab the bag. I turn the body over a few times, under a dozen, but it feels like an eternity. I dispose of the excess plastic in my dumpster as it would be a usual item to be there, look at my watch and see it is after 8:00 pm. The garbage will be picked up in less than twelve hours. I have no idea what happens after that, I have never had to imagine what would happen to a body or the garbage. Once back inside I need to come up with a plan for the dog, he cannot come to my house. How would I explain where I got him? What if he is chipped to Mrs. Peterson? I fret about the options for Remi, being an animal advocate, I will not leave him at a shelter or just turn him loose.

After returning to the bakery Remi was happy to see me even though he didn't know me. I place him in the dining area, thoroughly cleaning the kitchen, feeling more remorseful by the moment. Just knowing Mrs. Peterson is in the alley is more than my conscience can handle. I have never been faced before this moment with any misdealing that I have created. Phillip was a different case as he was going to cause harm to Everett and Logan. Guilt overwhelms me as I clean the floor, even washing down into the drain so as not to leave any traces of my crime. I feel the need to look at the contract again. It is not signed by Mrs. Peterson, only me, now what to do, I could blame this on her age, she simply forgot. I still do not know what to do with the dog, suddenly it seems it will make all of this go away if I take the storage blankets from the back room and sleep in the kitchen with Remi.

After a cold, uncomfortable night on the tiled floor where Mrs. Peterson had laid, I walked the little beast at 3:00 am feeling sad for him. He knows his master is gone but will walk with me as I decipher a plan for his little life knowing I will not keep him. Every time I looked at him, I would think of Mrs. Peterson. We return after our alley walk, staying out of sight. I hear the garbage truck in the distance knowing it will not be long before contents of my round black bins in the alley will be disposed of. As I put the key into the lock I see just to the right of my rust-colored steel door Mrs. Petersons purse. Her handbag, pocketbook, clutch all the purse words flying through my head when I am forced into this discovery. Instinct tells me to place it in a can now, but I stop just before touching it, running in to grab a towel to pick it up so my prints will not be visible. I leave the dog in the kitchen, pick up the purse just as the garbage truck rolls in the alley illuminating me holding a purse with the towel. I quickly pick up some other ever-present rubbish and place it all in my dumpster. Making the story up as I went to work as usual 3:00am to start baking and took the shrink-wrap out, which I hope was still there from last night, that was when I found the empty handbag. This was a true story, but I am not entirely sure the purse was empty. I was shaken to the core and had not even thought about anything further than knowing someone had opened the bag with Mrs. Petersons body, another human knows she is dead. Most likely they have her driver's license and the rest of her identity that was located in her handbag.

I return and start baking like this is a normal day. Today has appeared exactly like any other when that is so far from the truth. Remi is a help, and I discover he likes strawberries as I bake the muffins. He is happy to help with all the tasks, following me to the ovens, dishwasher, and display case. I just remembered, there are far too many pieces to this undesired puzzle, I do not know where Mrs. Peterson's car is. After finding the dog I forgot to look in her garage. I am not an experienced criminal. At 6:45am, just before Elora arrives to serve the customers, I transfer the blanket, Remi, and dog gear to my car. I need to protect my seats from muddy footprints and evidence the dog was ever with me.

Returning to the bakery alone, Elora arrives, I run errands as she thinks but I see a look in her eye and know she suspects something. Our relationship has been similar to mine and Mrs. Peterson, we know virtually nothing of each other's personal life. Seven years ago, during one of her initial days employment, there was an incident where she attempted to assist by removing a tin of 24 muffins. Misjudging the weight, she almost dropped them but managed to catch the tin with her other hand, burning herself in the process. Upon noticing, I promptly grabbed a towel, dampened it with lukewarm water, and laid it on her burned hand to prevent further damage. As I briefly touched her wrist, it was like fire or some power I had not felt before. I knew then to back away as I do not form any bonds with anyone. She did a great job with the customers, but I did not want to know any other part of her story. She came in this morning, walked around taking deep breaths, checking the kitchen, looking at me, which felt like an hour of interrogation but was only a minute or so. No questions physically asked but her eyes telling me she knew something. There was no way she could even begin to guess the truth. She put her coat under the platform where the cash register is located and went to work as usual. I raced to my Subaru worrying about the dog being alone in the alley of an enormous city, just realizing Mrs. Peterson was no longer with us. The facts racing with me missing crucial pieces of the story. I get in Remi greeting me as if I am his, we head north to North 46th Street turn right off Aurora entering the alley slowly so as not to make any noise. I need to check the garage for Mrs. Peterson's car. It is a relief the gray Fiat is in its place. If anyone asks why I am here it is to get Mrs. Peterson to sign our contract. I noticed from the corner of my eye a light just turned on in the laundry room where I had found the dog food. I saw someone walking through the house. I proceed to the front, glad I put all the dog products in my trunk, let the dog out with me, his red leash trailing on the sidewalk, dreading my next lies as I knock on the door, contract in hand to ask for a signature. Remi bounces around glad to be home, after his city adventure and me suddenly happy he is not able to relay his discoveries. A man I have never seen before answers the door quickly like he had been on the other side before I rang the bell. I am not sure if I should acknowledge the dog was in my car or come up with the story of it running up to me outside. The man doesn't look at me first thing because the dog jumps up as the man grabs him calling him by our name, making this awkward. Holding the dog, he asks me where Lucine is and why I was walking the dog. A lady appeared from the kitchen telling me they had just returned to town after a business trip and Lucine, Mrs. Peterson, had been dog sitting. They returned and she wasn't here. Remi was gone along with his food, bed, and toys. I knew I was not producing any of those items, glad they were safely in my trunk and the blankets on the floor of my car so I could stick with the story I was building with each moment.

They asked if I had been walking the dog. Turns out the leash being attached was helpful to my part of the investigation. They think Mrs. Peterson was close to home on a dog walk. I told them he was outside when I pulled up. I grabbed the leash to get a closer look at his tag for a phone number or other contact information discovering his name is Remi, I started to laugh. They both look at me and say, at the same time, "who are you? I showed him the contract needing the signature of Mrs. Peterson, asking if she was in. Then I say my name is Remy. They look at each other more puzzled than I can imagine. Their entire beings turn to concern at this point, them wondering if Mrs. Peterson has taken the dog in the car with all his belongings, which doesn't make sense. Me almost piping up saying the car is in the garage but catching myself in time and making a deal of the dog and I having the same name and talking to him as if we just met and had not spent the night together. The couple runs out to check the garage for her car, Remi following them. I stand in the entry way and decide to walk to the back door to look out as they look in the garage. Realizing this is a good reason for my shoe prints to be through the kitchen and laundry room. This visit has solved a couple of my dilemmas. Now to make an exit from here once we have a plan to find Mrs. Peterson, I offer to drive around looking for her and later I will locate a place to dispose of the dog essentials. I feel guilty Remi will not have his favorite stuffed gorilla squeaky toy which resides in my trunk at the moment. I will try to figure a way to leave it for him.

They return quickly stating her car is here, Remi lifting his leg on the large maple tree in the corner of the yard. Me already knowing I will offer to look for her, they walk through the house seeing if her coat is there, keys, purse, all gone but do see my check and the contract on her desk. I swap contracts while they are looking around discovering the other copy has her signature replacing it with the one, I brought. Not being positive whether that was a good idea or not since I had told them why I was there. I leave, petting Remi on my way out, collecting a business card from Eric Stuble, Project Manager with his cell number in large letters across the bottom. I agree to call within half an hour, them going home to call hospitals and the police if needed. I report back in thirty-seven minutes, sitting on the steps placing Remi's stuffed gorilla on the porch, I realize I didn't have to get out of my vehicle or know where the Stuble's lived but relieved and being sure they did not see me take the dog last night since they were out of town. They answer before the first ring is complete, I tell them who I am and that I saw no signs of Mrs. Peterson along my route. They informed me the hospitals have no admittance of anyone matching her description, police say there have not been any crimes reported with anyone elderly in the past several hours. Eric says Remi could not have been out long since he was not dirty or had any debris on his wiry hair, but he does have an unusual smell of some type of cleaning product. Now I know I need to dispose of my bleaching solution, the blankets, and the dog gear.

By the time I return to the bakery Elora is her usual self, it is a normal day, all is well and back in place except my mind will not break off the unexpected endless loop of events that have happened in the past twenty hours. Just as I get to my office and relax a bit the front bell rings and I hear a man talking to Elora, I assume. She comes back to the office saying a cop is there to see me. My blood pressure rises past healthy levels, but I know I need to act concerned. I only had what maybe fifteen minutes of peace in the past day. Well actually twenty-four hours ago all was well I was just paying off the bakery, check written and ready but then the unfortunate chain of events started.

In walks an officer, he shakes my hand introducing himself as Detective Muncer. We both stand facing each other as there is only one flour covered chair in my office. I ask if he would prefer to sit in the eating area with me while we talk. I am not sure my legs will hold me up since they are shaking as I look down and see my trousers quivering from nerves of this unwanted meeting. There is also a dog toy sticking out from under the rolling table that holds my prized assortment of rolling pins, a marble one from my grandpa with wooden handles. I look back suddenly at Detective Muncer who is staring at me, then he starts the slew of questions as if I am guilty. He tells me he assumes I am the last person known to have seen Mrs. Peterson. He doesn't say seen alive to my relief; I am not entirely sure if I could have composed myself at the mention of that word. He asked when I had seen her last. I told him here when she brought the contract for me to sign.

Then he asked if there was anything different about that meeting. I stated she seemed a bit sad for the purchase to be final knowing the bakery she had created was not hers any longer. I state she took the check and handed me the contract and left. He asked if she had a dog with her, if she had been driving, what she was wearing. My answers were there was no dog with her that I saw, I don't know how she got here usually she takes the bus even though she could have parked in the alley, she was wearing her usual camel colored wool coat, dark pants and black gloves that she placed in her pocket as she entered. He said he had talked with the Stuble's and knew I had been there about the contract and the dog had arrived with me. I told him the dog appeared when I pulled up at Mrs. Peterson's house. He asked how frequently I went to her house. I stated only a few times a year to make the monthly payment, sometimes we met here if she was going to be in town. He seemed satisfied with my answers, told me he would be in touch then to my relief for this meeting to be over he started to leave, then turned and asked if she had a leopard print pebble leather handbag with her. It had been a gift from Sharon Stuble from a recent business trip to Norwalk, CT. I answered yes but kept a puzzled face, brows cinched together as if thinking. She kept her coat on only unbuttoning it with her purse hanging from her right elbow as we spoke, that is where she placed the check I had given her for the final payment. I recall it was a rather large handbag for such a little lady.

Josephine Plummer

Laughing at my memory, reassuring Detective Muncer, I would let him know if I thought of anything else. He turned to leave as if he was going to say something else but to my relief he just waved. Later I know he is on to me but not sure where I slipped up if at all. Relief flooding my entire being, suddenly I am exhausted with the last burst of adrenaline leaving my body.

Chapter 14

December 2024
Elora

All this sneaking around makes me nervous; I am on edge at home not knowing what Niko will do and at work being unsure if the Seattle PD will bust through the door wanting Remy or thinking that I am part of this scheme. I have been working here for ten years so it would make sense I know the practices here, but I stay in the dining area and Remy has the kitchen all to himself. I don't do any cooking or have anything to do with supplies being delivered.

Niko has been on me to blackmail Remy for this crime he committed. I need to know more about him; where he lives, where he goes, who he associates with and what he is actually up to when he is not present here.

As time goes on and the police are all over this place if only for coffee and a quiet place to stop on break, I feel the pressure mounting. Everything including Niko has set me off and his ideas. Without anyone knowing I purchased a GPS mini tracker for Remy's car so most of my questions about his whereabouts will be answered by my phone app. I have been concerned about cameras from neighboring buildings in the alley or Remy coming out for a trash run and seeing me place the GPS tracker, so I haven't done it yet. It must be today. This whole thing could explode, and I could be an accessory even though I am not and had no actual knowledge of the crime until Niko sprouted off and convinced me saying, "I know it is him." My suspicions have been on the rise for a while about something, but I generally try to keep my head down and just do my job.

I have studied the guide for the installation of the tracker and while it is still fresh in my mind it will be installed today. Remy has taken on the routine of walking around the block the past week or so, always at 1:30pm. I need to be ready when he leaves and turns the corner at the far end of the block and be back in the dining room serving customers as if I had never left.

Seeing him round the corner I open the alley door with a gust of wind almost knocking me over and so cold it nearly takes my breath away. With my hands shaking from the fear of being caught and the sudden cold I managed to install the device and return to the dining area just as a customer wants a refill on his coffee. All that stress happened in a matter of two minutes and I am the only one who has any idea I was not here. I was like a vapor who morphed into the alley and back again. Just as I am imagining that, while pouring coffee, in walks Remy through the front door, which is unusual for him. He looks at me like he suspects something, but I am positive he didn't see me.

After work I return home leaving as usual. I pull out my phone to see where Remy's car is on the app. He is over on Fairview Avenue. His vehicle does not move all night. I have the notifications on for anytime he travels. About 3:30am I see him traveling towards the bakery, knowing this will be a harder day than most since there is something to hide now. Before I just had the weight of Niko and his suspicions.

After work I decided to stop at the library on 4th Ave. I am not sure why I chose this location other than it is a warm place to be. I don't read much but will check out their sale section so I can buy a book to have on hand in case I need distraction while out on surveillance. Once I am seated under the grid of light coming from the glass ceiling, happy to have come here, being more comfortable today than I have in a long time. I know Niko will not be sitting next to me putting pressure on me to do something like when I am at home. I am enjoying the book cover and carpets that resemble the outdoors when my phone vibrates in my coat pocket. I see Remy is home, my curiosity will not be satisfied until I can physically see where he lives. I almost ran out of here, thankfully I have already purchased my book since there is a long line now. I hit the sidewalk running back to my car for no reason at all but drove towards Fairview Avenue wishing I had consulted my map before just taking off. There is no hurry for me to get there, last night he stayed in one location all night. Tonight, he will probably do the same, he is a man of precision. Just as I turn onto Fairview from Roy Street, traffic being heavy at this time of night, my phone vibrates again. I pulled into a Public Storage parking lot and tracked his location; he has just passed me on Fairview Avenue. I know I need to be more careful now. I hadn't thought he would leave home again tonight. I decided to stay here and read for a bit then go see where he was parked last night, hoping to find a place to walk to his location undetected. I drive north on Fairview Avenue, an area that I am not familiar with, the addresses aren't as visible as I would like. The early darkness that comes this time of year, and all the traffic of the evening rush hour doesn't help. People driving here act as they belong. I saw a brown sign for a park on my way north, turn around at Pete's Super Market taking note to shop here sometime soon. Going south I find the park on my right side and just before it the address Remy was parked at overnight. Where he lived had not ever occurred to me or truthfully anything about him. He always appeared put together and every step intentional.

After checking the GPS tells me Remy is in Renton just off 405. I hadn't watched his movement since I left the storage parking lot and had not received any notifications. I get out of the car in the parking lot that is not street side. Since the weather is close to freezing, not many people are here but I can clearly see most of the house boats through a spot up by the trees where I wouldn't be seen either. I checked the App again, this could become an obsession, stalking someone I don't want to have anything to do with. I think of the first few pages of my newly purchased book as I wait for Remy to arrive home. Knowing I am hidden enough for him not to notice me. Even if he did see me, I would just say I was meeting a friend, hoping I would be convincible. About twenty-five minutes later, none too soon, I am not dressed for this adventure. I see the GPS dot is right in front of me. My heart races having somehow missed the tone he was on his move north, then there is a slight turn left into his parking lot. I am so close I can hear his car door close. I decide to stay in this position a bit longer, not being good at this I realize that is the best decision I have made all along. I see him turn and go onto the second dock, three houses in and he is gone, out of my sight. I didn't realize I was holding my breath for so long, releasing it with a mist of steam from my now troubled lungs. It is starting to get dark, so I make my way back to my car, thankful for my book to keep my mind off this mission I am stuck on. The GPS stays quiet until 3:30am right on schedule for him. Today at work I know things will be awkward but only on my end. Remy doesn't know of the actions I have been taking.

I get up tired from rising at 3:30am and not being able to get back to sleep, my mind racing and the constant checking on the app to see where he actually is. Today will be long I know, just as I get into the shower I hear a crash, knowing Remy is onto me. I ran out of the bathroom in my towel, shampoo still in my hair, water pooling on the hardwood floor. It is Niko who is far past sober again. He looks at me and laughs saying something about being a bubble head. I return to the shower without a word to him knowing no matter what I say it won't make a difference. My actions from the past couple of days have been alarming to my peace of mind but I must know if there is another side to Remy. One I have suspected all along.

Work is almost normal today. Remy is baking and whistling as usual. The flavor of the day is chocolate, I know our crowds are larger on our chocolate days. That will at least make the day go faster. Remy cleans the kitchen faster than normal and comes to sit in the dining room with his chocolate cupcake. This is not entirely unusual but today it feels as if an eternity passed before he returns to his space. He does leave fifteen minutes earlier than normal saying he will be meeting a supplier which is also a routine event. Most of our supplies are delivered but some products he retrieves from spice shops in various parts of the city.

With the day wrapping up and all our customers having returned to their places of employment I sit at a table in the dining room, read my book, have a cupcake and watch the app as Remy drives home and parks. It is so good to read again, taking my mind off the strange happenings that I didn't ask for in my life. I figured he would remain home for the night, but he is back in his car on the move as if he is coming here. I don't need to

see him again today. It is time for me to close up. I
check to be sure the back door is double locked, turn
the lights off, slide the picture over next to the front
door to reveal the alarm pad and enter the same
number I have used for the past ten years, exit and lock
the front door. This routine, done five days a week, felt
like it took forever this time. I walk two blocks to my
car. As it warms, I check the app and see he is almost
past Renton again but continues south on East Valley
Highway just entering Kent.

   Suddenly I have a great idea to go to his houseboat.
This idea is so foolish like it is almost not mine, but I
continue on my route north and pull into Remy's
parking lot not seeing his vehicle. Realizing I need to pull
in at the park next door in case he returns home so he
would not see my car there, I pull out on Fairview
Avenue, turn right and park in the interior parking space
at Terry Pettus Park. I leave my vehicle, walk down the
road with great speed and slip into the stairway
unnoticed, I hope. I didn't even take time to look for
cameras in the parking lot. I know he entered the slip on
the left or right third houseboat in. They have made it
easy for me, his having the name Morilli on a stained-
glass plaque with a simple blue sailboat right next to the
front door. I look around a bit, notice his window is
open a crack, there is no turning back from here. I enter
through the window losing my grip as my tennis shoe
slips and nearly fall into the water with only my shoe
becoming wet.

I entered without anyone seeing me, the parking lot was empty when I came down, Remy was still in Kent and had stopped at a park. I took out my phone again and saw he was still at the same location wondering what his business was there. Making my way around this house that is ever moving, I open cabinets, drawers, doors being careful to use my sleeves to not leave fingerprints. Opening the old cedar chest, I smell the fragrant wood filling the room, also the odor of ink. It is filled with numbered files thirty-six to be exact. I hear the alert on my phone knowing he is on the move, seeing he is venturing into Kent aways behind the park I quickly pull out two files and read as fast as I can. He has parked again in the neighborhood. I check the address on Google Maps just out of curiosity and also see the park having no idea what he is up to, if anything at all. Each file I scan over has newspaper articles and perfectly handwritten miscellaneous facts, almost like an old library check out card with dates of filing in place. I look at my phone when I was alerted to his movement. There is so much information to take in, no way to read it all but I quickly snap pictures with my phone and realize I have stayed here too long. I watched him as I quickly closed the window while looking at the app and seeing he is on Fairview Avenue already. I exited out the front door like a wished upon visitor, locking the bottom knob and walking as fast as possible back to my car without drawing suspicion. I entered the parking lot and got into my car just as my phone alerted me Remy had stopped. I am not sure how we did not see each other in our passing but I can breathe now knowing he is home, and I made it out of there. I realize to my horror I have left evidence that I was there, a stupid mistake, one I should never have made. One file left on the round wooden table you could tell Remy eats at often. Salt and pepper shakers, napkins in an old plastic holder, a perfectly set place mat and silverware as if he is waiting to be served each meal. I am not cut out for this type of mission and am relieved I will never have to go there again. Now to act normal at work each day, which should be easy. I may even delete the app.

Chapter 15

December 2024

~~Remy~~

I leave home this Monday morning just like the other 1040 Mondays. The start of a new week. One closer to me departing this scene. Baking, baking, baking, that is what I do and what I am seen as, the baker. I feel resentful that my potential is not realized by all who take me for granted. Most people don't even have contact with me, they all talk to Elora who my gut feeling tells me I can no longer trust. I am not certain if I am being paranoid since I saw her at the table with the police. I have always had a rule to stay above the law and they won't make contact but now they are onto Niko and assume he has a connection to my establishment. This angers me to no end since I am attempting to make a smooth get away.

My parking spot in the alley is vacant but there is something against the back exterior wall of the bakery like it had been run over and blown up here. I am drawn to it instantly, touch it with the toe of my flour encrusted work boot and see Mrs. Petersons face on her driver's license. A piece of identity that I have not been privy to before this moment. Has it been blowing around the alley all this time, a few months? I will need to look at the contract for the exact date of her last appearance.

I stand in shock knowing I should grab something from the car and be rid of this piece of evidence when a spotlight hits me, and I put my hand on the latch to open my hood. The officer speeds the rest of the way up the alley, parks behind my car and gets out demanding I freeze and put my hands in the air. I had not seen this officer prior to this, he must be new. He barks orders at me asking questions on speed dial like they taught him at the academy, and he feels he must get them all out in sequence. He doesn't even know my name or why I am here, but it is positive he has caught me in the middle of his next big bust.

I get him calmed down enough to show him my ID, business card and that the keys I have in my hand open the bakery and my vehicle which I make the mistake of opening the trunk which holds the remainder of white bane berry. He relays to me at a right rate of speed not coming back from his surety of locating the murderer that there was a woman they think was murdered in this alley. I assure him I am here Monday through Friday every week and no one has been killed in this alley that I am aware of. He points to the dumpster across the way, tells me she was killed here and left in a large lawn bag in that dumpster. I ask if they know her identity, he looks at me as if he doesn't believe I don't know she was there. He tells me she is the owner of this bakery,

Lucine Peterson was left in that dumpster. I replied to him I was aware she was missing but not that she was dead. Last I saw her was when she showed up for my final payment and signed off on our ten-year contract.

He still does not believe my side of the story; his body movements tell a story of my guilt. I invited him in, he wants to meet me around the front possibly not sure of entering a building alone with a murderer. His motions are slower as if he is pondering my story coming down off the high adrenalin scene, he thought he was entering. He strolls back to his squad car, then pulls out of the alley rounding the corner. I leave the driver's license where it is for now, open the back door, go through to the front. I am not sure what he wants from me, but I need to bake for the regular customers today and the special orders. I ask what he would like to eat, if there is anything else he needs from me and explain I have to bake. Inviting him into the kitchen so we can visit, if he feels we must. I am acting almost normal but should throw him a piece of information in case he feels I am not being truthful. I rub my brow once I get my gloves on, shake my head and look at Officer Stanley with pain on my face. It is not a pain that is from Mrs. Peterson being dead, I have recovered from that already but an anguish all new to me. Maybe I will be caught. I wonder how they knew of her in the alley here. What is the coincidence of Officer Stanley showing up on the same day as Mrs. Peterson's driver's license?

He stands in the doorway between the cash register and the kitchen. I can feel the wheels turning in his head, he is new and wants to solve this crime but not today. There is no evidence, he finishes his muffin and takes his orange juice to go. Both Officer Stanley and I know of my guilt but only one of us can prove it. He thanked me for my time, giving me his card with his direct cell number written on the back in red pen and leaves.

Once he is gone, I lock the front door, check the back door which I failed to lock. I lock it a couple times, hoist the bowl from the mixer up onto the counter, make the precise scoops and realize I have not preheated the oven. His visit has put my morning and mind on another level. Once the cupcakes, which are forty-five minutes late, are set in the ovens I clean, get into corners like never before, under the metal industrial table I find a link, one that used to belong to a bracelet or necklace. This double checking was right on task for the day.

Elora shows up and has stories of Niko, ones I do not wish to hear I already have enough on my mind. Why did we go from many years of hello, how was your night to woes of Niko? I have not expressed interest in her life, nor do I wish to be confided in. This time Niko was arrested downtown, drunk and disorderly, harassing people for money in an aggressive way and taken in with pills on him. This is not the first time he has been in this predicament Elora says then states she is not bailing him out again. Life is peaceful during the moments when he is not her responsibility. I have the feeling Elora is thinking about escaping this area, running away to another city. I can see her mentally packing up and leaving. This job is a job but not a career and is one she could obtain anywhere. I ask if she is from here, she nods yes but states she doesn't have family anywhere. I never want Elora to leave as she fits my front counter position quite well, but I also feel with the Niko business being brought here I wish for her to go. She has become all too familiar with my business and ways, then there was the dog toy. I will not lay her off yet but hope she decides to move on. With the holiday season in full swing and extra orders this is not the time to make this decision.

My mornings arriving at the bakery have put me on edge once Officer Stanley interrogated me. Since the first day he showed up thinking I was a suspect he has been by frequently. Maybe not frequent to him but I see him as he passes through the alley at least three times a week, waves and turns the lights on for a brief second. His actions are startling every time I see the nose of his squad car turn down my alley like he is coming to visit a friend. I am filled with anxiety. Questions race through my head a zillion an hour. Will he stop and ask questions? Will it be the spotlight or colored bubble gum ones on top? It could also be worse than such simple things. I do not know where he obtained the information about Mrs. Peterson's body being across from my establishment, but will he come in one day and know the entire story? He stops about once a week with another officer, sometimes four five of them at a time. This is getting to be known as the place for the SPD to hang out, it is good for business and will help in the sale that will happen soon. They order a muffin and coffee on their breaks; radios squawking, filling up the lobby with tales of the streets. They always greet me like an old friend, like they actually know me. No one knows my secrets now that Mrs. Peterson is gone. With her confrontation that at least gave me options. If she had just reported my actions to the authorities, I would already be locked up. Right up the road and behind bars.

 After the first encounter with Officer Stanley I waited until 2:00 pm to go out and retrieve Mrs. Peterson's driver's license in case anyone else was watching or he was still here due to suspicion. That day I started a new habit of walking around the block looking for any more stray pieces of her life. I picked up the license with an old rag, added the link from the jewelry I had found in the kitchen and the forgotten dog toy that had been nestled under the right drawer of my desk and placed them into a bag that had blown down the alley. After finding out Mrs. Peterson had been discovered here, I am not comfortable throwing this new piece of evidence away anywhere in this vicinity. After work I will drive to Kent and take a hike to locate more of my Poison Hemlock. I have all the equipment I need at home to harvest enough until I can be gone from here forever. There are two gas masks, four heavy duty gloves, and two hazmat suits left. I purchased them all using cash nearly fifteen years ago and my calculations have been correct for the need I would have of each piece. They are always disposed of before arriving home and in a secure bag. I have been preparing for this last mission; it has been a regular ritual of mine for all these years as much as arriving for work before the city is awake.

I will leave a bit early today being antsy with this extra package stuffed under my trunk liner, return home, grab my gear and fully charged burner phone leaving my regular cell phone on the table so I will not be tracked. As I go through each day that is closer to the end of this part of my life, I feel I am on the outside watching since each task I do has been completed the exact number of times I calculated from the beginning. My life has always been a work of precision, and it could not have been that way if anyone else had been involved. It is like a doctor's orders saying you will need twelve treatments, and you know exactly what to expect by the tenth or eleventh. I am worn down, carrying a heavy load, my files are full, the gear is almost gone, the last part of my mission will be fulfilled in a few months, and I will be long gone on a beach with rays of sunshine and no more care in this world. Except it is all crashing in on me now. How can it be so controlled and exceedingly chaotic with all the extra pieces popping up all at the same time? I don't live this way, each move on my part is intentional, it is the rest of the world that is out of order.

I drove home with the bag of incriminating evidence under the floor mat of the passenger seat. It is ready for disposal when I get gas in Renton, since it should not be discarded with my hazmat suit making any connection to my other side job. I am not a criminal, a murderer or devious in any way. I own an upstanding business, run a clean blog that benefits the residents and businesses of Seattle by attracting tourism, I even returned Remi to his owner, the poor little guy who got caught up in this mess. Me being thankful I didn't have to make any decisions on what to do with him after sleeping on the floor with him in the bakery kitchen shows I am not on the wrong path. I do have a heart and wish no one ill will but people like Phillip and Mrs. Peterson should not have tried to stop what I am protecting. It is my mission, they simply got in the way.

Traffic is heavy as I knew it would be this time of day going southbound. Blending in is always the best, even if it appears I am just on an errand which I am. I get fuel in Renton just off 405 right before the I-5 exchange, it feels as if I am being watched. I know that is silly, but I am not comfortable fishing out the bag from under the floor mat. I paid cash, got my receipt, which is a stupid idea, more evidence of my route. That paper places me in this neighborhood but that doesn't exactly matter except I am at home with my cell phone and not here. I place the receipt in the garbage can next to the pump as a wind gust lifts it up to fly to the next pump. A very attractive lady wearing expensive office clothing catches it, walks over to me, looks me in the eye and asks if I could pump her gas. She has a story I didn't ask to hear about this being a loaner car since hers is in the shop due to an accident. I pump the fuel, wishing to be free of her but she has seen me, checked me out and could identify me. I am so extremely agitated at the actions of that business lady ruining my plans for the day. I completely forget about pumping my own fuel and leave unsure if I should continue south with the rest of my calculated journey or go home. I get back on 405 northbound smelling the stench of beauty bark just beyond the ramp my planned route diverted, a routine path chosen years ago and now her involvement has made me waver from my operation.

I pull in at home all tucked into my designated parking space feeling agitated but knowing tomorrow I must go after work for my final trek south. Following any rainstorm, I take the stairs carefully as they are steep, watching my footing and thinking of my brothers, mother and Phillip using this same entry way. I feel joy in knowing the brothers are safe now because of my actions. When my foot hits the bottom of the stairs and I transfer to the dock I am comforted by the movement of the water underneath my feet, know I am home and safe from any trouble.

When I enter, I see the newspaper story on Officer Dufort lying open on my kitchen table. I know I looked that one over last night before bed but do not recall it being out when I came home to gather the equipment for my journey today. I am surprised at my carelessness, of course I have never had so many out of sequence things happen before. Too many people, Mrs. Peterson with her so-called knowledge of my actions, Officer Stanley and his repeat appearance, Remi the dog, whoever was in the alley and discovered Mrs. Peterson's handbag and body, the lady at the gas pump. It is all their fault, even Elora with her insane brother that has brought the police to my establishment in the first place. Then I remembered the bag with all that evidence in it is under the passenger seat of my car and I did not get fuel. My worries multiply, do I even have enough gas to get back to the bakery in the morning?

I sleep as if I am on an airplane with turbulence. There are far too many unplanned occurrences. I got up at 2:00 am, half an hour early to get gas and rid myself of that bag in my car again. There is an AM/PM gas station on 4th Ave just south of Lumen Field. I pull in, the bag in my pocket to dispose of and get gas this time using my debit card. The cashier wearing his black emblemed apron approaches me outside while he is changing the receipt tapes on the pumps, probably part of his daily shift but why now? The only other person I see is an unstable person saying he wants to put gas in his stuffed giraffe so he can go to Paris. With two witnesses I decided not to dispose of the bag of evidence here, knowing the longer I have it the more probability I could be connected to Mrs. Peterson's murder if I am not already. The driver's license now burns a hole in my pocket but this time of the day anyone out will be watched even if they are an upstanding citizen and simply going to work. I will dispose of it on my journey after work to Kent, taking a different route so as not to run into the lady that increasingly makes me mad.

I am grateful my morning is progressing along without too many hinderances. I pull in the alley, hear the garbage truck but then realize the bag in my pocket that I could dispose of quickly before picking up has my fingerprints all over it. I pull out a pair of disposable gloves, retrieve the license, look at Mrs. Peterson one last time, get out Remy's toy and drop the link on the floorboard. The garbage truck is nearing my alley and not being able to pick up the link in time to place it in the large black dumpster I leave it and run to the one across the way where her body had been disposed of, carefully placing the dog toy in almost with regret. That is my last connection to that cute little dog, I did enjoy my time with him. He helped me get through the night from the shock of Mrs. Peterson's death. I close the lid, dispose of the gloves in my own dumpster and go back to get the metal link and it is gone. After searching for quite a while in the car and the alley I went inside to bake. The routine of that part of my morning is soothing; pouring, mixing, pouring again and then baking is a precise science to me and fits my personality.

I hear Elora enter, she generally pops her head in and says hello but not today. I peer around the corner to ensure she hasn't brought trouble to our doorstep since she is obviously having an uncivilized dispute with someone on the phone. I have never heard this tone from her in all the time she has worked here. She doesn't know I am listening to her. I hear bits and pieces of this side of the conversation. "No, I will not confront him, I need my paycheck, he has no idea I know, no he is not hearing this conversation." Now I am more uneasy about everything. What does she know? Is it Mrs. Peterson? Did Elora come in during that fight we had? Had she returned to retrieve a forgotten item? Is this what she knows? Is it even about me or could it be about one of my other secrets? I am rattled and have forgotten to take the morning muffins out of the oven at seventeen minutes. They have been in the oven twenty minutes but will have to work since I can't take it anymore.

Elora walks by the kitchen entrance and smiles. Doesn't even say good morning. I know her secret even if she does not know I am onto her. If I fire her she will proceed with turning me in for whatever it is she thinks she knows. I do not believe there is any evidence anywhere near here except the link that must have been stuck in the tread of my shoe since it is lying on the floor between Elora and me. I stay where I am not looking at the link and comment on the weather hoping Elora will prepare the dining area for our early morning customers. She does not, she enters the kitchen and says the muffins smell different. I told her I may need to get the ovens checked. She leaves while looking at me as if she doesn't trust me or maybe it is the one up look like she has something on me.

Once she has left my area and is back on her own turf, the dining room, I retrieve the link placing it in my pocket and clean the area. A couple more hours and I can leave. Now I need to worry about Elora and if she will steal from me, have me tailed or if she is giving information to someone, someone who already knows something. What is she telling them? Why is she backing me in a corner? What does she want? She is too visible to just be rid of and after Mrs. Peterson I don't need any further investigation. I will keep a close eye on Elora, maybe hang out with her a bit to make her uncomfortable or possibly observe something.

I jumped in my car almost peeling out in the alley. I realize my actions just as my tire catches from the spin. I don't need to draw attention to myself with the hazmat suit and now the link. Why won't all the evidence leave me? I take I-5 South to Renton and drive further south on East Valley Highway thinking of Elora and forgetting I was going to take another route today. As the road nears downtown Kent and turns into Central Avenue, I hear honking and see in my side mirror the lady from yesterday approaching in the right lane. Traffic is too backed up for me to gun it and get into the left turn lane. Thinking this is abnormal to see her again but check the clock on my dash and it is the same time as yesterday. She was next to me waving and honking. I turned up my radio before she was parallel with me and started bobbing my head as if listening to heavy metal music, not seeing or hearing her. Why is she here, I never asked to meet her yesterday and surely did not want to see her again. At the next intersection I merge into the left turn lane, luckily my light changes as I get there, turn and then turn right on the next block and enter a parking lot to ensure she is not following me, this crazy lady. I do not see her anywhere, but my nerves are rattled, and I know I am doing the correct thing for me by selling and leaving here forever. There is getting to be too much pressure from every direction.

At the next intersection I wait to cross four lanes of traffic during rush hour. Then pull into the parking lot, get my backpack out of the trunk with all my gear and walk deep into the woods where the trees bring shadows and light is let in through the evergreen branches as the wind pushes them about. I threw the link into the woods finally being rid of the third piece of evidence. Possibly the last connection between me and Mrs. Peterson. Placing my backpack on a fallen tree I get into my suit to harvest in my usual area, being careful and precise not making any mistakes. A feeling of sadness enters me as I place the rest of my harvest into the container, this being the last time I will ever be in this location. Years of my ritual are all behind me. I know it is pertinent that I stay clear headed during the next month or two while I wait for the bakery to sell and organize my move without anyone knowing I am leaving. The houseboat will sit forever, I don't care. My car left on the side of the road; my precious, organized files burned in a fire at a city park BBQ grill the day before I slip out of town. Everything is in place, removing my suit being careful not to contaminate myself I place it in its own bag and smile. As I near the garbage can closest to my car I see her, she is wearing spandex this time and not business clothing but there is no way around if I wish to return to my car I have to pass her. I act as if I do not see her. I can see out of the corner of my eye she has stopped stretching and is looking at me smiling. I open my backpack then I think I cannot dispose of this suit here with her watching. I am stuck with this now, there will be no throwing anything away with her observations. She is in front of me smiling as if we are long lost friends. I look up as if I had just seen her and smile like all is well even though nothing is ok.

   She held out her hand and introduced herself as Tanya Murphy. I shook her hand hoping I had not brought any of my harvest back on my hands. She stares then says well what is your name. Robert Edwards is the first name that comes to my mind, a simple and safe name. She gets in her car, reverses and starts to pull out, me thinking go, leave already so I can dispose of my final bag, and she rolls down her window says, "hi Robert I was thinking, I have a small issue at my house with my gate. I have been parking on the street since I cannot enter my yard. The gate is stuck, and I am not strong enough to lift it. Can you help me?" I do not know what has come over me yesterday or today, but I agree, following her the short distance to her house. It is an easy fix to lift the long chain-link gate back onto the roller. I am done in a matter of seconds. She is smiling, asking if I would like a cup of coffee for my troubles yesterday and today. I explained I will be late for a meeting if I don't leave now. She thanks me, says she is happy to meet me, and I get in my Subaru and wave. As I drive away, I think to myself she should not be so friendly with strangers. I would never harm her, but someone could. At least I didn't reveal my true name and hoped to never run into her again. I contemplate stopping at Denny's on my way home but drive back to where I belong and without any chance of meeting new people. I am unloading not adding to. Between the past two days my mind has not been in the right place, and I still need to get rid of the bag in my backpack. I see the park next to my house and almost turn in to dispose of this last bag but remember the garbage comes at home tomorrow morning. That feels easiest at the moment, but I know it will be a decision I regret later. I make a dinner of stew from my freezer and drink hot chocolate while I wait for it to warm up, gather every piece of garbage, clean out my refrigerator a ritual of mine on Wednesdays to take to the dumpster in the parking lot. Also putting on gloves to retrieve the bag in my car and deciding to dispose of the backpack too. One more secret gone from me. I felt content tonight as I descended the steps to the only home I have known and elated for a new future in the sun.

Chapter 16

December 2024
Detective Muncer

With Christmas season in full swing crime is up, monetary issues create strife in any household or neighborhood, and people are on edge having real or imaginary expectations placed on them. All the extra commitments, tension running higher in the home is spilled onto the street resulting in shorter fuses. All the extra activities required of us, though they may be fun, these activities are stressful at the same time. Parties, shopping, time to bake, acquiring the perfect gift, wrap presents, spend time with family, loved ones or trying to avoid relations with others that don't mesh well. This creates a toll on society, all the way down to street level. That is where I come in. The call at 3:07 am to have a conversation with someone who was planning to be at that exact location or not but now are required to be present, at least physically, and remember what happened in the worst moment of their life. Most witnesses don't see the crime scene the same way. Almost everyone says the person was wearing a different color clothing, driving another vehicle, height, weight, and direction left are all on levels almost as if they all witnessed several crimes but not the same one. Once a statement is made, they cannot go back and change it. Most of the time there is one witness and if there were more, they have fled the witness in attendance as I call them, not even sure of the direction the others departed. People who were not planning to be involved in a crime are not the best witnesses, they don't know the individuals involved, had only seen them for a second or two and did not know prior what was about to happen. Many witnesses are in shock and forced to be out in the dark, cold or rain waiting for the police to arrive. Truthfully, I am not sure why some call in about what they saw and stay at the scene of the crime to give a verbal report. If they actually don't know anything about what happened why are they involved? People who are not accustomed to the streets and find themselves in the middle of a crime scene may actually just be doing what they think is required of them as a citizen.

At any given moment in every major city, Seattle being included, crimes are happening, more than are reported, most never cross the desk of anyone. People look out and see something, but it comes out of their mouth for their own personal safety that they saw nothing. I learned many years ago, while still on foot patrol in Pioneer Square, that the one who says "I didn't see anything" is the one who knows exactly what happened. We, as a police department, are supposed to solve the crime but most of the time, we do not have cooperative witnesses or suspects that are caught red handed are released to commit more crimes right after processing to report to a later court date that they do not show up for. I do my job to the best of my ability for the safety of the people of Seattle. That is what I have been hired to do and will continue this mission until I retire.

Detective Martinez had some files he was working on when he was injured, one of the last days he was on the clock there was one file in particular he was certain of solving. I do not know where the files were kept as they would have been considered personal property as he had his own side investigation going. Getting a hold of Hector will be the best for now and see if he can meet me downtown to ask if he has run across the files since his grandpa's passing.

I return to headquarters entering through the alley, debris swirling by on this cold December night, badging in the door, and entering my code it does not open. It has been quite a while, at least a few days since I have entered here, not going in as often since I can email files directly. I wonder why I have been banned from this establishment. I need to enter to look up Hector's phone number. As I try again pulling the handle at the same time someone else is exiting it takes us both by surprise being used to using force to open this steel door. With one of us pulling and the other pushing it is opened in an exaggerated manner. Both of us were shocked at the result, her exiting and me entering.

Hazel is leaving for the day from her shift, and I am just starting on duty always preferring the night shift. We told each other at the same time about the door not opening on the first try. That's when we realized one of us was attempting to enter and the other exit at concurrent times and the safety mechanism designed for our protection worked. Hazel returned to her office saying she has seen Hector lately almost daily at the courthouse. Hazel always wears a Navy Pea Coat and has her military issue, dark blue backpack slinging from her shoulder. She retrieves Hectors number for me in an instant as if she knew exactly where it was, of course she is the records keeper and has a photographic memory of current cases and past unsolved ones. She can move from this moment to years ago, her mind being sharp and detail oriented. I had figured she would retire after her journey to see her friend in Eastbourne, but she came back as if she had never left, vaguely mentioning the trip or the friend she had gone to be with. I often wonder about that visit and her other short trips but do not invade her privacy. She takes a Monday or Friday off here and there. I am not sure what she is up to or maybe she just needs rest. I was imagining Hector having a cell phone recorded with us, it is for sure a land line that I recognize from the prefix. Hector has not been in any trouble, but we are all familiar with him as he grew up here, stopping in with his grandpa, frequently always excited and as intuitive as Detective Martinez taking everything in.

August Island Rike Paper Company

Thanking Hazel and walking out with her I returned to
my cruiser not remembering what else I was going to do
while in my office. Being only 7:00 pm I decided to call
Hector about the files. Second ring and the machine
answers, "August Island Rike Paper Company business
hours are 8:00 am to 5:00 pm, Monday through Friday.
Please leave a message. For a directory of departments
please press 1." I do not leave a message not knowing
which department Hector works in and not wanting
anyone to assume he is in trouble with the police
calling. I am surprised by this phone being listed as his,
this leads to other questions about what Hector may be
up to these days. Last I heard he was contemplating
joining the force.

The next morning, I finished my shift around 7:30 am
and decided to stop in to see Hector. I waited in the
parking lot, behind the large tin looking monstrosity of a
building, but Hector never arrived. By 8:00am I call, not
identifying myself, and am directed to the warehouse.
Hector answers and is surprised to hear from me
especially at work. I explained how I received his
number, and it was the only one on file, and he softens.
Then I tell him of Hazel mentioning seeing him at the
courthouse, he stalls as if he isn't there anymore. I can
feel irritation through the phone line as if this is a
sensitive area for him. Possibly other officers have been
contacting him about his timeline, when his time should
be as private as he wishes. Then he says he is studying
for a course and wishes to meet with me, he has news

of a new decision saying although not new to him. We agree to meet tomorrow morning, 6:00 am at Einstein Bros. Bagels on 4th Ave. It will be good to catch up with Hector. I am glad I did not ask Hector about the files on the phone, in person there are many other layers of a person to read. He seemed to be in the conversation then out. He was pulling back, possibly hiding something. I head north to Eastlake Avenue taking the scenic route home to Fremont as the traffic increases southbound into the city. I recede to my duplex ready for rest, dinner, and music; the necessities that keep me sane in this job that makes no sense. I had already cut into my me time waiting for Hector and wondering why I did not see him arrive, I had fully planned on meeting him outside. I cherish my days sleeping and have worked the night shift so long no one ever expects to see me in the daylight hours.

I arrive before 6:00am after another long shift with no answers to what happens overnight in the city. I spotted Hector sitting at the end of a brick planter box just to the south of the parking garage, he hasn't seen me yet. I park displaying my police credentials on the dash and come up behind him, startling him out of his intense thoughts. He was clearly sitting on 4th Avenue in the dark on a cold morning but wasn't mentally here, not the demeanor of Hector I remember. We entered and I offered to pay. He says he comes here often and always orders the Texas Brisket Egg Sandwich. It was his grandpa's favorite, said it reminded him of his grandpa growing up on the farm before arriving in Seattle to work for Seattle PD. Hector said he never went to the farm but always felt he had been there from the vivid stories. I ordered a basic egg and cheese bagel and some orange juice. Hector has coffee as he is starting his day, and I am on the downside of mine. They call for our food, Hector jumps to retrieve it. As soon as the tray hits the table Hector says, "I need to talk." Me thinking he will tell of his courthouse visits or some other big trouble, but he simply says, "I am not going to join the police force, it feels so good to get that off my chest." I don't know what to say. I thought he had a big story and had not even remembered this morning about him planning to join the police force. He devours the bagel like it is his last meal and wants to get away from me, looks at his watch, something most people don't have any more and says, "thank you for breakfast and understanding but if I am going to make it to work on time, I better go. It is over a mile." Then I realized Hector was on foot and I had not asked about the files. I offer to give him a ride, he agrees but not to the parking lot saying August, the new owner, has been following him to the courthouse at lunch and doesn't wish to be seen with the police as he is not in trouble. He prefers not to look suspicious. He does not elaborate on the courthouse, but I will take note of that if needed at a later date. Sometimes the facts are not delivered in the proper sequence and need to be sorted out and reorganized. Hector tells me of the private investigation he is attending on the way to his work but says he will not be a private eye either. His grandpa signed him up and paid for it, so he is going but enjoys the family he has at Rike Paper. I asked before I forgot about the files, did he see any around, notebooks with case files, some sort of file box that wasn't personal? He looks at me as if not sure how to answer, stalls a minute then thanks me for the ride and says he would look but I can tell from his hesitation he knows where they are and has read them. It makes me wonder if a case has been solved or if Detective Martinez had a hunch about or was onto before his disability retirement. Maybe that is what Hector is doing at the courthouse. Now August, Hazel and I know of his activity. I will have to investigate August too since he has been watching Hector. I phone Hazel leaving a voice mail on her work line asking for her to report if she sees August or Hector at the courthouse since she goes daily at apparently the same time as them. Also, I ask for a records report on August, realizing at that moment I only know his first name. Then wonder if that is his name on the sign and he is a Rike.

Heading home I feel I have a larger mystery on my hands than when I started the day, but this one is unraveling backwards. I have the facts just not the cause of them at least everyone involved does not have a record or is not dangerous I don't think. Hoping Hector is not putting himself in jeopardy studying cases Detective Martinez was onto. We as police always have our eyes on things that could, would or will happen at some point. August suddenly arriving here after his dad's death may be coincidental, but I don't know him. Does he have family besides his newly deceased father located here, how does he know how to run that company if he just arrived, where was he before this? I will have to look up the obituary once I get home to see what information that will give. Taking the short way home today, music in my head, words flowing, lyrics beating I arrive home happy that I have eaten so I can go to my studio and get these bars out of my head. Now to synchronize with the music once written, my notepad in place for the first scribbles as it flows from my brain into reality waiting as if in cue to exit out of speakers into the air and be in the wild. The words penciled in, suggested chords and beats put together and I am spent. The day gone, pieces of me on the streets, on paper, in the music, in the air, the water ripples outside my window, diesel fumes from the boats passing through to Portage Bay. I am ready for rest heading downstairs to my residence remembering the obituary I was supposed to read and that I had a text from Naomi overnight to respond to. She is probably still awake, I think, as a smile is planted on my face coming from within. Most of my emotions do not include a smile or any actual happy thoughts. I do wish everyone the best, but my occupation does not show them in that light. I text Naomi with the last of me for this day, falling asleep in the recliner mentally designing the interior staircase I need to build from my studio to the kitchen.

Chapter 17

December 2024
Remy

The past twenty-four hours have been tiring, perhaps the most stressful period in my life. I keep it simple after the chaos of my childhood; work before anyone is up, home before rush hour. No one lives with me, so my clean houseboat stays that way. I eat the same meal every Monday, Tuesday and so on. I prefer order, my own order, no other input or additions to my schedule or system. When I opened the blog, I was the one to suggest it and decide when to add entries. Mrs. Peterson's accusations threw my strict schedule off and now I have more tasks to complete in an expedited manner. I didn't clean the kitchen today on my way out with a preoccupied mind. I have trash bags and a box knife to purchase to get rid of the dog paraphernalia, the packing blankets, then the box of bags so I will not have that brand in my possession and the box knife. I am not comfortable thinking with the mind of a criminal. All my life I have had to be responsible, be the authority as mom was gone most of the days doing something other than taking care of me, Everett, and Logan. I daydream for a while about some of the antics we pulled; three young boys without structure, me the oldest, supposed to make order in our newly found life after grandpa passed away. Mom seemed to be relieved she didn't have to make rent anymore, she almost disposed of us three on the houseboat leaving the majority of our belongings in the old rental unit that should never have been occupied. The walls peeling from mold, rodents scurrying, sometimes running over our covers at all hours. It was a one bedroom, upstairs behind an old store that was no longer occupied but was a roof for the four of us. With mom in the living room, if she came home at all. Dad never lived with us, nor do I have any recollection of him. My life has always followed a strict agenda: ensuring Everett did or didn't do certain things. Logan, being younger, observed Everett's troubles and stayed close to me, still needing guidance at a young age. Everett was always into something, taking this apart or trying to add parts from the dryer to the deck fencing or some other inane caper. A boy that needed constant supervision. Mom would bring food home weekly sometimes on a day other than her regular Thursday schedule, but it would have to last. We didn't know when our next meal would be or if I knew how to cook what was brought to us. Most of the items were retrieved from the food bank, dried beans, peanut butter, canned goods, even socks or a book occasionally. Everett moved out at sixteen after getting a job at a pet store. I am not sure where he lived then or now. Logan is married and happy. He stops by the bakery now and then always at the close of the day to visit with me. Showing me pictures of his wife, their new house, their newfangled black, curly headed dog, a doodle of some sort. He is attentive to his life and to me as we visit, sometimes silently. He has thanked me for showing him how to be a man and survive in this world. Me always being proud that Logan made the right choices. All of our lives could have gone the wrong way.

These are all items arising in my head like files when I should be on with my tasks of disposal. As I have thoughts of Remi, my night with him was pleasant as I have not had any evening company in years. I feel fortunate to have left my phone at home so tracking will not be an issue. I drive south to Kent, stop at a convenience store to buy lawn bags and some scissors since they don't sell box knives, paying cash so as not to be tracked. Drive further south, turn into a park with trails. I get out, put on my gloves, cut the dog bed up and place it in four bags with a toy in each. Seeing a homeless encampment just around the first bend, the peaks of tents looking as if they were garden flags from this angle. I have an idea to leave the dog food and toys in one bag, the packing blankets in another. That is the bulk of my disposal gone here in one stop. I drive across the parking lot to drop the bags when a scruffy gentleman approaches me asking for money. I gave him the change $8.12 from the convenience store, asked if he would like the blankets and dog food, he smiled saying his dog is back at the camp with Snowflake, his girlfriend. He is pleased with his money and newly found warmth. I wish him well, thanking him and appearing overly anxious to be giving away something.

My next stop is a Union 76 gas station, this is where the first piece of dog bed is disposed before getting gas, me realizing that the lawn bags are not the most intelligent idea. Who tosses lawn bags at a gas station, this is where you get rid of car garbage not yard waste. I am proving to not be an experienced criminal. The next is tossed easily at another park off Central almost in Renton. I stop at Lake Washington, Gene Coulon Memorial Park wishing I had my camera, the Nikon belonging to grandpa I found in an oak cabinet that was a custom install to the houseboat. It is what I use for all the blog pictures. I should get an updated camera with memory cards and stop using 35mm film, it has been an obsession of mine to get the pictures developed, not knowing which shots will be the stars of the show. My followers have increased twenty-fold since Amazon became a fixture in Seattle, having to up my game with the photography. I felt the need to buy a small aluminum motorboat to moor at my place so I can get to the real life of the lake and not just my alley of houseboats. Prior to being serious on my blog and it being just a hobby I would take pictures from the locations I drove. I am not sure where that train of thought came from, I need to concentrate on my mission at hand. I dispose of the next bag here in a trash can before ordering Ivar's fish and chips. It is entirely too frigid to be eating outside but I find a spot undercover with picnic tables that are flipped up against the wall for winter storage not wishing to be close to people in the small restaurant, hoping no one sees the guilt on me as I pass them. I feel guilty about disposing of Remi's toys and bed but glad I was able to leave his gorilla on Mrs. Peterson's porch. I lean on the rail eating my dinner watching the planes land on the lake, with a splash and start to glide. Ducks part the water knowing what happens here, the planes have priority. The boats float by at a slow speed since this is nearly the end of the lake. All in all, surprisingly it has been an enjoyable day as I never get away from the city. One more bag to go and I can relax like the past few hours have never happened. I can feel the stress of it all unraveling from my body. The last bag is disposed of at the end of the walking trail. I head north, turning the radio on quietly, knowing the silence will bring back my endless loop of events, reveling in my newfound peace. With the window open I smell the scent of Lake Washington, the last mile on this road as a train inches by to my right swaying along. This may be a newfound serene feeling in my life. I was satisfied before with the quiet predictable schedule but now I know that chaos can happen suddenly in a day, but I have controlled this situation just like any other time when events went wrong and brought it all back into alignment.

After a peaceful night at home, everything appears to be back in sync with my prior life. There are moments that create a crack in our timeline like bad news, a car crash, health scare that we refer to time as before and after. This is one of those days, not an event but an entire series that escalated with me turning into something and someone that I had never imagined. It makes me think of the world differently. You hear of people saying, "they did what they had to do." Looking back, I could have just said Mrs. Peterson slipped and hit her head, but I was not positive she wouldn't wake up and tell her story that may or may not be worse for me than this predicament. I feel this option is controllable on my end anyway.

The bakery looked the same as when I rolled by the front to park in the stall assigned to me down the alley. Somehow, I thought it would look or feel different. I remind myself I am the only person who knows what happened and with the leash attached to Remi everyone thinks Mrs. Peterson is lost in north Seattle. Entering, turning off the alarm my guilt returns, I look at the floor knowing she was there and regret not clearing up this mess. I panicked and handled it wrong, too late now to change my story or any events.

Today is Thursday, we always have a variety of cinnamon, strawberry, lavender, and licorice cupcakes. I pull out the laminated recipe, not for the batter but for the amount of flavoring. It hits immediately the sight of Mrs. Peterson's strict flowing writing on the recipe card written in fine line pen. Her initials are at the bottom right corner of the card. She is all over this bakery, the tools, recipes, colors, customers, pretty soon the word will be out that she is missing, and everyone will be asking me, talking to me about her. I need to hold up, keep my face straight, concern showing, matching their feelings. I am more concerned about my wellbeing, but they don't need to know that part of the story. It is possible this crime will not be solved. I come back to the kitchen mentally, pouring the ingredients in the Globe industrial mixer that I had just purchased, butter, eggs, and all the other ingredients added without thought. I have done this every day for twenty-three years, the batches larger as business picks up. The revenue is picking up as word of mouth gets out. I consider hiring another baker, but I am in fear the superior quality would settle to just average. I am positive Mrs. Peterson had these same thoughts when she considered hiring me, my interview Italian Cream cupcakes won her over. I am not sure I am ready to bring someone else into this mess at the moment. I bake about 50,000 cupcakes a month and the extras for the display case then the occasional sheet cake but that is approximately two thousand a day, which is manageable. My new Waring ovens each have five racks, I can bake 240 cupcakes at a time, with three ovens the task goes easily. I am done most days before Elora arrives and can leave but I don't. I don't want her here alone, not because I fear for her safety which I should but deep down I do not trust anyone to be here alone especially now. While she works, I stay in my office and calculate how to cut costs without decreasing quality, now I think of Remi wondering what the little doggie is doing.

  I am startled by Elora as she stands in my office door just like every other workday but this time, she hands me the dog toy I had forgotten about when Detective Muncer was here. She simply hands it to me along with the proceeds of the day and says, "see you tomorrow, Remy." I am rattled to the core again, my stress level going from calm to off the charts in an instant. I cannot believe I missed another piece of evidence. Thinking back there has been some events that are critical in the past couple of days that may be incriminating, or I may be overthinking. Who waved at me as I had just exited the Metro bus, did the garbage man see me with the purse or was it covered by the towel, were there any cameras at any of the locations I disposed of the dog bed? Suddenly I realize I still have the small box of lawn bags in my trunk and scissors with threads and foam caught in the piece where they come together. Part of me wishing this could all rewind; seeing the dog bed go back together, Mrs. Peterson telling Remi goodnight and her being alive.

  Before leaving I get the scissors and bags into the front seat and keep them in the console at hand so I can dispose of them first chance that becomes available. Another piece of this story created. It is endless and tiring, I like everything repetitious and predictable. Now I have loose wires flapping all over, each with a current that could burn me and a story I need to keep believable. The scissors I place in an old bag from under the front seat. I park around the corner from the bank on 4th Ave, tucking my deposit in my pocket and carrying the bag with the scissors and place them in the metal mesh looking garbage bin connected to the bus stop for the 400 series busses: 402, 405, 410, 412. I need to leave so as not to look suspicious. While waiting in line at the bank I realize I am over analyzing my actions, standing at a bus stop is normal behavior. After making the deposit and returning to the car I open my console ready to be done with the last piece of the mess I created. I roll down the passenger window as someone honks wanting me to give up the much sought after parking spot, ready to throw the box of bags out the window and see a police car in the rearview. I turn on my blinker, wait for him to go by and ease out of the spot with my box of bags.

Chapter 18

December 2024
August

 Monday, arriving at the warehouse in the dark and
dreary calendar blocks of December make the days
long. I approach the building well before sunrise nearing
on the darkest day of the year and hear the faint tones
of Christmas music playing. Upon opening the door
there are white lights strung all over. These were not
here when I left on Friday. Cards are displayed on string
with clothes pins. I must find out who was here over the
weekend to decorate. Patricia in office management
answers the phone like it is connected to her. I pictured
her with the purple headphone attached to her the
entire shift. She informs me everyone comes in on
Sunday two weeks before Christmas to decorate. The
ornaments and lights are stored in the warehouse, the
cards have been collected for years. I say thanks and as I
hung up part of me is offended to have not known this
activity was happening. What if I had wished to
participate, suddenly happier I had decorated my
second tree and laughed at the first one disappearing. I
am getting a schedule of events from Dustin in HR so I
know and can attend other events if I wish. Maybe even

install a whiteboard calendar in the lunchroom so no one is left out, especially me. My blinds are closed again, the paperwork I left on the desk is neatly stacked to the side and there are v's on the carpet from the vacuum. All this is going on here at my company and I wasn't informed. I am not generally irritated and don't know why but at this moment with things being different than every other Monday I have arrived it bothers me. I must find out when the decorations will come down. I think I know what is wrong with me. I don't belong anywhere specific; this is my company with my name on it and I wish to be asked if I would like to be included if there are any celebrations happening.

Dustin emails me the schedules, one for company activities, another for deadlines like orders, taxes, when a job is complete anywhere in the company it is recorded and moved from ordered to finished automatically. All birthday celebrations, company parties, picnics, are consolidated by the month. Dustin is quite efficient to have this completed for 2024. He is the perfect employee for HR, he has a system for everything, a file basket of urgent, to do and to be delivered. He takes the mail downtown to 3rd and Union on his way home checking his own P.O. Box daily. I stand here wondering when all these traditions were put into place and needing to know if they still work for everyone.

Today everyone talks of the Christmas party last Friday comparing it to other places they have been held. It is quiet this time of year, most orders have been processed, cleaning and organizing are the focus. My main goal is to expand the website and get more orders out of state. Blake will be going to Idaho with an order and samples after the first of the year. The week feels long as each day stretches out and me waiting to see Willow on Saturday. I still do not know where the other man I recognized is from. I will have to ask about him, hoping she will know as it feels important to me. I call mom on Friday telling her I will be out on Saturday, so she doesn't stop by but offer my availability for Sunday if she is open to having lunch or dinner. She texts back a couple hours later explaining her work schedule and we agreed to meet on Sunday.

Friday night I shop as usual but closer to home this time. I get a new sweater for my outing tomorrow. It will be cold, but I will be warm inside knowing of the future of my new hobby and friendships.

I drive across town on 80th Street as it turns from NW to North and eventually to East. The neighborhoods pass by, me picturing our group as it was last weekend, hoping I did not forget something like the ornament again. I pulled into a virtually empty parking lot knowing I was early and remembering I needed to purchase another vehicle. I get out and walk around suddenly self-conscience of Willow knowing that I am driving a family man vehicle, even though it wasn't my choice to be single I am and wish to appear as if I am. I walk the path not too far but just enough to be separated from my vehicle. I see Willow pull in but not anyone else. She cannot see me from my vantage point, it appears there is something bouncing in her brown beat up car. I had not even thought of this prior to now but could she have a child? She exits the vehicle, I can see it better as I walk closer, it is a Nissan of some sort, rust all over the bottom half as if it came from the Midwest, suddenly making me feel at home when this is where I belong. Here I go again standing here and thinking about my newly discarded life. I have missed what Willow is doing, and she is almost upon me when I was daydreaming.

We walk towards each other at a brisk pace, her being pulled by an eager rather short, brown and stocky pit bull. She smiles and says I hope you don't mind Daisy joining us, as Daisy rubs her large mouth on my knee leaving strings of slobber around my leg. I am in this for the afternoon so do not mind at all, I ask where the rest of the photography group is. Willow says she thought I knew that it would be just us, asking if I mind. This actually makes me happier than the group, shows me Willow wants to see me and only me, not sure if she trusts me bringing her muscular dog who appears to want to walk in front of me. I don't have much knowledge of animals since I have not owned one but do believe Daisy is showing her dominance over me by leading. Willow hands me the leash and we proceed on, stopping for sniffing breaks along the way. Willow explains the brown dog with one white spot on her tail and a pink nose belongs to her neighbor who is out of town for the weekend.

   Willow talks about pickle ball to me all the while saying, volley, kitchen, sportsmanship, explaining how it is one of the fastest growing sports and has a long-playing season here in the Pacific Northwest since our weather is mild. She asks if I would like to learn the basics before the season gets underway. Then I would know if I wanted to play or not. Offering to meet next Sunday, the 30th, if the weather is not too bad to at least get the feel of the court. Saying there are other indoor courts, but she prefers the one at Green Lake. I am just getting used to walking Daisy, being alone with Willow and now I am interested in pickle ball. In my last life there was socializing but not any activities or hobbies, these will help me remain limber. I must research to see what clothing I would need for this new sport. I am picturing it as bicycle gear, spandex of course not a helmet. I better do some research so as not to show up looking silly. I have never worn spandex before. After walking the entire loop of the park past the playground and water tower twice Willow asked if I would like to get some lunch. She explained she can't leave Daisy in the car alone or she would eat the seats so they would have to eat in her car. She offers to drive and bring me back; this leaves my newly found embarrassment of my vehicle in the dark still. I gladly accept a ride from her when she informs Daisy of her backseat assignment, Daisy clearly rides in the front.

Josephine Plummer

Willow explains she doesn't want the dog in her vehicle so there is an agreement with the neighbor if she watches the dog since she can't leave it alone that she must borrow the car too. She also explains that Daisy goes to day care at Downtown Dog Lounge since her owner Marshall works in an office building close by as an accountant.

We drove around a bit looking for something suitable both of us cold and not wanting to eat outside, deciding on McDonalds choosing a cheeseburger for Daisy all the while she clearly wanted my burger and fries. Willow says she has to get the dog back for her scheduled visitation with the other parent and takes me back to the park. I have a strange feeling realizing neither of us has revealed anything about ourselves. She hasn't asked about me then I think possibly she thinks I am not interested in her since I haven't asked anything about her except how she is. I have not dated in over twenty years, being with Alice was easy, we knew each other, could read, and feel the other but this is new. I will text her later and thank her for today, letting her know Daisy was a nice addition to our outing. Truthfully, we probably wouldn't have walked as far if she hadn't been there. It was too cold for a walk, and we were almost the only people at the park, it was so cold. Then we are going next week, I head north after the park with no other plans for today, a smile on my face thinking of my relaxing afternoon. Stopping at Dicks Sporting Goods on my way home and browsing the different areas of pickle

160

August Island Rike Paper Company

ball gear. I don't purchase anything except a dog toy, not even knowing if I will be seeing Willow or Daisy again but if I do, I am prepared.

Chapter 19

December 2024

August

As the new year arrives without any commotion the reality of my dad's death finally hits me. My dad is gone, he will not be entering the year 2025 or any other stage in my life. I wouldn't be here if he had been, or would I? Where would I be, somewhere in Florida or a small town in Kentucky? I had not thought thoroughly about my destination and never would have dreamed it would end up here, right where I started.

Monday morning rolls around too quickly but not fast enough. I will meet Willow next Saturday to discuss pickleball. So far, I have only done a bit of research and discovered it was invented by three men on Bainbridge Island. My two priorities this week are to study the rules of the game and get back to the monthly files in my office.

Even though this month's birthdays are Andre and Paul, why can't we start celebrating the other January birthdays of prior employees? They were in on this system too whether they knew it or not. It will be nice to find out if anyone here knows the previous people and has memories.

By Friday I have researched all the pickleball rules and wonder if Daisy will join us on our outing. If not, I will leave the toy with Willow to deliver. I hadn't realized I actually don't have any attachments and how much I have thought of Daisy this past week. I don't even know this dog, where it lives or even what part of town Willow lives in. We have not asked any personal questions or revealed anything about ourselves except where we are employed. Could she be married since she only wishes to meet on the weekend. Now I have many questions about her.

This afternoon at the birthday party I propose the idea of putting the names and dates of employment on paper and placing them in a jar. If it is your birthday, you draw a name and tell what you know about that person and others can follow. I had already created the concept, explained the theory and placed the jar in front of Andre, who had chosen chocolate cake. He drew the name Garrett Rike, September. The room went silent, and each employee turned to me not knowing what to say. We all missed him, on some days speaking about a lost loved one can't happen. There is just silence. After the silence and the cake being served Andre stood and started talking, almost tearing up. "Mr. Rike, Garrett, he was so separate from our staff and seemed to want it that way as he stayed in his top floor office most of our shifts and would emerge walking around with his clipboard checking off orders. I never knew what he did up there, but I believe he somehow knew about us and our lives outside of here. One year when my children were smaller, and I broke my leg, Mr. Rike delivered little league equipment for the team I was coaching to the school my children attended. Enough for the whole team. I was going to start a fundraiser but being in the hospital prevented that. I had not mentioned this to anyone except my wife who never came here. I am not sure how Mr. Rike knew what was needed but he showed up with everything. He came to the first practice and showed the team what to do. He didn't show them what I had scheduled but had them out stretching, tossing the ball, getting the feel of the mitt and running bases. Basically, he showed them how to be a team just like us here. Mr. Rike was a true leader; he would show up at games that I was not aware he had a schedule for but would root for our team as if they were his children."

I was almost not able to speak but felt I should thank Andre and tell some back story on this. My dad had signed me up for little league but truthfully, I was not good at it and wished to quit the team after the first season. Dad was disappointed as I could tell even at that young age but simply took me by the hand and exited the field. On the way home we stopped for ice cream, him getting his usual butter pecan double scoop and me never being able to decide which flavor to try. That day I chose dad's favorite too; he had been generous to me and my wishes so I would see why he liked that flavor so much. There wasn't any conversation at the beginning of our ice cream. I was only six or so, but dad turned to me seriously and spoke like he was in a business meeting. He asked, "If you don't like baseball what would you like to do? Everyone needs a hobby, and you may as well get started now." I had to think about this for a while, that felt like an eternity while dad sat and patiently waited. I finally came up with photography. We stopped on the way home and bought a camera, went to the waterfront and sat waiting for a bird. Dad said, "photography takes patience, and this is what you asked for." I believe that day changed the course of my life learning about changing directions, not giving up, doing what was right for me and teaching patience. The room was silent again for the third time today. I am positive there are many more stories about dad. I will start compiling them in his September file.

Saturday, I woke up ready to go meet Willow at the pickle ball court. Around noon, just as I was pulling out of the carport she texted asking if I would mind picking her up or meeting at Rhein Haus instead. I opted to pick her up so I would know where she lives, and I had no idea where Rhein Haus was or what even happened there. She texted me her address on Phinney Ave N. saying follow the signs to the zoo and you'll find me, I'll be outside. GPS took me down 65th, it was only about a ten-minute ride but just long enough to realize I am still driving the family vehicle. Willow will for sure see it today. I had not even asked her what we would be doing just knowing we would be inside due to the temperature change.

I pull up in front of a tan two story building seeing the address located above the side entrance. Pavers line the alley alongside the rear of the building for resident parking. I do not see Willow then she comes jogging from one of the vehicles in the parking area. I wish I had seen which one. I know part of our agenda today will be to discuss vehicles. We head south with traffic creeping across the Ship Canal Bridge. Seeing as there is a Husky football game today, I suddenly miss the excitement of crowds; the majority of my time here has been alone or at work. I realize Willow and I are not talking about anything. I ask if she likes football and what will be happening at Rhien Haus. She says she would watch a game on TV but probably not attend one. Then she goes on to explain Rhien Haus is a restaurant and has bocce ball courts. I have never even heard of bocce ball but am willing to go see, another new activity added to my repurposed life. We get to Capitol Hill, a neighborhood I haven't been to since attending high school. I see the growth and familiar places, a cold Saturday afternoon with sidewalks full of bundled up people in a hurry to get to their destination. I am suddenly ready for lunch, not knowing how much further to our destination. Today my lunch is late, I have not had a precise eating schedule since high school as my time was set by me in

Milwaukee but now, I eat when the rest of the employees do only, they congregate in the lunchroom, and I head to my office upstairs. We are seated and I notice the dark wooden old-world style décor. The menu has a to share option, we decide on the Cheddarwurst Sliders, House Salad and beer. As soon as we order I hear people hollering with excitement. This noise was possibly going on when we entered while I was taking in the extensive woodwork of the bar and furniture. Now it is unmistakable, excitement in the air but from what? Maybe this is a sports bar too. Just as I turn to look in the direction of the noise coming around the corner is that man, I could not place from the photography club. He is walking towards us, and I figure he knows Willow. He walks up and stops, talking to Willow, angled with his back towards me. Possibly we have gotten off on the wrong foot somewhere, I cannot remember where I have seen him before. Then Willow introduces him as Remy from the photo club. I know there is more to this but do not let on. He pulls up a chair from another table and they discuss the topic of next week's meeting in the park. The month has gone on so fast it hardly seems possible we were taking pictures of ornaments not too long ago. That means I have known or met Willow just over a month ago. This month's topic will be snow or frost. I was doing it again, not paying attention to where I am. When I focus our waitress has brought our lunch. After lunch we go to the room with the bocce ball courts. There is Remy again, he appears to be the star of the court and possibly everything else. I may have to learn about this sport too. I look down at our table where another beer has been delivered and see Willow smiling at me. I ask if she is from Seattle. She smiles and says no, Chicago, but this is my home now. That statement caused more questions than answers to run through my head, I think of myself leaving Milwaukee and here I am.

Willow did not elaborate anymore on how she ended up in Seattle, at the camera shop or why she left Chicago. I decided to tell her of my times visiting Chicago, she seemed to withdraw with fear in her eyes. I then asked if she wished to hear how I ended up in Seattle secretly hoping she would open up to me about her journey. I started this conversation with growing up here, the paper company named after me that was started many generations back, moving to Milwaukee for college and only going to Chicago for special trips and training with work. I told her about being a Mechanical Engineer and inspecting the buildings on Lake Michigan. I stop she seems to have come out of her corner that she had wedged herself into and began to relax a bit. Then I started back up talking about the plan I had to discuss something with her but wish to tell her the rest of the story first. I tell her the story of Alice, now Alli, and how she lives in Milwaukee. We are divorced, my road trip, the call from mom and that I am staying here indefinitely.

Then I look at Willow's emotionless face for a minute or two and she starts to laugh. I am not sure of her reason, tears flow from her eyes, and she is smiling much to my surprise. She started opening up saying she had not told anyone her story since moving here saying her life has been horrible, scary in fact. No one is looking for her, but she had been raised in the foster system in Chicago from birth living with one family then the next in Cabrini Green Housing. She quickly learned to run fast, get perfect grades that would pave the way for some sort of scholarship. She started spending as much time with the guidance counselor in high school as she could and landed a full scholarship at The University of Washington. She said she was terrified of a new city but quickly found out Seattle was friendly, and her dorm was more accommodating than the public housing. No one here knew where she was from or that she didn't have parents, occasionally she went to her friend's home for Thanksgiving but never Christmas. She would check into a motel on Christmas Eve and stay a couple nights so whoever was left at the dorm would think she had family. Always returning with a new sweater or book saying it was a gift. She may have purchased it at a close-out sale the year before and hid it to be able to afford it, but it was hers and so was her story. She met Marshell, who owned the camera store, at one of her lectures. He left his card she is positive to draw business into his store. The following Saturday she took the bus to Kenmore and visited the store, upon entering she saw a man and Marshell in a heated discussion, the man flew by her almost knocking her over. She was surprised at the scene she had walked in on but not scared as she had witnessed much worse in foster care in Chicago. She loved the feel of the store with the cameras and all the other equipment, tripods, camera bags and such. Marshell apologized for the commotion and asked if he could help her. She showed him his business card and stated she had attended his lecture at the university last week. He said nice to meet you even though she had not given out her name. He asked if she had stopped by looking for a job. That is not why she came here but she filled out the application with no work history other than the on-campus bookstore and he started telling her all about the job as if she was hired. After a couple of hours, he said we close on Saturday at four o'clock and open tomorrow at ten. Can you make it back then? She just went with the schedule never being told she had the job and that was twenty years ago. Marshell doesn't come in much anymore only to fill in on days she was off or Dallas, their weekend employee is unable to make it in. She tells me she has a confession to make, she chose to talk to me because the first day I pulled into Kenmore Camera she was looking out the window and thought my Volkswagen Atlas was safe looking.

That is when I told her about my idea to trade it in for something else that better suited me since Alice had picked it out. She shook her head and said no, that vehicle is why we are sitting here now.

August Island Rike Paper Company

Chapter 20

December 2024 / January 2025
August

Tuesday morning, the last day of 2024, I wake up with many thoughts weighing on my mind. A new year will arrive for me and not my dad or the police officer whose funeral and guests shared the cemetery with my family. Grief is not something I have thought about prior to this. No one I know has passed away. There is also my entire life gone, erased, a life I was satisfied with and had built to last, retiring had not crossed my mind, nor had divorce. I loved Alice and probably still do; the shock has not worn off yet. Dad passing, my new occupation, being single, a different up-close relationship with mom, the new apartment and Willow. My camera sits on the small table by the kitchen in a space too tiny to be considered a dining room. It is the start of my new life, the miniature black box with memory cards and accessories have changed my life. At 6:00 pm I will pick up Willow and take her to dinner at a restaurant of her choice. In Milwaukee Alice and I stayed home and hosted a repeat party every year, the same people, the same food, the same night, the same ones who drank too much and stayed over for breakfast. Every New Years morning I can still see Paul as I came down the stairs entering the kitchen with a big breakfast cooking. Sausage, eggs, hashbrowns, pancakes. I had never thought about where he had gotten the food to cook, he must have brought it with him and planned his morning meal. Now I wonder where all those people who attended our party will be tonight. Our house was always full, twenty or more close friends or at least New Years Eve friends. Will Alice have people over to her new place? I shouldn't think of that if I am here, I should be here.

I must have fallen asleep because it is after 3:00 pm and I have so much to do before picking up Willow not realizing there will be tomorrow for chores. I wear a button-down shirt and bring along a flannel, not knowing where we will be dining. Willow is festive when I pick her up, wearing a shirt with sequins and sparkles. I have never seen her hair curled or wearing much make up. She asks if I am ready for dinner, then wonders if we should have made reservations. I ask where to, she says it doesn't sound like much and there is good food at a place called Victor Tavern. I started to laugh. We have only briefly spoken since my company Christmas party. She asks what is funny, should we go somewhere else? I tell her of the recent party and my experience with this place. I know I will have the Victory Burger again; it takes a while for seating and service being as it is New Years Eve. I didn't mind, not at all. his gave me a chance to get to know Willow a bit more. By 11:00pm we headed west on 5th Avenue to the Space Needle and waited with the high energy crowd at the base. It has been a casual easy night, I am content to be in Seattle, and to be next to Willow.

At 11:45 pm or so the drone fireworks show starts. The night sky lights with colors and shapes unreal in a fireworks show. Neither of us have been to a display like this. Willow says she used to watch fireworks over Lake Michigan for different events but never New Years Eve. She looked reminiscent and far off while she shared the story and a tad bit of herself with me. Possibly like she missed Chicago, that is where she grew up and was familiar with. I suppose it was home to her as much as Seattle and Milwaukee are to me. Her story was of the barge she could see the fireworks being set off from and the danger she envisioned the pyrotechnics people were in all for the sake of others entertainment. She said the summer she saw the Fourth of July show was her last one before leaving there. She had been frightened to go back to her foster home and felt they may have been onto her departure for the University of Washington. Since she was a ward of the state at that time, she did not have to reveal any information to Mr. and Mrs. Culver about her future plans. She had overheard them talking one night through the heater vent in the drafty old Craftsman house. She would be eighteen soon and their pay would end, and they needed to fill her room. They all knew she would become a burden on July 27th once she became an adult. She was worried about returning home and her meager amount of worldly goods would be on the sidewalk or in the old metal trash bin in the alley. She returned to find her key still worked but found Mr. and Mrs. Culver sitting in their tweed matching recliners with the arms even worn the same way, the identical expression on their faces. Willow turns to me and says, "I knew on July 29th I would be on a bus heading west to Seattle. They were unaware of my story, so I sat calmly and listened to their preplanned speech. It didn't matter at all to me what they said as long as I didn't have to go today, that was the worst they could do to me and then I would stay in another home for a few days. They explained all I had overheard from the kitchen smoothing over my departure like I was a piece of discarded unwanted furniture to just be gone. Thankfully there were no questions about where I would be relocating just the fact, I needed to make arrangements to depart no later than July 31st. They gave me a slip of coffee-stained paper with my case workers phone number and email address, even though the email address was formatted wrong I didn't care. I continued upstairs feeling fortunate to have been housed for four years, all the way through high school in one home, still thinking of the wonderful fireworks display and feelings of freedom and hope. I never told them goodbye, just left at 4:00 am to catch my bus leaving a note of thanks, a bag of candy and a clean room ready for the next person."

I find it odd we were on the same lake a couple hours apart and would not have met if it weren't for our mutual moves to Seattle. At midnight Willow grabs my hand and gives me the slightest kiss almost on my mouth. I put my arm around her, so she feels safe knowing I have a need to always protect her. We linger on the corner not ready to leave the scene we had just created. People stroll by with blankets, scarves, mittens and lawn chairs that look out of place on this windy night. Some people we saw were rigid from the cold barely above freezing at this hour. Me just content with our conversation and that we didn't opt to stay outside as long as the other people did. We turn and walk up the hill towards my VW Atlas both silent and lost in thought of our past times on Lake Michigan with fireworks.

I open the door to let Willow in the passenger seat, she smiles ever so slightly and asks if I will drive by the Space Needle one more time so she can savor this memory. We park at McDonalds across the way on 4th Ave. and order a milkshake and fries. Still silent but comfortable, I may not have been this relaxed in my entire life. It seems I should not be with my dad passing, the sudden move and divorce and learning how to run a large company. I asked Willow if she would like to see where I work since it is not far from here.

We travel south on 4th Ave a little over three miles to Lander, turn east and see the monstrosity right in front of us. She recognizes it immediately, points at the huge sign with her mouth open, unbelieving and saying this is your ship? Your middle name is Island? She wants to drive through the alley, around the block, still not believing what she sees. It is quite an unbelievable site at this time of the night. I discover someone sleeping in the small indent with the heat exhaust by the back door. She finally asks for the whole story. For some reason it starts with Hector, the shipping department and the courthouse. It is past 2:00 am when we head north to Willow's apartment. Me only telling none of the actual story yet.

We decided to drive past the Space Needle one more time and head north on Highway 99, I realize I must not have been paying close attention to directions prior to this and not being familiar with the area just followed the signs towards the zoo and Phinney Ave N, asking for specifics once we were near her apartment. We pull up, me nervous to let her go alone to her door at this time of night and equally disturbed at asking to walk her to her door. She sits in the car after we park while I process my dilemma, then realize it has been a few minutes. I jump out, run around and open the door, making space for her to exit. I explain I am worried about her safety at this hour and wish to walk her to her door if she is ok with that. She smiles, nods and says she is tired. She leads the way, gets her keys out, opens her door, I ask her not to say anything. She smiles, relieved, I kiss her on the cheek, wait for her door to close with locks in place. She looks out her front window and waves. I drive home calmer than I have ever felt.

Chapter 21

December 2024 / January 2025
Detective Muncer

New Years Eve at the Space Needle I attended alone this year. Deciding to take the extra shift I was on duty, undercover there to keep eyes on the crowd and occasionally seeing someone who has a warrant out for a heinous crime I have been trying to solve shows up. They end up getting arrested in front of their family or other loved ones. Some walk away quietly with me while we wait on a patrol unit to take them in for processing while others dart through the tightly packed crowd knocking innocent people to the pavement. Most holidays are workdays for any law enforcement or bail bonds agent. People good or bad tend to return to family on holidays.

How different this year looks; I am remembering last year's New Years Eve party at the penthouse with Naomi. Me wearing my leather band clothing from another era I can't seem to shake. The music rolls through my head all day and night. It is what keeps me on the streets, rolls me through town to see some of the worst stories that could be imagined and brings me back to reality. All to help someone. Families of known criminals who loved them unconditionally all the way down to innocent bystanders who were one eighth of an inch in the wrong direction and became a victim of a crime. Some of the crimes are fabricated with great precision, I think back on Pearl and her crew of criminals. All their plans concocted so carefully across the country, a syndicate of madness. Then there are the opportunists who see a vulnerable spot in someone's life and take advantage of that one second. I meet the families, talk to the victims and perpetrators, they all sit in the same spots telling pieces of the story. Mostly pieces I do not need, and it clouds the picture of reality. I do not need to know they attended a symphony a week ago just because it was something they always desired to do. I need to know who they are associated with, why they were where the crime happened and what their plans were after the event happened that they will not be attending now.

My mind returns back to my present location. It is a Tuesday night, the crowd not as dense as many other times I have been on duty here. My eye catches a glimpse of a distinguished beard with a hint of red about ten people deep in the sea of people. I have seen that particular person in footage I have viewed in connection to Randell Rinwell aka Stu. Footage I have watched hundreds of times for one sliver of information. Nothing has ever stuck out as abnormal, it was routine, just people leaving the stadium. All just patrons visiting the stadium to cheer on the Seahawks.

August Island Rike Paper Company

I took out my phone and snapped a few shots of the guy with the beard and his accomplices. I narrowed down the footage from the night of Randell's murder on January 2nd if I recall the date correctly, right after the game against the Arizona Cardinals with the Seahawks winning. I am almost positive at least one of these other males are in that footage. Wouldn't that be a twist of fate to solve that crime with no leads for over a year. Fleur Fensby, Randell's longtime girlfriend, called me every few weeks for the first months after her shocking discovery of Randell's death and learning of his other identity Stu asking for updates on the case and then she just stopped calling. Vada and Amos stopped in almost weekly asking for details of the investigation. The truth is I didn't have any information. Randell was an upstanding citizen that was killed while out having fun. He was an icon in this city for many years providing pep outside of every football game year after year. He was an asset to this city, in the realm of business and entertainment and each person connected to him deserved an answer to this crime. He was left to lay behind Lumen Field while people passed unaware. His only involvement in the day was being there. It was not a provoked fight on his end, Stu was in costume when he was murdered but was a mild-mannered man both in costume and real life. He never deserved this treatment, and it is my job to bring justice for him.

As midnight draws near, I am cold, elated I took this assignment but only wish to be at the precinct or at

home to watch the footage of Randell's last night. I
need to identify this man and his posse. The minutes
tick by slowly, finally fireworks and a wonderful drone
show that I cannot fully appreciate due to my train of
thought and sudden break in this tragic case the time is
now to start 2025. Ten, nine, eight, seven, six five, four,
three, two, one. Happy new Year Randell Rinwell. My
detail at this location is set to end at 1:00 am, this may
be the longest hour of my life. I turn back after the
lights and fireworks have stopped and the entire crowd
has shifted, the highlight of the night over, the new year
started, and the bearded man gone. I will find out his
identity soon, one of his friends will break as soon as
they are taken into custody as accomplices if they were
truly not involved. If they helped with the murder, it
may be harder to break their silence or the story they
will tell. Truthfully, I am relieved there is more than one
person to interrogate and observe on this case. Most
people that attend games are working people who have
a life and people they care about not just a run of the
mill criminal. These guys should break open the story
rather quickly.

By 12:30 am most people have left the viewing area
around the Space Needle. Of course, we still have some
revelers on course for the new year. Party hats are
strewn, beer cans and liquor bottles thrown and
broken. I have never understood the mentality of a
crowd. They all unite from different walks of life and
then merge into a solid group of people who would

never do something like break an empty bottle of rum at the base of our iconic Space Needle. It is the deep parts in people's souls that reveal their true self. Some people would never commit a crime but as a set of circumstances line up, they become a murderer or bank robber. We all know there is a lot of money in the bank but with a slim piece of society they feed the thought of all the money. They start watching the system, find excuses to frequent the bank then know enough not to be seen there for a considerable amount of time. Then when they think the time is right reappear and rob the bank now going from a dock worker or office worker to committing a federal crime.

I watch as the last of the people file out, mainly due to the cleanup crew being everywhere. Garbage is strewn in places people don't even go. I spent my last few minutes here talking with the patrol officers and Seattle Center security. Keeping my eye out for the bearded man but know he is gone since he was one to leave the football game early to beat traffic. One of his traits being an impatient man.

I text Naomi a Happy New Years message as soon as I get into my cruiser and head north on Aurora Avenue. The road cannot be behind me fast enough. It may be nearly 1:30 am but this is my time, when I am at my best and do the deepest investigation. I exit at the first off ramp after the Aurora Bridge and anxiety over comes me. My only plan all evening was to come home and research the footage from the night of the

Cardinals game and it is the beginning of New Years Day, a time when I could get called away to interview or observe another crime. All I want to do is solve this one and keep the image of the bearded man in my mind before another case obscures the sudden lead.

I pull into my street parking spot even though it is on the street it is mine. Everyone knows I keep odd hours, and no one ever parks in the spot right in front of my house. The city is quiet, tire noise from the Aurora bridge echoing overhead and an occasional voice or horn cut through the air but it is peaceful. 2025 starts off with promise.

My usual time to arrive home is 7:00 am so my schedule is off. I normally eat and go upstairs to write lyrics or just listen to music unwinding from my nights of grit accumulated during my shift. I decided to stay downstairs this morning, so I am not distracted. I watch the start of the camera footage from the beginning almost as a build up to the actual piece I am after having seen it numerous times I know exactly where to stop. I am not sure what in me needs to see Stu walk by the location one more time and then again. I rewind and see him he is alive. I see him as Stu on the footage, but I knew him as Randell Rinwell the business analyst from my face-to-face dealings with him. Either way he is an icon of the city but in his real life as Randell he helped clean up some agencies and saved business owners, the city and county money they never would have realized was being wasted if not for him. He was

184

August Island Rike Paper Company

also an invisible man, one who no one seems to know in either of his life roles. Each person who thought they knew him learned a bit more about him after his death.

Chapter 22

January 2025
Detective Muncer
Detective Rubio

It is nearly 4:00 am I have searched all databases for facial recognition on the gentleman with the straw-colored hair and square beard, longer than most. He does not give off any indication that he or his friends are criminal in nature, or violent. He is not in any database that I can find. It takes more than my clearance to search the Department of Licensing without a name. I am looking for Agent Fred Ford's direct line, his card is here somewhere on my desk, a desk I pay all the bills for both duplexes from. I started this when I lived upstairs and only paid my bills back when checks were the only way to pay but after Mrs. Johnson left me the two identical duplexes and the care of Everett Sunshine, I moved the green wood-stained desk downstairs and continued the habit. Now mostly I check the various bank accounts for accuracy as Everett and his household are run from a trust account left for his care. I do not find Ford's contact information and am just about ready to exhaust my abilities on the bearded man when my phone rings.

August Island Rike Paper Company

Detective Rubio simply says again, "they are back. Can you meet me at Golf Drive South, northbound side of the street, right on the edge or Lewis Park. I will be here, lights off, having called you before calling this in. Our client has been here a while and cannot be anymore deceased." I gather my keys, radio and put my vest back on, all this being a rewind of when I returned home less than two hours ago. As I leave being heavier from the weight of my gear my mind is burdensome also. What did he mean? I know him well enough that he would not be willing to discuss who the "they" are on the phone or radio. It is me alone he trusts. I proceed into the cold night, in the couple of hours I have been home a thin film of ice has developed on my door handle, and I hear the door unseal from its frame as I open it. The city requires a detective to wear dress pants that do not go with any season. I feel the chill coming from the leather and stitching on my well-worn seat through my trousers as I get in and drive towards I-5 southbound on auto pilot merging onto 1-90 and exiting on Dearborn St. I loop around and see Rubio's cruiser up on the left, the street lit up, but he has found a spot without the streetlight blaring at him and giving him away as King County Sheriff. The cars we drive scream *I am the police*, there would never be any undercover work in them.

I drove by him, so he is aware who is here, turn around and squeeze into the sliver of darkness he has found in a city full of lights. We get out, me more cautiously than

Rubio being as I have no idea who is deceased or who has returned. He walks about 30 yards to the south and right there on the edge of the sidewalk two feet or so in is a deceased female, Rubio says it is Stephanie Thomas. I look at him while filing through the rolodex of my mind and have no recollection of Stephanie Thomas. Rubio shakes his head and turns to me with a grimacing look on his face, me still not following his lead as if I was out of the game not playing on the same board. He spills parts of sentences out. I pick up his train of thought and what we are dealing with when he says Daniella Harper from the motel on Aurora. I know exactly who is back now—Little Mel and his crew. Stephanie is his running mate. Last year a group we had been watching for manufacturing methamphetamine had a prominent member of their clan pass away. He was who we had most of the connections on. We weren't ready to go in yet but then a few days later tainted product had been sold in high quantities from a motel in north Seattle. It had been distributed as far south as Thurston County and up to Snohomish County, that we are aware of. We met with other agencies then all the leads dropped off. Donny was dead, Don flat out disappeared, Little Mel was selling scrap metal, and his cohorts were hanging out collecting what they could from odd jobs and food stamps living legal or so it appeared. Even Daniella, the prostitute from the Aurora Avenue motel, was gone.

We called forensics to tape off the crime scene and collect any evidence. The medical examiner showed up to cart Stephanie away, I turned to ask Rubio how he knew her body was here. He says a CI knew they were back at it, and this is where she was laid. The odd jobs didn't pay enough to cover their habits and actually working was not worth it when they owed back child support or collection debt to take over any legal money they would make. The art of being an addict does not allow for a consistency of daily employment. These people do not follow Little Mel's recipe that is cynical enough but add their own chemicals to create a larger batch. Little Mel expects approximately four pounds when done and with the new method developed by Don another pound can be added to that. Meaning Don would end up with the four pounds Little Mel expected and have an extra one. This left Don with a considerable amount of product and funding. They had to have disposed of the waste from manufacturing close by their site. Donny lived in the shed connected to the garage, being so close to the county line and not exactly in the city it would not have been turned in for a code violation unless someone informed the county Donny was living there. That was the last thing we wanted during an active investigation. I leave and go to the precinct asking if Rubio would join me to dig up the files on Don, Donny, Daniella and the deceased from the previous bad batch that is coming into play again. If I recall 124 lives were lost in three counties when all our leads had suddenly gone dry, deaths had stopped, and Little Mel looked like an upstanding citizen. We decided to take some notes regarding the previous files, Rubio has been unusually quiet during this time. Then he tells me this is the fourth body he knows of in the past 24 hours from this product that almost dissolves the fingernail and turns them green. Four individuals were dumped in the south part of Seattle/King County and suspected to have been linked to Little Mel or at least one of his crew.

Chapter 23

January 2025
August

Even though I had been up nearly all night the start of a new year I was wide awake at 6:00 am, woke up, had breakfast, got dressed and was ready for work. After locking the front door and heading to the carport I noticed practically all the neighborhood cars were still in their stalls. I look at my phone and see it is Wednesday, January 1st, return to my apartment and turn on the computer feeling foolish to have done a dress rehearsal for work on a day almost everyone has off.

With the start of January, I am trying to be ahead of everything that comes up. I need to talk to Dustin in HR about the process of getting payroll final information for 2024 to the accountant to prepare the W2's. I don't know how dad kept up on all of this but since I have been thrown in headfirst at the opposite corner of the United States than I was planning for, or maybe not planning, I will take on each task in a timely manner. I am still convinced this company could run without me.

Opening my email, I see one from the Seattle Photographic Society. The meeting will be January 11th at the Washington Arboretum. There are instructions on this month's topic: dew, frost or flakes. I automatically think of last night and Willow, how we had spent such a casual night. There seems to be no expectation on her part except safety and on my end I am ready to just spend time, have someone to share a meal with or outing. She has gotten me out of my regular routine. I am looking forward to warmer weather, pickle ball or possibly bocce ball.

The temperature today is only 31° at this hour. I am full of energy and need practice with my camera. I haven't even picked it up since our last meeting. I feel I am not serious about anything, am just going through the motions of each day and need to be more intentional. I decided to go where I know it will still be cold when I arrive. Jump in my car, the VW Atlas feeling fortunate I have it, I take my usual route as if going to work but hop on eastbound 1-90 and cross Mercer Island over the floating bridge I see the glass towers of downtown Bellevue; the land becomes open again with farmland and fresh air as I head for North Bend. I don't think I have spent any time there before so it will be an adventure all my own and on a whim. I see a sign for Tennant Trailhead Park, feel confident I can hike a bit with my newly acquired clothing and shoes, park and get out just as the sun is shining through the trees from the east showing off the dew evaporating. I get a few shots with different settings of steam rising off a log and fern. I am too inexperienced to change lenses and adjust my settings in time for this scene not to be over. After many shots at different angles, I realize it is extremely cold but sit down anyway despite the lack of temperature and set my camera to capture images close up and test out how to back away from an image, practicing on a rock in the middle of the path.

I head deeper into the woods down the dirt path that is frozen under my feet, I realize I may be the only person in this park on New Years Day at this early hour. As I round a corner, I see frost sparkling like a prism with a sliver of sunlight shining through the dense forest. I stand there absorbing this scene so long the frost that I had intended to photograph has melted and my moment is gone. I head deeper into the woods as the path dips and climbs, the forest becomes darker and my chance at capturing frost or anything of the sort are slim. Just then I hear voices, many of them laughing and sounding as if they are on horseback. As they round the next corner, I see there are indeed no horses but about fifty people. They appear as surprised as I am, stopping to tell me about their New Years Day walking tradition. They act as if they know me and recount their walks from other years. They are just happy today there is not snow but say it is close. Then they leave in the opposite direction of where I am heading, happy to have seen people and now know I will travel further east to capture images of snowflakes which will become my New Years Day tradition.

I walked a bit further into the woods, amazed at the different types of bark and the towering height of the trees, the smell and cold air are comforting. I headed back towards the parking lot with a few shots of ice and dew. I realize how cold I am once I turn the heater on and travel further east. I don't want to travel all the way over Snoqualmie Pass, so I follow the signs to Kendall Katwalk Trailhead and walk the trail knowing I am not dressed for this adventure even with my new Pacific Northwest outfit and wish for the clothing I had worn in Milwaukee. I quickly capture a couple shots of frost, snow or anything frozen I see and get back to my vehicle. I saw a sign on the way here for The Issaquah Café knowing I need a warm lunch as it is past noon. I head west missing the exit but catch the next one and turn east on Gilman Blvd pulling in knowing I am a changed person from this morning. I'm not sure what has changed or that I was trying to make any variations, but my load is lighter, and I am more confident in my ability to operate my Nikon. I ordered Grilled Veggie Hash and a chocolate milkshake. I sat and read the menu for a considerable amount of time after I had finished with my meal savoring the milkshake and making plans to bring Willow here in the near future. Now to get my photos printed to have something to show, even if I am an amateur. Pulling out of the parking lot it hits me, the feeling I have is that this is where I belong. All the years after I graduated high school and lived in Milwaukee, I did what was expected through college, with my inspections at Greene Mechanical, my marriage to Alice. I floated through all of this over twenty years doing what was expected even though the majority of tasks were what I wanted or was willing to do. I loved my wife, my job, our home, and my circle of friends and was satisfied with it all. I gave each item an honest and from the heart shot, but they were things to be suddenly left behind and this right here in the city of Seattle where I was raised is the spot it has all come together.

Chapter 24

January 2025
~~Detective Muncer~~
~~Detective Rubio~~

It is nearing dawn on January 1st the day had been packed so far; all the files are on my table relating to the bearded man and Randell Rinwell. This is not something I wish to discuss with Rubio and am ready to be alone and for Rubio to get back to his own jurisdiction. I follow him south to complete one more task. It is a case I worked alone in the beginning. I was the one who connected his vehicle, Stu and the real identity of Randell. I have always felt a twinge of guilt for not solving this case. I understand the grief of the family after mine disappeared too many years ago to count.

We decided to pay Little Mel Scriptnor a visit this morning, before the sun rises. His name and address are Stephanie Thomas' emergency contact for her Oregon ID card. I know she has resided here in Seattle for well over a year and has unpaid DWLS tickets dating as far back as five years written by SPD. Why had she kept renewing her ID in Oregon? Who was there that would not be listed as an emergency contact? Rubio drives

south on I-5 while I pull up King County Parcel Viewer,
Melvin Scriptnor owns the property located almost as
far south as you can call Seattle and still be located in
the city limits. We go over the Duwamish River on the
First Avenue Bridge, get on 509 and head to Melvin's
house. This is a day just like all the others for us, but I
bet Little Mel, who prefers to lay low has not had
company like us who showed up in the middle of the
night before. He may be still awake from days gone by.

   The six-foot chain-link fence that encloses the half acre
of property did have the green, white and gray privacy
slats, at least in the front section. Now they are broken,
faded or gone. It is as if they stole or found them along
their journey and inserted them at random. I could see
the small white house through a cross in the chain link,
two Dobermans walked around the yard but didn't
bark. The ivy-covered gate had a regular padlock
attached. I could see two people in the yard on the side
of the garage to the right of the house. They looked up
when we were discussing our entry and entered
through the back door which we could see through the
front window. People were milling about as if in unison
just behind the yellowed sheer curtain that made my
stomach turn thinking about what was on that piece of
fabric. Back and forth they went in unison. Suddenly the
front door opened, the screen door was pushed open
with force like she was shoved outside. The designated
one to talk to the police. It was a lady, approximately
5'7", extremely short black hair as if a bathing cap was

on her head. She had a graceful movement about her. Her appearance resonated guilt and she acted as if she knew us. I have never had any dealings with her before.

Introducing herself as Raven Wells, she shakes our hands, looks us both in the eye and then stands there. No other words from her, the gate still locked with ivy touching her face as she peered out. We ask for Mel, Melvin Scriptnor. Raven turns without a word, steps up to the porch, reverses and returns to the gate like she is the bodyguard to this short older man. He could be anywhere between 50 and 80 years old. These drugs and lifestyle do that to people who start out with potential and the next thing they know they are living in a group of others in the same condition. Melvin Scriptnor was balding on the top; his fine long wavy hair blew up in wisps off his shiny head in the cold morning wind. He shivered and went to draw his nonexistent coat around his slender body. His eyes were too wide for his face and may have fit before he had lost all the weight, like his wide leg brown corduroy pants that pooled around his ankles in folds. They may have belonged to a taller person and Melvin was simply wearing a piece of donated clothing obtained at a clothing bank. He was observing us as much as we were checking him out. Only silence, mist from our breath early this January morning and tension filled the air.

To put them at ease I break the silence by telling Melvin and Raven we are not here to enter his property, do not have a warrant but need information. He backs away fast right into his fence shaking his head and saying," I am not a rat. I won't tell you anything, no warrant please leave." My suspicion is that he has not been to bed yet, maybe for a few days. I observe he is stressed and curious at the same time about our sudden visit. I pull out a printed full sized ID card photo of Stephanie Thomas. Melvin briefly looks at it and states she is sleeping, not feeling well, been in bed for a few days, maybe two or three looking at Raven to back up his story. She is a lady of few words an observer. After looking Melvin up and down she turns and goes back in, starting to lock the already locked gate from habit. Melvin becomes concerned, a grimace on his face knowing he has been snubbed or at least dismissed by one of his own. They are to do as he says, they all live with him and on his property, he is the boss and now Raven has turned her back. She has done this once before when he told her to take Donny to the hospital so he wouldn't die here. She didn't and an outsider came in to take him. That was her first strike. All this running through his head. We stand there waiting for more from him, all of us knowing Stephanie is not here sleeping. We know of her fate. Melvin is unsure of her location or trouble. He insists she is sleeping in the back room, we ask to talk to her, either in there or out here. He refuses our entry, starts to go in, I tell Rubio we should get back to headquarters to request the warrant. Little Mel shrinks into himself and asks what she has done to bring you here, she doesn't even reside here, she lives in Oregon. We all know that is far from the truth, but it doesn't matter where her residence is. I tell him she is at the morgue and needs someone to identify her body. He truly looks shocked at this information, most likely thinking she had been arrested and given information on his operations, trusting no one at this point and wishing to believe his story of her being inside asleep.

He agreed to meet us there but not come with us. Entering his gate, locking it and peering between the ivy leaves longer than expected, we eventually see the front door open and close. Little Mel back in to lead his people. We waited down the road to follow him, he comes out from the rear of the house wearing a thick flannel that I had seen before. It was distinct with the mustard-colored suede patches on the elbows and worn collar detaching from the neckline. This was a jacket Donny had worn when we followed him last year. Little Mel most likely absorbed all of Donny's possessions. He unlocks the large roller gate, opens it all the way, walks back by the garage and returns in Donny's truck. He exits the property with his head hanging, fully engulfed in the task he is about to do, starting his new year with this, betrayal and his best man Donny gone.

Running the plate tells me the truck is still in Donny's name with the license tabs expiring two years ago. Melvin Scriptnor is driving a truck he most likely doesn't have permission to operate, and he isn't licensed to drive in front of two detectives. You have to give him credit for being cooperative and brave enough to get right out in front of us in his situation and identify the body of whom we believe is his longtime girlfriend. He does the speed limit, merges onto 509, then I-5 and gets off at Dearborn Street turns on James Street and heads up the hill just like he does this every day. Me wondering how he knows where the King County morgue is. Upon leaving Little Mel's house I had forgotten how far north we had to travel. I feel as if we have been on the road for a century. I have been away from my paperwork and main mission of the day, the tension in the car radiates between us as the police radio chatters but not for us. We discuss once in the garage how cooperative he has been and follow him to the first level, us taking a police-only space and waiting for him to return and walking through hospital screening with us. Not just weapons or contraband to be discovered anymore but temperature taken, questions asked about symptoms and whereabouts before entry. The guard looking at us with questioning eyes. I am sure he wonders why two detectives are here with this man who is clearly not under arrest, but we all enter without answers. Proceed to the bank of elevators, hit the down arrow when Melvin gets agitated. We are at ground level he says, "I am not going in the basement." When the car arrives and the heavy metal doors open, Mel gets in and proceeds to the back wall hanging on to the support bar. He wants to get off at the first floor down we explain there are surgery floors down here also and we need to proceed past those. He nods, being nervous, and gets off as soon as the doors open passing between us, realizing he doesn't know where to go. Stops and says, "come on," we lead him to the location of Stephanie's remains, they barely take the sheet off her head, and he says, "yes that is her, he knows by the mole on top of her head" then proceeds back to the elevator realizing he needs credentials to get out of here. We ride the elevator in silence, follow him outside and ask if he knows what happened to her. He nods no now genuinely grieving since he has seen his lover and friend dead and turns to leave. He is not a suspect at this time, so we thank him for his cooperation and let him go on his way giving him privacy as he leaves.

Chapter 25

January 2025
Detective Muncer

 Melvin Scriptnor does not drive by us when leaving the parking garage. He has to have a lot on his mind, and I am positive it includes if we will pull him over, arrest him for driving while his license is suspended and impound Donny's truck. A piece of his friend that he could never reclaim as he does not have the right to possess the vehicle. It should be daylight in a couple of hours, and I wish to be home to peruse over the crime scene photos and reports from Randell Rinwell but there is one more thing I need to do here. I left Rubio on the cold corner this New Years Day and tell him I can catch up with him later, turn and enter the sliding glass and aluminum doors for the second time tonight with a smile on my face this time. After all the thoughts and cares of the city of Seattle where my loyalty has always been I have a piece of me that I need to be true to.

 I badge through security, turn right to pass the same elevators we just returned from and walk down the corridor with urgency, entering the ER from the back side one not used by the public. It is chaotic here tonight as usual; noises not heard in other establishments, security needed in room 16, radiation techs, physicians, nurses at the desk keeping order in all this and there sits the reason I am here, Naomi. I see her red hair as soon as I turn the corner. It has been a couple weeks since our schedules have synced up, but I will get a minute or two tonight. The first day of 2025 and Naomi will be part of it. She looks up, signs out, leaves her station and says she is on break and asks if I want coffee.

 We enter the partially open cafeteria like hospitals have. A small part is open at all hours to accommodate the staff but mostly it is a break room. After getting a soda for me and coffee for Naomi we sit side by side in a plastic booth as if we were at a diner and smile. No words are able to come out after our separate but equally stressful events full of emergencies all in the past few hours. She says, "someone blew their fingers off at midnight, I have a bay full of DUI suspects that need to be processed. I am so happy to start my new year right here with this small surprise moment with you." We mostly sit and unwind, laugh a bit at the coincidence of me being able to be here on this night when we are both on the clock. She asks why I am here I say the morgue; she nods and rests her head on my shoulder. I remember our date at Green Lake where we had breakfast and slept. Knowing we cannot sleep here, just a few more minutes and we are back to solving the problems of Seattle. Naomi must have fallen asleep thinking she had overextended her break. She woke with a start and jumped up asking for the time. It had only been six minutes, and she needed the other four to get back to her station. As we meandered out of the cafeteria, I spot the top of a head I recognize across the way behind a partition. It is Melvin holding a paper coffee cup with steam coming out, but he is not drinking it just staring into space. I decided to walk Naomi back then return to see if Melvin was alone.

After leaving the cafeteria that was technically closed and the lights off in half the area we slowly zigzag down the corridor. Naomi was already mentally with the patients she had left behind making mental preparations for the next step to take. Me thinking about my pile of paperwork at home, I return to the cafeteria and see from this entrance that Little Mel is alone and debate my option to leave him alone. He looks up as he sees me approaching from about fifty feet way, stares at the dividing wall next to him and doesn't look at me. My instinct is to leave him alone, his emotional state is not my business, but I see he has a wet line on his cheek just one line as if from a single tear. He turns to me and says, "I don't know how to leave Stephanie here. I brought her from Oregon fifteen years ago and she has never left not even for a day. How can I go home with her here?" I don't have an answer for him. All I can do is sit with him for a while. I get another soda and pull up a chair to the table next to him giving him distance. There is silence between us, but I am sure in my decision to stay until I need to leave, or he is prepared to go. We sit for the better part of an hour then my radio directs me to my next destination. Little Mel gets up and walks away, saying thank you under his breath, probably unable to speak in a normal tone as he is on his way to the steps in his life that will be different. That timeline started the moment Rubio, and I showed up at his house on SW 119th St.

I wonder when there will be a break in the case of the miscalculated batch of methamphetamine. How much does Mel know? Although he runs an illegal business why is he allowing product to come out that is killing people? We have not seen this exact miscalculation, there have been many, and the spread of the product is stopped fairly quickly. Dannielle Harper got off last year for her part in the spread of that tainted product with her detailed information on a couple higher up rings that we had been watching, not connected to the downtown groups which are usually smaller and deeper in use than business being made.

I am being summoned to Bud's House, a local pot shop that has had numerous robberies. Twice in the past month and now this. The 2004 Ford Taurus is hanging halfway out of the building, the driver is slumped over, with his head on the passenger's lap. Without checking I know they are gone; my first suspect is the owner who is tired of this. Just wishing to run his business and being targeted again. After calling the emergency contact on file for this business I discover the owner, and his entire family, are in DC for a family emergency.

It isn't very often that the burglary suspects are murdered unless someone is protecting their property or there were more people in the vehicle who turned on their accomplices. Nothing appears to be missing from the store, the owner gives us his local contact information to secure the building, the password to the surveillance system and permission to check it. He states the last two robberies they took almost all the product that was left out in jars. This time it appears nothing is missing. I enter the office and watch the camera feed while Forensics, Homicide, the Medical Examiner and tow truck do their part to unravel this. Making the phone call to the local handy man to be here to board it up when we are all done, I see on the video a stocky man about 5'10", hockey type mask, green work jacket, large caliber weapon come out of nowhere. He rounds the corner about the time of the crash through the window, fires off two precise shots, leaving a pair of young men dead in his path. Now to locate which group these young men came from and see who they had double crossed to solve this murder.

   While sending the file of the murders to my email for evidence my phone rings. My mind instantly goes through what, where, who and why mode. It is the Medical Examiner with the results of the recently deceased methamphetamine findings; they all have a commonality of samarium in their system. He is more technical than I need. I am not even sure any of what he has told me is helpful to my investigation. I call Rubio who meets me a couple blocks from here saying there is another one. Telling him of the Medical Examiners report he pipes on about magnetics, electricity, the heart and how iron levels can turn your fingernails green. I am always surprised at his Rolodex of facts; samarium is a manmade product and a temporary magnetic substance. This information doesn't appear to help any of the investigations I have open currently. I am hoping to go home and find Fred Ford's phone number for contact in a few hours. I am ready to sleep; it has been an eventful New Year's Day. Following North 34th Street onto 4th Avenue N I am almost home it has been a long night, lengthier than most and there is my hideaway, the sweet little spot, my piece of the pie on Euturia St. Someone is in my parking spot, this never happens. I can't write them a ticket but can sure watch to see who it is. Someone new in the neighborhood I suppose.

Chapter 26

January 2025
Detective Muncer

Daylight cracked the sky from the darkness that had set in the city overnight. On the first day of this year, I am saddened by the succession of crimes committed, mysteries made, people and property destroyed, Randell Rinwell's killer still on the loose but hope in recognition. My phone shrills breaking the silence of the morning. I should be sleeping since I was tending to business all night while others were sleeping it off waking in the new year, resolutions broken. That is not something I do; goals are set in my head, but life is always unpredictable. Each day holds a mess of its own. This morning it is the identity of the two victims from last night. I pulled out my phone and send the file to my computer from last night and the camera footage of the shooter.

Angel Maverick, nineteen years old, five foot seven inches, brown hair, hazel eyes. The second victim, Jordan Bruno, sixteen years old, six foot two, blond hair, brown eyes. I want to sleep after only a couple hours but now my mind is placing the city in order with plenty of questions, most without answers. I watch the footage of the shooter again after turning on my computer. He has a slight limp on his left leg, work boots, and surprising speed for such a stocky man. His uniform jacket gives the appearance of his neck being nonexistent. I run arrest records for both Angel and Jordan. Surprisingly, only Jordan has a record, a violent one, stabbing someone on the metro bus, punching another person in the bus tunnel, a restraining order from a female named Haley Cummings and two criminal trespass orders one from a bar on Queen Anne the other from the UPS Store in the 1700 block of 7th Ave. That is a lengthy list of charges for the teen to have acquired. I start my investigation with the first charge and see who he is associated with, all the way down the list no one was arrested or charged with him except at the UPS Store Haley Cummings was there. The report states that he chased her in the store knocking over racks, pinning the employee to the counter when she attempted to intervene. One moment calculating the cost of shipping, the next assaulted. Jordan never appeared in court as scheduled, released to his parent, Richard Bruno, who appears to have spent the majority of Jordan's life in Walla Walla State Prison. Where was Jordan during that time? I am surprised the records didn't rest on Angel. He is nonexistent in our system except for a red-light camera ticket a couple years ago on NE 80th Street and 5th Ave NE. After checking the compounding file that had been started early this morning just a short time ago, I see a Seattle Central College ID in his wallet and paperwork from the trunk for Graphic Design. Notebooks and binders with extensive notes from each class and pencil sketches drawn of the city from all different angles. On the inventory sheet, there was a lawn chair, an attachable umbrella, many expensive sets of pencils for sketching and multimedia tablets. All from a box in his trunk obviously knocked over upon impact with the brick building, both the storefront window and windshield shattering simultaneously. Two young people possibly thought they could make some fast cash from the inventory at the Bud's House pot shop. They thought it would be a smash and grab, but the tables were turned on them by someone who took matters into their own hands. With the store owner out of town the investigation on his end will start with the scenario since he had been hit twice before hiring someone to stay inside to protect his establishment. Although from the footage it appears the stocky shooter came from outside.

  With all my pages in order and my mind racing, I go upstairs, looking out at my cruiser up the block where it doesn't belong, vowing to install an indoor staircase from my residence to my studio. Sleep is the last thing on my mind as lyrics flow through my head. I sit on the 1970's flowered rocking chair in the corner with my tablet to take notes and fall asleep at 11:00am. This year is packed with new crime scenes already with last years on the top of the mix.

Car door noise wakens me 6:00pm, I looked out and the car that was in my parking space had moved, the space empty, oil left in a rainbow puddle on the street. I put on my suede slippers and retrieve the cruiser, park in my spot and place the Seattle Police parking designation on the dashboard which does not do any good but may deter the rust-colored Oldsmobile next time. I return upstairs, wet from the storm that feels like snow is on the way and look at my scribble of lyrics. Go to the computer and pick a title to match. My plan is to sell enough lyrics to retire. I am starting to hear more and more of my music on the streets on my assigned tour around town.

Bad Batch Green

Verse 1:

Seattle overnight, rain's pouring down,

Detective on the streets, huntin' clowns in this town,

Little M's lady in the morgue, we don't play with life,

Found a bad batch of drugs, cuttin' deep like a knife.

Thugs flexin' on the block, thinkin' but they're fallin',

Unthinkable crimes, hear the radios callin'.

Buds stacked high, but there's blood on the floor,

Seattle streets dark, but I'm ready for war.

**Chorus:

Ladies actin' tough, but they're soft as a feather,

Rain falls heavy, we the storm, we together.

Morgue vibes lurkin', can't escape the pain,

Bad batch blues, drownin' sin in the rain.

Verse 2

Seahawks fly high in Lumen, but we on the ground,

Chasin' down the truth, every lead that we found.

Makin' moves like chess, kingpin of the crime,

Got my eye on these criminals, runnin' outta time.

Record every step, yeah, the plot thickens,

Line up the suspects, we breakin' these chickens.

Gangsters in the alley, thinkin' they can hide,

But we police with a Glock, if we must take 'em out
with pride.

**Chorus:

Bridge:

Ballin' on the edge, livin' life on the line,

Flexin' on these haters, watch me shine, watch me grind.

Detectives in the zone, every clue we find,

Bad batch in the city, tweak your mind, rewind.

Verse 3

So, we roll through the darkness, shadows full of dread,

Crimes unthinkable, but justice ain't dead.

Rain keeps fallin', but my heart's made of steel,

Seattle city's anthem, livin' raw, keep it real.

Streets talk louder than the chatter of snitches,

Hold tight to the truth, we dig with no glitches.

From the morgue to the block, yeah, we makin' it hot,

Bad batch green, but now I'm givin' it all I got.

**Chorus:

Outro:

So, if you step in this game, know the rules that apply,

Seattle's heart beats strong, watch the truth never die.

August Island Rike Paper Company

Little M's story twisted, but I'm chasin' the light,

Bad batch green fade, we will conquer the night.

#MunDet J #DJMuncer # Seattle Strong

Chapter 27

January 2025
Detective Muncer
Detective Rubio

It's two twelve, I have been on shift three hours and twelve minutes and Rubio calls only saying, "now, meet me at 2476 Westlake Ave N." The body of Raven Wells is lying in the ivy and appears to have been discarded at the bottom of the hill. She is unmistakable from her cropped hair; we had just spoken with her approximately 24 hours ago. The young woman of few words now is silent. Her dialog was filtered in life and nonexistent in death. The fingernails greener than Stephanie's, they both have been poisoned by Little Mel or one of his crew. We wait for the Medical Examiner and Forensics just like every case. It must be done by the books to be thorough. All bases covered, each case file in the same order, every step taken precisely the same, but leads aren't delivered this way and there will only be evidence at the top end of this crime scene pertaining to Raven. Anything at the bottom of this cold vegetation-covered hill will belong to her. There were no ropes, bags, or tape, just her body and clothing with ivy sticking out here and there as if she had inserted decoration in a wreath. Once the Examiner had loaded Raven, who I now feel sorry for, she did help us in retrieving Little Mel. We walked across Westlake, got in our cruisers, and circle around to Newton Street turning onto 8th Avenue N. Rubio takes the lead, even though it is not in his jurisdiction I let him think so. He has not spoken much since he called me, only a couple of syllables, grunts and nods. He pulls over by a shopping cart loaded with aluminum cans, window screen frames, and a screen door sticking up almost to the power lines. He gets out, looks at the cart and cuts through a condo parking area. Standing behind the building on the edge of the cliff someone sleeps on the other side of the wall we are walking by. We clearly see the indentation where Raven Wells' body broke through and flattened the vegetation on her self-created path down towards Westlake. We are on a gravel pathway; footprints would not be visible but there are three cigarette butts and a spot someone sat, and someone lay at the top of this hill. I suspect Raven was already gone by the time she was here unless it was in this building she passed away. Whoever was with her and decided to push her over the edge clearly thought about it while smoking, wished to spend a little more time with her, had remorse or other motives. We placed the Camel cigarette butts in evidence bags, Rubio is still silent. He normally talks to me nonstop about all cases, not just the one we are on. He is hard to keep up with on most days. This time I follow him around the back of the worn-down building, up the cement steps, around the front past the moss-covered cedar siding towards the hill. Nothing stands out, we do this with the next and on the wooden stairs and see the moss has been wiped away all the way down on the east side of the steps, there are footprints from Nike Air Force shoes. I recognize the six circles inside of each other from another case in South Seattle last year. It appears Raven or perhaps a bag or box of something was drug down the stairs. We climb the stairs without disturbing the side with evidence after taking pictures and calling the Forensic Team back out. The trail of whatever was pulled down the stairs came out of apartment C. What was confusing is the trail was on the balcony that held a small table and blue striped umbrella, which was now covered in moss except for one chair that held a butt print. The evidence shows the body most likely was rested here or Raven sat for a while prior to or during her demise. This is twenty-one miles north of where Raven resided. Why was she here, was this a hide way for her, did she know the person who resides here? It would not be likely she would have another supplier unless she was introducing these drugs to a new client, or another drug added to her needs.

Rubio turns to look at me and I see something in his eyes that has not been there before. He turns further towards me, speaking so quietly I had to strain to hear, and says, "Raven was my contact, my CI. She almost had this case solved and the plan was to meet here at 2:40 am. That is how I knew when to be here. I am not trying to lay tread in your territory. I know we work together well and don't want to step on your investigation, but this one is personal to me. Now she is gone with all the evidence still in pieces in her head rolled down the hill." He turns and beats on the door of apartment C, the door opening as he is still pounding as if they had been watching all along. A lady about 50 years old in a flannel nightgown opens the door at such a high rate of speed Rubio almost tumbled in. We ask her about Raven who she claims not to know, states there have been people out on her balcony frequently and she has not been sleeping well. Her name is Nora Boyer, she is a nurse at Harborview and mostly works nights on the oncology unit but the past two weeks she has been on swing shift and has come home to the carts out front and twice someone on her balcony smoking, using her table and chairs like they own them. She has asked her son to remove them, but he can't be here until the weekend. We talk to Forensics who will be taking the moss-covered table and chairs for evidence anyway. Nora then asks why we are here. We tell her of the crime scene, ask her not to use the stairs until we are done, and I leave my card in case she has any further trouble or remembers anything. She looks me in the eye and says, "it wasn't like this when I moved here twenty-two years ago. I used to enjoy the view, my balcony and my neighbors. Now I am scared to open the door to leave or not know what I will be facing after a shift on Pill Hill. There is enough to unwind from there, home should be peaceful." Shaking her head she is clearly disturbed by the news of a body on her balcony. We know Raven was not alone but did not relay that information to Nora. We inquire for Forensics to fingerprint the aluminum-filled cart. It is the only thing in this entire scene that is out of place as if this is our actual witness, an unhoused person making a living who stumbled across this murder. Despite our noise and multi-person investigation, not a light has been turned on and no one has even noticed we were scouring their territory, except the person or animal across the alley who we were not aware of until I turned at the snap of a twig, then two. I ran over commanding for whoever was there to stop. I had not seen them, only heard the pounding on the ground possibly a dog or coyote. About thirty to forty feet in I see the imprint of a pair of Nike shoes just like the ones from the crime scene in a small puddle of mud, a signature laid at the scene in perfect form. The killer is out here in this stretch of woods and I am not leaving until I find them. Rubio comes in from the south end of the alley-like road and me from the north, calling in backup to contain the area with a foot pursuit. Neither of us see or hear anything until we meet in the middle. K-9 was called, followed a lead for about a mile but then nothing. A stretch of water coming down off Queen Anne stopped the scent. Our killer is gone but we have a long list of evidence, the cigarette butts, furniture, the body of Raven, and a perfectly assembled imprint of the Nike shoe.

Chapter 28

January 2025
August

Returning to work on Thursday everyone is tired, I still have not studied the financials of the company and have no idea if this is a good suggestion or not but call a company meeting at lunch. I don't wish to study the paperwork up in my office that is needed to grow this company. I need quiet and room to spread out, peace to think. At lunch I ask about any pending orders and their due dates. Allison assures me all orders have been fulfilled for the year; some final paperwork needs to be entered into the system for inventory and year close out. Hector states the current orders are all packaged and ready for pick up this afternoon. He appears irritated and asks why, don't I know all orders have a due date and we strive to ship at least two weeks early. I wonder what his hostility is about. My suggestion is once the orders are on their way everyone take Friday plus the weekend off for all their hard work and return to work on Monday, January 6th. Everyone appears relieved it wasn't notice of a closure, no one here totally trusts me yet, it has only been slightly over three months since I have been running this show and feels like an eternity.

My weekend that started on Friday is full of spreadsheets and accounting details. I see we are making a profit that has enough leeway to give everyone a bonus at the end of each year. I do not feel comfortable giving everyone a raise just yet. The profit margin will be stretched thin with the bonuses and expansion. Our newly designed online store, that can be used locally and nationally, will catch on in time for a raise by next year. After Blake, our sales rep's trip to Idaho later this month, I hope to send him out for a few days to Oregon with samples of our products for expansion from our other local accounts. The next week trails on without any incidents. Inventory is having been completed without too many slip ups, the orders are trickling in slowly, but we are ready for the February rush.

Saturday, I wake up with my mind racing from the day of numbers and possibilities. My camera is ready for our photo shoot, that is when I realize I never printed the photos from my trip to North Bend as intended on the way home. After some research online I found Panda Lab on Warren Ave N. Their website says they can process my order this morning. Being antsy I cannot just sit in the waiting room, so I head out and walk the grounds of Seattle Repertory Theater. I wish I had brought my camera to capture the angles of the building and the grounds, the architecture of the wood jutting out below the windows and the building across the street with the contrasting industrial brick and metal styles. I sit for a while deciding if I should purchase tickets when I come upon a red door with an ornate frame that appears to be leading nowhere. On the top of the frame is the name August Wilson Way. I take a photo with my phone, go to their website and order tickets for Blues to an Alabama Sky on January 30th at 7:30 pm. I continue to wonder, stop occasionally to read more information about August Wilson on my phone. I became so involved in my new knowledge I almost forgot my time frame on getting to the Arboretum.

The photos were ready upon my return, all tucked in the envelope only used by photography stores. Once in my vehicle I smell the chemicals used to develop, not being sure of my ability to photograph I am frightened to take the neatly stacked photos out of the packet. Surprisingly they are great. I am learning about exposure and shutter speed. Happy I had asked for two copies I quickly found a drug store and bought Willow a blank card with a farm scene on the front to give her a set. This will be the first thing I have ever given her; I opt for a frame for one shot of deep frost and prism of light shining through it. It is a simple frame with four more pictures inside. I shall just include them without saying anything. I sign the card, lay it on the seat and head east on Mercer Street, turning north on Eastlake Ave to Lakeview Blvd. E continuing east then south to the Arboretum. I am not sure this is the most direct route, but I am still here ahead of schedule and earlier than most people. I recognize the small green Toyota pickup truck from the 80's and older gentleman who is standing by his grill taking in the splendor of the bare trees. Hector shows up on the bus again, this still does not give me any information as to where Hector lives, and I forgot to check his personnel file. The bus displays 1 Line -Lynwood on the reader board. Surely, he doesn't travel that great a distance from work every day. I am not sure why I need to know anything about him as I do not feel this way about any of the other employees. He catches me staring at him and veers away up a side path making me feel as if I am invading his space again. Truthfully, I have stopped following him to the courthouse and have not hung out in the shipping department. All this happens so fast I look up the path and see Willow talking to the tall burly man again. I exited the car, leaving my gift on the seat and being glad to see Willow, it has been ten days I realize. I start to head that way, knowing Willow must not have seen me then feel maybe I am invading her space too since this has been her hang out and Hectors too. I have been so confident in my days since my trip to North Bend and now I am unsure of myself and all my actions. Suddenly I remembered she invited me here and turned up the gravel path on this freezing morning to greet her.

As I approached the bend on the path, and I hung back for a few seconds recalling the last time Willow

and I were together, which went well in my mind but
was it ok with her? We have texted a couple times over
the past ten days, but I have been the one to make
contact, our messages ending in a smiley face emoji,
there didn't seem to be any tension. I increase my
speed and catch up to the burly man and Willow who
seem to have a long-time connection. They are talking
about the February meet and finding hearts in nature.
We are quite a way down the path when I hear
someone announce there is dew on the underside of a
fallen branch. There was so much going on in my mind I
had not even taken note that we were supposed to be
taking pictures, mine were in my car and now I am
unsure of even showing Willow. We all congregate
together next to the dew, like this park doesn't have
any more options. Everyone takes the same shot except
me who ventures on past the crowd, as I go Willow
follows and says she should have asked beforehand, but
her friend dropped her off here and she was hoping we
could go to lunch after. Maybe find a place later to look
for hearts in nature. I am happy and don't feel as antsy
as I did this entire adventure so far, after we go to Cloud
City Coffee on Roosevelt Way NE again. This seems to
be the place everyone prefers to go after the photos
have all been taken to compare shots and discuss
angles. I look around and see the wooden chairs and
tables giving the feeling of being outside. Some of the
club members are talking cameras and lenses, some
have even brought photographs to share. Willow pulls
my photo and card from her bag; she immediately takes

the frame apart looking for the stock photo that comes with the frame. She says she has a thing about other people behind her pictures. She is going slow as she looks, I am not sure what to say or even if I should interrupt her process. I had figured someday she would discover the extra photos not on day one with me observing. She looks up and smiles saying she sees I have gotten out some.

Just at that moment Hector walks up and asks if he can have a word with me outside, he still remains cordial but perturbed. I excuse myself wondering what Willow remembers of my story on New Years Eve about Hector. We walked out next to the Little Free Library in a retired phone booth. Hector reading the titles and not looking in my direction making this moment awkward, when he turns to face me saying, "Bossman, I may not have a job after this, and I love working there but please stop following me to the courthouse or anywhere." I am shocked and embarrassed that he knows. I apologize, assure him he is not in any jeopardy of losing his position and tell him why I started. I could not imagine why he was there so much then my curiosity just kept digging at me. He never told me why he was there, but I know if I am to observe any more of his actions it best be behind the scenes as my curiosity is more peaked now than before. We go back in I sit with Willow, not able to act normal anymore wondering how it will be at work from now on. I have for sure crossed a boundary of privacy. Willow has been studying my photos while I have been gone. She asks me to see my camera and lenses, she sets each photo out and numbers them on a napkin with shutter speed and lens type written next to each. I am happy I have developed a set for myself and know on the way home I will purchase a frame for them all and include the note, so I don't forget.

Willow says she knows of a small park not far from her house. We leave, travel over I - 5 and Aurora onto 85th Street N and arrive at Greenwood Station Park. The community patch is overgrown and past its season. We sit and pull weeds as if it is our own, looking for hearts in nature. At the bottom of a puddle, we find a leaf preserved in the water that is heart shaped, also where a limb has broken off a tree in last month's storm there is a heart in the existing trunk. We come across an arch with a metal cut out of a train car and take our first picture together one in front and then get someone walking by to take another with us looking through as if we are on the train. I wonder if we will develop this one and somehow already see it on my round end table.

We are both cold and tired after our morning outing. I drop Willow off at home tell her I would like to go to that park every month to see the changes, she says she has always wanted to reserve a patch to grow something. I imagine zucchini taking over and a single sunflower towering over us. I would enjoy some gardening. I shall look online to see how to reserve a spot for later in the year. We made a couple of long-term decisions today to reserve a spot, come here once a month until the planting season to look for pictures on the subject of next month's club meeting. I almost forgot about the tickets I had purchased, didn't even remember the exact name of the play but asked Willow to go just before dropping her off.

On my way home I stopped at Fred Meyer. As I parked, I am still laughing about the Christmas tree that had gotten lost. Entering the store, I see an apple in the shape of a heart, putting it the cart and a few other items, enough to get me through today and tomorrow. I don't plan on leaving until tomorrow to pick lunch up for me and mom. Now to find the photo section of the store. Seems like every time I am here it is for something different, and I have to learn where it is. The perfect frame with five 4" x 6" frames connected is right in front like it was waiting for me. I put it in my cart along with a couple other frames in case Willow approves of our photo being developed.

The rest of Saturday and half of Sunday are spent on the spreadsheets, at 3:00 pm I leave to get dinner for me and mom. She likes Italian best I think, I am not entirely sure as I didn't follow her likes and dislikes while I lived away from here and now that I am back, she appears to be an entirely different person still. When I would visit, or they would come to Milwaukee it was never just mom, always mom and dad. Since I was born that is how my entire life has been, except the past four months. Now mom is lighter somehow, another person, not half of mom and dad, maybe it is distance in her, she may not know how to relate to me. Dad always ran the paper company, and I am sure they talked around the dinner table every evening about their day at work. She has not asked me anything except if I plan to stay.

Checking the clock, I better hurry to Metropolitan Market, I hear they have a great selection of premade meals. I leave realizing halfway there I forgot my list and park somehow close but not actually, more like up the road and around the block. I am thinking of mom and the conversation we should have this evening and then the Space Needle comes into view just behind me and I recall New Years Eve, the night Willow and I spent getting to know each other. I snap a photo with my phone and send it to Willow with a smiley face. No expectation, just letting her know I am thinking of her.

I enter the store under the glass and metal awning, grab a cart and head towards the deli. Knowing I need to hurry I grab a couple lasagnas, a salad and a six pack of Tangerine San Pellegrino. I pick up a couple more dinners for later in the week and a cake from the bakery. Upon checking out I noticed the table decorations and bought a snowflake tablecloth and candle holders.

Mom arrives at 4:10 pm, right on schedule, she doesn't waste a minute anywhere. I need to get to know her. What does she do with the time she is not with me? I already have the lasagna reheating, the salad and dressing in a bowl on the table with the tablecloth. Mom sits and watches me as if I am a stranger, she gets up and slowly walks over to my newly framed photos on the living room wall. She asked if I had purchased them at the Farmers Market. I leave the pan on low with the lid and pull my camera out of the cabinet next to the refrigerator. She is surprised that I have taken them. Then says, "I don't know you anymore. It has been years." She has a sad look on her face, me knowing she misses dad and has probably missed me, her only child, for over twenty years. I nodded in agreement, telling her I have felt the same way about her and decided to have a sit-down sort of home cooked meal. I wished to tell her about my plans with the paper company and its expansion, ask what she knows about any of the employees specifically Hector, what she knows of the file box and strange birthdate hiring process and see what plans she has for herself. Maybe she will share details of part of her days with me.

She sits at the table as I serve her, looking a bit more relaxed. Then she draws her eyebrows together and looks at the two empty frames on my end table. She asks what I will put there. I pull out my phone, tell her I am not sure if the photo will be developed or just live on in my phone but show her the photos of Willow me at Greenwood Park. She smiles and takes some bites then says, "good, that is good, beautiful lady." She has never pried in my life and always waits for whatever information I choose to give. We finish eating, I load the dishwasher with our two plates and bring the cake over and tell her of my plans to expand the company and about the new website. I pull out a tube that has the spreadsheets and let her know I gave everyone Friday off and came home to crunch the numbers. Then I ask what she knows about the employees. The only information she has is about Allison and Laura and their job share. "Dad and her never talked in depth about their work," she says. Truthfully, she says she loved dad deeply but didn't want to bring either of their workplaces or coworkers into their home. I decided not to ask about the birthday files. It was dad's family who set up the paper company so she may not know even as much as I do.

I ask about her and her job, she has worked there for over 30 years and says she will continue, books are her passion if she has any left and the library is a space she is used to. I didn't get any more information from her about her life, so I told her of the photo club and the pictures she was looking at were from a trip to North Bend. She still does not open up but decides to leave and asks how I would feel about her selling the house. I am shocked by her question but need to act normal since it is her house. I ask her to think about it for a while if she wishes then said I may buy it if she sells it.

I walk mom to her car, wave as she drives off and know it will all be different from this moment on. What else is mom thinking of changing? Would I want to move to the house I grew up in? Three bedrooms isn't huge but enough space for me. Maybe I could get a pet or plant. This is different than when I bought the house on North Hawley Road with Alice. We had plans, now it is just me, maybe I don't want a yard or a couple floors. I have enough responsibility at work with that monstrosity of a building and all that goes on inside. A chill runs down my back as the wind whips my coat away from me and I realize I am still outside by my carport and mom is long gone. I don't think I wish to buy the house but will think on it before I make the final decision. As I return to my apartment and see the door is wide open, I clear the cake and plates off the table and open the tube saved from my mechanical engineering days imagining the spreadsheets as blueprints to what I am building currently.

Chapter 29

January 2025
Detective Muncer
Detective Rubio

Rubio and I both agreed it was time to pay Little Mel a visit again. We dropped my cruiser off at my residence and rode together. I already know I will regret this decision while parallel parking in front of my place. He listens to that stuff on the radio, slow music with barely a beat. I find myself tapping my toe wanting the music to go faster as we gain speed down I-5 but it never does.

We go south on I-5 back to Little Mel's for another surprise visit. Five in the morning they may still be up, or everyone will be passed out at once, they work as one. We pull in not in front as before since there are a few extra cars parked on the street. The lights are on, and we can see movement through the yellowed sheer curtain. They have seen us; all movement has stopped. The front gate is locked as we knew from before. I try the large slider gate that is used for vehicles to exit. It slides open, we enter the property from an angle they cannot see from the front window. As soon as we come into view the door opens and Raven exits, she is distraught but does not give us any indication of her source of angst. We are stunned as to why we are here, since we arrived to talk to Little Mel about Raven's body being discovered and she is standing alive right in front of us.

Little Mel walks out asking why we are here again. He is in a foul mood, unlike the prior visit. He doesn't wish to answer our questions but gives generic answers instead. He calls for Raven to stay with him while we talk. We allow him to falter for a while then he asks why we are here again. I told him about the body we thought was Ravens in North Seattle. He falls back as if in shock catching himself on the metal rusted handrail. He whispers, "Not Meade." Raven is walking in large circles in the yard, distraught as if she already knew something was wrong having the twin connection formed before birth. We ask them to explain what is going on, do they know the lady who looks identical to Raven?

Raven passes by uttering partial syllables about a twin, she is missing, went off with Don who showed up out of nowhere last week, always with a plan to get rich fast. Now we understand. Don had been in our first investigation with samarium mixed into the batch of methamphetamines that was on the streets a few months ago. They explained they were having a party for Don since he had just arrived back in town. We asked if Don was here, he had not been talked to after the last batch because he simply vanished along with

Donny who we have since found out passed away about the same time. The investigation came to a standstill due to overuse of the drugs and heart failure. Don is not here; everyone shakes their head no in unison. He left with Meade last night to go to North Seattle for a boat ride. He said they always had a not-so-secret love affair going on. He was driving a newer maroon pickup truck. Meade and Don had been dating for quite some time prior to him leaving for a family matter down south somewhere, they informed us.

Rubio is quite relieved his informant is alive but cannot talk with her here to blow her cover or put her in danger. He feels she may be playing both sides of this game. Loyal to no one and now her twin sister is dead. We left with another helix set of circumstances than when we arrived.

Back at the precinct we lay out the files and make a sketch on the whiteboard of each person and who was connected to who, then and now. The story hasn't changed much except Donny, Stephanie, and Meade are gone. We know for sure Little Mel has a couple of his crew use the back of the garage to cook the product. It is an area that doesn't appear to be seen from the street. From our last surveillance video, you can see a truck parked there all the way to the tool bench on the back wall. You would never know there is another room behind there. Also, Donny's old apartment on the far back exterior and a space with all his equipment for almost any job imaginable. It is an ideal property for many types of operations and is maintained well due to someone always being awake there. We believe the garage as we see it from the street used to be a large one-story shop or barn. We can see places along the edge that are propped up and repaired with general maintenance done by amateurs at 3:00 am.

Raven needs to meet with Rubio, send pictures, and give us a better run down on what happens there before there are any more victims. It has only been a few days, and the cases are racking up here in King County. Where else and who else is being affected by this? Who does Little Mel have cooking his product? Is it always the same person? Is he involved? I think he is not aware of the side business playing off of his watch.

Chapter 30

January 2025
August

The weekend has been quiet. It was so cold I didn't want to leave my apartment, Willow worked both days, and on Sunday evening we met for a late dinner at Jay's Café on Bothell Way NE. Neither of us were hungry but still wishing to see each other. Me being tired from lazing around all weekend with this being my only commitment and Willow from working all weekend. Surprisingly the camera industry is active this time of year with after Christmas sales, people gearing up for senior photos and thinking of spring break and summer vacations. The café was cozy except for the door opening with each customer entering and leaving, bringing leaves in with every swing of the heavy door. Both of us bundled up Willow chose to keep her black and white hounds tooth coat on. Me glad I wore my winter coat and scarf which nestled on my neck. We chose to split a Blue Cheeseburger and fries, neither of us saying much, just as I was wondering if it was a good idea to meet this evening, Willow looked up and smiled, handing me a French fry with a perfect line of ketchup on it hugging each crinkle. That's when we knew our silence was comforting.

I had completely forgotten last week after setting up the extra scheduled meetings due to the new online accounts and travel arrangements for Blake being made. Mom is selling her house, maybe. It has finally hit me now, right this minute, my childhood home could be gone. Willow looks at me with concern as I almost choke on a fry. I tell her about the possibility of the house sale and my contemplation of the purchase. She is silent with a look in her eyes, wanting an answer on my decision but not pushing. I don't have one, the only answers I have now are of the fear of both options. Willow says someday she may own a house but has not been faced with this much pressure and not having a family home to think about makes life easier. I told her I should have talked to Mom this week but haven't since all the items were added to my schedule. She laughs and says, "this is a grown-up decision, and I am not sure I will ever be grown up." After paying we stand in the parking lot for a minute, but the temperature is near 20°, we are both shaking, a quick hug, and proceed to our vehicles. Willow waves and signals to drive west as I follow a short distance, her waving at her turn-off for home. Me with a smile on my face and relief that I have a friend in this city. I stopped at Metropolitan Market again for my weekly groceries. My new comfort food store. The idea of premade meals is easiest during my busy schedule and adjustment to my new life. This evening, I will text Mom to ask if she wishes to get together this week for dinner.

It is Monday morning again. I am starting to get into the routine of being in Seattle. After so many years of being emailed my schedule for the day and working in the field, I can't lie being in a large warehouse has taken some getting used to. It is still dark out with winter in full swing. My mind is going a million miles an hour with the expansion, website, Blake's travel plans and running a company that is new to me. This is the start of my fifth month being back here in Seattle. I must have been on autopilot as I am on 4th Avenue and almost to work. The light changes to red in front of Spinner Records, through the large paned windows I see three individuals moving about at a high rate of speed toting crates to the back door. Suddenly another person enters, one much larger than the other three who appear younger. To my amazement he shoots all three of them, runs to the back knocking stacks of crates over, and leaves out the rear door to the alley. I can see the green neon sign with the exit left open and no one standing. Just as I take all this in, he runs by me, his face covered, and he is stocky with a green canvas-type work coat. I am on my cell with 911 describing the scene. They ask if I am in danger or need medical aid, nodding no then I realize the dispatcher cannot see me. I hear sirens coming from all directions, the first thing I think is I have never dealt with the police before, I haven't even had a traffic ticket.

Detective Muncer arrives on the scene. I am still in my vehicle, too frightened to get out or to drive off, there is a shooter on the loose, things you hear about on television. The dispatcher tells me officers are on the scene and ask what I am driving so I can give a statement. I immediately regret having called and being connected to this. Muncer walks up and asks for my statement, calling me by name. This makes me uneasy. I have always been under the impression that you don't want the police to know who you are. I give my statement, and answer their questions, not wishing to see inside the floor-to-ceiling windows, forever grateful for the crates along the window to block my view of the horrific scene inside.

I get back in my vehicle, heading south to the warehouse again, wishing I had not left home this early to get work done when I have not done any. Only putting myself in danger. I pull into the back parking lot, just like every other day, but today I am anxious. I park right next to the back door, grab my backpack and lunch, and open the door looking for the shooter, rationalizing with myself that he most likely isn't here and didn't run in this direction. Thinking about Sven, having left a couple of hours ago and making my way to my clean office. I get inside the 10,000-square-foot warehouse and realize I am alone, which doesn't usually bother me but today is not like any other day I have lived. I probably witnessed three people being murdered. I did not see any ambulances at Spinners while I was being questioned so there was no urgency to help the people who had been shot.

Just as I take a few steps inside I hear a bang, then slam, it echoes through the enormous building. I climb the stairs staying against the handrail having something to hold while looking up and down safely. Just as I get to my door a text comes through, scaring me even more being on such high alert. Reaching my office at the top of the stairs I pull my keys out of my coat pocket trembling so badly I barely get the door open. I drop my bags, lock the door, and there it is again bang, slam with a greater force. I come to the reality that I am here, safely inside, and am the leader of this establishment so I must get it together. No one else will arrive for about another hour. I creep back down the stairs hearing the noise again, exit to the rear of the building, and see a piece of corrugated sheet metal has come loose on two corners, and with each wind gust it slams into the building. I return inside locking the door behind me, getting the aluminum extension ladder from the storage closet, some nails, and a hammer. The first thing that has felt good all day, doing something positive. Just as I am coming down off the ladder Patrick from shipping pulls in driving a full-sized Chevy Silverado and asks me if I am done. I nod and he grabs the ladder and returns it to its proper place like it is his possession. He says, "your dad sent me to Ace Hardware to purchase this ladder" and turns away with what I think was a tear in his eye. My morning story will not be shared with him. His head is full of prior memories. This morning, I am especially thankful my dad is here with me at least in spirit.

I take the stairs two at a time and return to my office, put away my backpack and lunch, and get back to my chair just as Blake shows up. Chipper and dapper, he is always positive, and eager to be on his way for the meeting scheduled in Idaho. That is why he does the outside sales. The box for his sales trip containing flyers, business cards, samples, and pamphlets is on the table only lacking four dozen cupcakes that were promised by 9:00 am. He is ready to leave, and it isn't even 8:00 am. Remembering my text I take out my phone and see it is Willow, who never initiates a text. I handed Blake a prepaid Visa for his two-night stay, fuel, and meals and sent him downstairs to load his vehicle and search for the cupcakes.

Willow asked if she could see the house sometime. I told her I would ask Mom about her plans for this weekend. The first normal thoughts of the morning bring a smile to my already used-up emotional state. Secretly hoping mom will be at work and Willow can have a comfortable tour with just me.

I know I would love to see Willow tonight even though we will be going to Mom's house over the weekend so she can see it. On impulse I text her

Me: Would you like to meet for dinner this evening?

Willow: a new place?

Me: Where?

Willow: The Unicorn 1118 E. Pike Street

Me: see you there.

Just as I put my phone away and hear Blake asking around about the cupcakes, I hear Hector yelling, "Bossman, bossman." I am quite surprised and envision an emergency. He has never, since I have been here, sought me out except after our last day at Seattle Photography when we were at Cloud City Coffee. He was quite clear he didn't want me meddling in his affairs.

He enters at a high rate of speed, returning to the landing equally as quickly, knocking as he goes in both directions and entering again. "Bossman, I need help. There is a box at my house, and I don't drive. Can you take me? If you do, I will need the box, which was my grandpa's, to stay in your vehicle and then be taken back to my residence at quitting time, or I can cart it home on a hand truck."

I am not entirely sure of what I am getting myself into but my curiosity about Hector still stands, even though he has asked me to stay out of his business. Just as we exit the building Remy, from the photo club, comes out from behind us getting into a Subaru in the parking lot. As far as I know, Hector is the only person Remy knows here so who else could he be seeing at this hour and why? Does he work for one of our contracts and is picking up or a supplier of a product we use? We got into my vehicle, Hector saying I was parked in a different space today. I did not feel this was the right time to share my morning with him, so I just took directions from him as we cut across town towards the water. He lives in Pioneer Square, explaining his grandpa left him this place to him after he passed away. He instructs me to park and says he will be right back. After a short while Hector returns with a hand truck and a large old box. He asks if the hand truck can stay or should he take it back in. I open the back hatch for him to place the box inside. When he gets back in, I ask about the leak. He looks at me like he doesn't remember that is the reason he is here. I ask nothing further just drive back to the warehouse. When we pull in Hector says, "Thank you for helping me, I didn't feel I could trust anyone else with this box. I will be ready to leave whenever you are today, please dock my pay for the inconvenience." I told him we all have emergencies now and then; this was no trouble.

As I surveyed the parking lot, I saw Blake's vehicle was already gone. I couldn't have made a better choice in picking the outside sales representative with his up-to-date fashion. Just like out of the store windows I see on my way home while driving through downtown. His attitude is just like he is aware his paycheck is connected to his sales quota, but he is genuine, always happy, looks you in the eye whenever you pass him and always asks how you are. Maybe I should know more about all my employees, listening at birthday parties should bring more information. I don't need to know a lot about them, but it is nice to create a connection. I

think I will add a whiteboard in the breakroom for
needs whether it is for yard work, a maintenance issue,
or a material product maybe we can all help each other
out some.

Chapter 31

January 2025
~~Detective Muncer~~

Monday morning, almost time to end my shift and duty to this city for the night. I am already composing in my head what the next beats will be, and a call comes through the radio. The reporter is August Rike, which reminds me I need to pick up the report on him from Hazel later today. Before responding I emailed Hazel asking for the report to be delivered to my private inbox. The in-box system seems dated, I check it every night before my shift unless I am called out directly from home.

Upon arrival at Spinners Records on 4th Avenue the patrol officers who had responded said victims were three down, shooter on the run going north. I enter the front door, which is wide open, every light in the place on so to see each detail more in-depth than I need to, surveying blood spatter and angles. The back door frame splintered but the lock had been drilled out as if they attempted to drill and became impatient and compromised the door. Stacks of crated records were stacked near the office by the exit as if they were taking them and got interrupted similar to the victims last week at Bud's House.

I greet August by name and ask for his statement, he looks irritated and scans the scene for the patrol officers. I tell him I know he has already relayed his story to them but not to me. I may see things differently than they do. I mostly focus on the shooter and his description. Stocky build and green canvas shop coat were the only two items I needed to know the scenes were connected. It matches the one from last week and so does the storyline but how does he know when these crimes will be committed and be there to commit and justify them?

This time there are three. Three wasted lives who decided records were worth more than their own lives. It looks as if they may have gotten away with this if it wasn't for our vigilante crime stopper. Javon Reid, 15 years old; Kendrick Minor, 14 years old; and Matthew Kolton, 17 years old. I always wonder about these tragic deaths. Did they happen because their lives would have been worse if they had lived longer? This was not a good way to die but possibly more painless than if they had gone on to become career criminals, I think of the families involved. That is why I return to the streets daily. At this point in the investigation, I don't have any background on these murdered young ones and the patrol officers will notify the families. I am curious about where the victims lived, and how they knew each other. Patrol says they all live in the same building just on different floors. This will be hard to deliver the news of these children's departure. Most of the time children will grow up in the same neighborhood whether rich, poor, or middle class. These ones probably had some history behind them and could have gone in a different direction, but this is where they chose to end it, where they were left to bleed out. Their story ends and mine has just begun on this case. There were no other clues in the pot shop case that have been made obvious in the past few days. Hopefully, there are cameras on the shooter's exit route that may reveal a vehicle.

I am done for this shift, going home with pieces of Randell Rinwell, Little Mel and his crew, the Capital Hill victims, and now these from Spinners Records downtown. My list keeps getting longer and the clues more unclear but eventually the story comes out. I pull up in my usual parking space, placing my police parking placard on the dash and go inside, change, grab a piece of bread, an apple, and head upstairs. The music runs through my head and must come out.

Solving Shadows

Verse 1

Seattle, where the rain don't stop,

Detectives grindin', always on top.

Murders in the alley, no time to chill,

Bakin' up this heat, like I'm whipin' up a thrill.

248

August Island Rike Paper Company

Paper company pushin', stackin' that crop,

Ladies' actin' shady, but I'm never gonna stop.

Flexin' on the streets, with the crew at night,

Got my eyes on the prize, bringin' truth to the light.

Chorus

Solvin' shadows in the city of dreams,

Ain't no haltin' this hustle, burstin' at the seams.

Thug life mentality thinks, we ahead of the game,

Caring for the fam, but they ain't playin' tame.

Verse 2

Crimes in the night like a thief in the dark,

Murder scenes vivid, I'm the one with the spark.

Bakin' pastries, but the dough ain't sweet,

Got a nose for the truth, can't accept defeat.

This city's playin' chess, I'm the king on the board,

Got my mind on my mission, my heart like a sword.

People trippin', but I'm never gonna fall,

Seattle's my playground, I'm rollin' through it all.

Chorus

(Bridge)

In the cruiser, got the heat on blast,

Criminal minds twist, but my visions steadfast.

Police sippin' lattes while I'm huntin' the kill,

Seattle's heartbeat, you can feel that thrill.

Verse 3

Unraveling the plot, like I'm snappin' a thread,

Every clue's a piece, put 'em all in my head.

I'm the shadow in the night, always creepin' deep,

All for the souls we lost, man, I promise I'll keep.

Real talk, we care, but it's raw as it gets,

Keepin' heads on a swivel, drownin' out the regrets.

So when the sirens wail, I'm the one they call,

Seattle's finest, I'm ready for it all.

Outro

So here's a toast to the streets, and the battles we face,

Seattle detective, I'm locked in the chase.

We the voice of the lost, bringing light to the night,

In this city of shadows, I'm ready to fight.

#MunDet J # DJ Muncer #Seattle Strong

Chapter 32

January 2025
August

This week has gone faster than the other ones where I had no idea what my purpose was. I am a bit nervous about taking Willow to see my family homestead tomorrow. Truthfully, I have only been there once since Dad's funeral. I am not sure of her reasoning, but Mom is aloof, just hasn't invited me, got used to being forced to live here without me, and now has chosen a time to not be at the house when I show Willow. Maybe she wants me to purchase the home so it will be easy for her. She will not have to find an agent, feel guilty about selling outside of the family, or worry about clearing out the place she has called home for longer than I have been alive.

I have an idea to bring Willow to see the house and order lunch to be delivered. Maybe even leave a meal for mom in the refrigerator.

Willow arrives at my apartment for the first time, this whole day is making me antsy. She knocks and I almost don't invite her in but grab my coat as if to leave. She has a paper bag in her hand from Kenmore Camera and hands it to me. I step back, letting her across the threshold into my space, she pulls out a chair and waits for me to open the bag. It is the photo of us from last month at Greenwood Station Park. I smiled and placed it in the empty frame from my end table that had been awaiting this photo. Willow asks if I am ready for this excursion as I grab my keys and coat.

I seem to not place my residence and moms in close proximity but go west on 85th Street and turn right a short distance ahead on 11th Avenue NW. Pulling up in front I realize neither of us has said a word on the short trip here. Willow turns to me as I pull into the driveway of the two-story beige house with white trim that has a freshly manicured lawn edged completely around. All the hydrangea bushes are trimmed, and not a leaf or weed in sight. We enter through the front door; I smell fresh paint, and this is not the furniture that was here the last time I visited. There is a red leather sofa and recliner, round hammered metal coffee, and end tables. The large family dining table in the next room has been replaced with a glass and metal table and industrial-looking chairs. I have not said a word since entering but can't help but think of Alice in her new condo replacing or covering up our lives and creating a new one. Willow proceeds to the kitchen, touching the finish on the cabinets, opening the refrigerator and turns to me asking what is wrong. I tell her this may be the house I grew up in, but it is not how it looked last I was here. She says she doesn't need to see any more if I wish to leave. Then I spot a central sound system and see the television is no longer front and center in the living room. I ask if Willow would like to have lunch here or go out. She pulls out a chair that still has plastic on it and sits at the dining table placing a cloth napkin under her elbow so as not to leave prints on the table.

We order Uber Eats; Willow says she would like to see the backyard and the bedroom that used to be mine. I had not been in that room since high school and at that moment I understood how disconnected I was from this house back then and now. Mom should sell it. It is not somewhere I wish to return to, but I want to think of all the happy memories that were made here. There are not three of us anymore, only two who are both starting over and I feel at least I need to move on.

We see my room that has been turned into a library and the back yard is as immaculate as the front. Mom must have hired a gardener; I do not have any memories of her out pushing the lawn mower. I see in the garage Dad's car; sadness covers me that he will not be driving to the paper company any longer. That torch was passed to me. I pulled away from the window and Willow looked in, seeming to understand why my mood had changed. We are both cold and ready to go. I wiped down the new table and left a note for Mom thanking her for letting us in and telling her about the dinner we left for her.

Willow and I chose not to go to the locks as it is so cold. A place saved for another time. We drive around aimlessly neither one of us ready for the day to be over. We both agreed that Sloop Tavern, on Market Street, would be an interesting place to visit because of the animals that have been painted on the side of the building, especially the unicorn. We find a parking space easily as it is still early on a Saturday. We enter, take a booth and both order a beer and split an order of fries. The tension has rolled off of me and Willow appears content. I tell her of the old furniture, and lawn that used to have spots where Dad removed dandelions, the paint color isn't even the same. She says she likes the house and is happy she could see where I grew up.

I look at my phone, see the date, and am not sure if I have asked Willow to go with me to see Blues to an Alabama Sky on January 30th. That is coming up in a few days. I showed her the tickets and apologized for not asking sooner but explaining I had forgotten She says she has always wanted to go to a real play and has only attended one while in high school. We discussed acting on television versus on stage, then I showed her a picture of the door with August Wilson's name on it and how I had come to find it. I could see Willow was getting tired. I don't think it's from her strenuous day but thinking about her workday tomorrow. There is always one Sunday a month she is required to work. We leave and go back to my house; she declines coming in as I already knew she would. One thing I love about

Josephine Plummer

Willow is she cherishes her solitude as much as I do. After a longer hug than usual, I close her car door for her and wave as she drives away.

I go in just as my phone rings, it is mom thanking me for dinner and asking if she can bring something over tomorrow. She does not mention the changes she has made at the house or ask any questions about my opinion. We plan for dinner at my place the next evening.

Saturday, I go shopping but don't worry about dinner as mom is bringing it, take my camera by the Space Needle and shoot from different angles remembering New Year's Eve with fondness. I come home and nap before our meeting, as I call it.

I guess I overslept this week since I am making progress in the company and my personal life, I have been more tired. Mom is knocking at the door as I am peeling the blanket off me, holding it as I answer. She had brought a great deal of food. I draped the blanket over the chair, relieving her of the bags as she looked on in question. We are having food from The Yard Café; a place mom has eaten frequently since working at the library. Today she brought a monster of a salad called Cardini Salad and the Yard Bird Chicken sandwich to split. During dinner we are almost silent then she tells me she has decided to remodel the house and then see if she wishes to sell but would like help in selling Dad's Buick. He loved that car and named the vehicle Vera

256

since it was a Verano. The tension was broken at this point and mom walked over to see the new picture in its frame on my end table. I told her I liked her taste in the furniture and would be there to help with whatever she decided. She yawns, puts on her coat, and hugs me, tired from the week since Sunday is her Friday. I wonder what she will do on her days off but do not ask.

Chapter 33

February 2025
~~Detective Muncer~~

I have never been good at keeping track of business cards and frequently lose contact information unless scribbled in my notebook or on a report as most contact is temporary. Once the case is closed, I no longer need the information, or if I did it would be in the file. I am thankful for Hazel who retains all knowledge. I also keep forgetting to ask how her friend Hal something in England is doing.

With Agent Frederick Ford being newly assigned to the Seattle headquarters, I am fortunate to have met and been introduced to him but I for sure have lost his card. Hazel can point me in the right direction. I stay up later than usual, 9:00 am or before is my normal retiring time each day. The traffic on the Aurora Bridge and boats in the Fremont Cut lull me to sleep. It is comforting to know I am not out dealing with all the masses of people who operate in this city during the daylight hours. When I have been out, I see them commuting on skateboards and buses, zipping through traffic on bicycles going faster than cars. Their lives are so close to the edge with these performances daily to survive. Backpacks full of clothes, books, and groceries.

I am overthinking my trip out this morning to stop at the precinct then over to 3rd Avenue and Seneca St. to find parking.

Being with the Seattle PD for so long I am privileged to find parking in most situations. Going to visit Agent Ford parking is not a given. There is only street parking and this time in the day it is at a premium. I grab some change for the meter if I can find a space.

Hazel is chipper this morning, as usual, she is geared up for her daily routine. I got the information on Agent Ford from her and asked her how the friend she went to visit some time ago was doing. She looks at me puzzled and laughs, then sits and laughs some more. This is not normal behavior for Hazel. She is always happy or at least cordial, but I have never seen her outright laugh before. Her personality appears to be between two lines that she does not cross, always staying in her zone. Thinking back, I have never seen her angry, not even when her mother, Vera, was murdered or at the killers who were caught. I am taken aback by this outburst of laughter but now that I have created this mess I have to remain here until she is composed enough to reply. I see she needs tissue from the tears of joy running down her cheeks. I retrieve some from the desk next to hers. She looks at me, apologizes, and claims she is fine then goes on to say her friend Halverson is doing well too.

She keeps looking at me out of the corner of her eye. Thinking she might not be done relaying her story to me even though she did answer my question without giving any details. I look back and Hazel is opening her desk drawer retrieving something. She hands me a copy of a children's book with a dragon and a gray-haired lady on the cover. Hazel tells me this is the friend she took time to go see. She explains about Halverson, her childhood, and how she brought the book on her travels to the stops she had made while in the Navy.

I leave with the gift of my children's book, Halverson, amazed that Hazel has had this secret for some time. We all think we know people, but everyone has secrets, good and bad. I call Agent Ford on my way out, he is on his way back to headquarters and has a few minutes to meet with me.

I get to 3rd Avenue and of course, I don't find parking; after circling the block a few times around I park at the Diamond lot on 2nd Avenue. It has been so long since I have used paid parking, I was looking for the pay box or attendant, but neither was present. There was a sign by the entrance with directions on how to pay online with my phone. After getting that set up, I walked over to FBI Headquarters arriving at the same time as Agent Ford. I have only met him on a couple of brief occasions so am not comfortable calling him Fred. He turns, smiles, and shakes my hand calling me Detective. I feel these are acceptable titles for us, agent and detective. We walked down the long, carpeted hallway to his office in silence.

I am surprised he does not have a desk but prefers to work as I do on a large wooden table. His is government issued too and possibly from the 1950s like mine, surplus from a time of war.

Being comfortable in his presence I pull out a chair and sit, pulling my files out of my tactical backpack. I ask if he would be willing to give me some input on a cold case from last year. Also, if he has time, give a rough profile on a current case. He looks at me with an unknowing expression. Most of my cases do not end at the federal level except last year with Pearl Swanson and her crew. He then smiles reminding me of that case and tells me of his input on it. Informing me that case is what made him choose to apply for this position in Seattle. He says he would love to help and has a few minutes but could make more time to talk first thing tomorrow morning.

I leave a copy of the photos I printed from the night Randell Rinwell was killed and the one from New Year's Eve this year at the Space Needle. He compares them saying, "it is the same male, 6 ft tall, look at that beard, it grows like the wind is under it." We sit back laughing, noticing our first meeting has been complete due to time constraints. I thank him for his time with the promise of being here at 8:00 am tomorrow. Reversing my trip back to the Diamond lot to retrieve my cruiser and then drive home in all these uniform lines of traffic.

I arrived home; my parking space is open. I see the offending vehicle up the block a couple of spaces. Entering something feels off, I search every room downstairs, go upstairs, walk around the building and see a green 1980s olive green Samsonite by the side of my house. It has been a few weeks since I have been out here. I noticed my basement door is open, just a bit. Maybe because the weather does strange things to that door, swelling and retracting with the heat and moisture. I can't even remember the last time I was down here, maybe in September when I put the lawn mower away. I pull my weapon, tap open the door, and announce myself as police before entering. As soon as I take my first footstep into the dark musty-smelling basement I hear movement from the corner near the shelves where Mrs. Johnson kept her wire baskets of gardening equipment. I announce myself again and a female voice whispers, "Jeffery it is Jill." I am in shock, not feeling danger but you can never be sure there are thousands of Jill's in the world, but not all know my name. My sister is here, I don't know why she is in my basement or where the rest of my family is, but Jill is here. I try to hug her even in her filthy state to bring her inside, but she flinches. The vibrant outgoing teenager who went to Mexico twenty-one years ago sits in that shell of skin and bone, but she is not the same person as the one who left. She kept apologizing, saying when they let her go, she didn't want to be a burden to me but had nowhere to go and never meant to park in my spot or stay on my property. She utters something about the suitcase being left outside and if she had brought it in, I would have never suspected her being here.

I am in shock still; twenty-one years is a long time to not have any family. My mind and body have adjusted but now this is different. It is too soon for either of us to get to the bottom of what happened all those years ago but right now I need to know if she knows where mom, dad, and Joshua are. She shakes her head as if in disbelief only saying they separated us all and I got away a few days or weeks ago. I need my diploma, that was my graduation trip, it was horrible. I put my hand out for her to take if she wishes. Leaving her plaid sleeping bag and old pillow on the well-worn shelf, she attempts to place the wire baskets up in the corner in order. I say no, taking her hand and leading her inside, grabbing the heavy suitcase on the way back up the hill. It has been a long night already and closer to lunchtime than breakfast, but I am awake and do not envision a time for sleep anywhere on the clock dial. I ordered a pizza, remembering Jill loved pepperoni and pineapple with extra cheese, and opened a beer asking if she wanted one or a soda. As she sits at the kitchen table that once belonged to Mrs. Johnson, I see my broken sister and, not knowing what else to do, I show her where everything is in the kitchen and take the olive-green Samsonite to the spare room. Happy Jill is here and go to sit with her turning the radio on a mellow station wishing I could remember which one Rubio listened to. Each day has its own twists, this one was an enormous bombshell. I sit and look at Jill sipping her Coke and start to tell her about Mrs. Johnson and Everett Sunshine.

Chapter 34

February 2025
Detective Muncer

Sleep is a required item on my list. It is well into the day. Jill sits here; I am positive she is wondering what to do. She says that her vehicle is out front sort of, at least the one she arrived in. She may not even wish to stay here; I am not convinced this would be a good location for her. She is my sister, and I will offer my spare room. I am still in shock over her arrival and will need to get a list of questions together for her but now I need sleep.

I handed Jill the remote, telling her she was welcome to stay and asking if she wished to remain here for the day or however long she may need showing her the bathroom and linen closet. Then it hits me what if someone is looking for her? I ask her and she nods no but I am not entirely convinced of this. She knows I work nights; I am aware that she would need a key if she were to stay here. These are all matters to work out when I wake up. I am uneasy leaving her alone for her safety, mine, and my earthly possessions. Truthfully, I don't know her or who she may associate with but know this is Jill.

Sleep comes fast, like the past twelve or more hours were a dream. I know I will be shocked when I wake up and Jill is out there. I have always lived alone since college and just having another presence in my space is throwing me off. I dream of my family, the last time I saw them at the airport, wishing I could go with them, we had always been a close family. Me newly hired at Seattle PD and the twins Jill and Joshua just graduated from high school. I could see us all in the dream, a time I do not visit mentally particularly often as there have not been any clues since my three-year exhaustive search until today.

I wake at 9:00 pm knowing Jill is there, take a shower, then go out to the living room. The television is on, but it is silent, Jill is curled up and covered in the old rocking chair. I remember now I took her suitcase into the room but never offered it to her. She stirs and says she is sorry she fell asleep; I ask her to follow me back to the guest room. She walks behind me, which is something that puts me on edge from my occupation. I work through that reasoning with myself, she sits on the bed wearing the blanket from the living room. This is awkward for both of us, I ask her to join me in the kitchen as I go through my usual preparations for my night on the street. She returns almost robotic like to the kitchen like she is used to being told what to do. I ask if she would like to use the guest room for a while, and she nods yes, if she has any plans for the future, she nods no. I see we are not getting anywhere, and my questions are making her withdraw deeper into herself. This will take a few days to get straight, but this is my house and my ground rules, I hand her a key that she does not take so I place it on the table in front of her, tell her if she goes anywhere to lock up when leaving. My one request is that she does not bring people here, ever. I know that sounds harsh, but I do not know her story or even who she has been created into. I ask if she is ok here alone since I work nights. She smiles, gets up, and hugs me. I know she understands my side of this twenty-one years is a long time to not see someone.

I proceed with my routine, lunchbox, icepack, food, drink, napkins, and a notepad. It is 10:00 pm, time to roll out into the streets and join the night crew. The weather is below freezing, I can't believe Jill was outside for at least a couple of weeks since first I saw the car in the parking spot. Something is not adding up, if she escaped from somewhere where did the car come from?

I head south; my plan is to keep an eye out for the stocky vigilante wearing a green work coat. He has hit twice now, both times around the downtown area between 2:00 am and 5:00 am. My guess is that he works nights as I do. There is no way for him to have known about the burglaries in progress unless he was one of them. What would it profit him if he killed each set of people and didn't take anything, or did he? Is there some other connection that goes deeper than pot and rare LPs? I drive by both locations, circling the buildings, and checking the alleyways. Behind Spinners Records I see a short Styrofoam coffee cup placed just behind the dumpster with the name James written with a heart next to it, I bag it and plan to take it in for processing. It may not have anything to do with this case but maybe the break we need to solve it. I circle the block by Bud's House, hoping for an identical clue with no such luck. I combed the alley, walking with my flashlight thinking of the way a police officer's mind works. Certainly not as the average civilian. We are who you call when something happens, we are not the callers, we are possibly the only ones who race towards crimes and ghettos when it is the most unsafe. I am not positive what has brought me to this alley at 1:00 am by myself looking for a dangerous man but I am committed to protecting the city of Seattle and its occupants to the best of my ability.

The precinct is always open to me at any hour. I carefully remove the evidence bag so as not to spill the remainder of the coffee. After dusting the porous material of the cup and finding a partial print, I run it through the fingerprint system, coming up with no matches. The cup only has the writing in pen on it so did not come from Starbucks or other big brand coffee stand in the slew of local coffee shops. This means that it is probably not from a breakroom but maybe a cafeteria that does not focus solely on coffee. All this thought and energy and this may not have anything to do with this crime.

I finish the rest of the notes on this case, copy any pertinent files on Randell Rinwell, and search the list of files relating to the murders last year from the bad batch of drugs. Adding the new ones to my personal note as well as the notes about the green-coated vigilante, then head out again.

I hope my meeting with Agent Ford can happen a bit early. I arrive and find street parking on Seneca Street, wait in my vehicle perusing the files until 7:30 am then call Agent Ford. He was available and glad I had called ahead of schedule. I enter the building through the front door showing my badge which I know is inferior here, walk the carpeted hallway to Agent Ford's office, and sit realizing how tired I am and how large this load is that I am asking him to help with.

He looks at me strangely, we are not friends nor are we even acquainted, and I just sat down without being invited. I tell him briefly about Jill's return and my exhaustion. He wishes to know more at a later date, which I am grateful for. He pushes my original file of the bearded man back across the table to me. I see there is writing on the back, turn it over and see the name Levi Maddox DOB 02/02/1986, North Dakota driver's license, address listed as Little Missouri River, Marmarth, ND. While on shift tonight I need to contact Slope County Sheriff in Marmarth, ND to process the warrant for Levi Maddox, Randell Rinwell's murderer. We talked about Levi Maddox in connection with Randell Rinwell and the warrant procedure of a processed warrant and put in a request for extradition for the coordination of both agencies. It will be out of my hands until I am privileged with the opportunity to visit with Levi and his wind-blown beard. I do not have time now to process the information knowing I need this time to talk about a profile for the vigilante. I am generally an accurate profiler, and my guess is almost always right on cue but since I am here, I may as well use his professional input. I give a condensed version of the cases at Bud's House and Spinner Records and briefly read the reports involved. Agent Ford asks a few questions about associations and then says he doesn't think the lone perpetrator is connected to law enforcement or the military. He has a sense of justice that only he can deliver, in his own style, performs his own surveillance, or happens upon these places by chance but that is highly unlikely. His personality is equipped with a short fuse that only he can control but needs outbursts with such a high level of stress in his life. Most likely a dissatisfied individual in their mid-40s to 50s, blue-collar worker, not from the city originally, experiencing cultural shock or not used to crime on the scale of a large city. This gives me quite a bit to compile on this case. I thank Agent Ford and rise to leave. He asked if I would like to meet later in the week to talk about my family and that cold case. I am relieved he shows interest as that was not a case I was here to share. I tuck the file back into my backpack pertaining to Little Mel, not addressing this case, along with the newly acquired notes on the green-coated vigilante and

August Island Rike Paper Company

Randell Rinwell's killer. Levi Maddox, now I have a
name. Agent Ford says he will call later in the week
once his schedule is cleared. I am hoping he will not
want to meet in the middle of the day as I need to sleep
but am grateful and will do what is needed for my
family and the city of Seattle.

Chapter 35

February 2025
August

It is always a shock to arrive at the warehouse and see everyone performing their job, the boxes of orders ready to ship and be delivered. I am still not used to this, not being from a contained world and working in the field for so long.

As I walk up the stairs, I see a note taped to my door simply addressed to me. I open it as I sit at my desk. It is a notice from Lori who works in the mail room. She states she is sorry but will not be back. She had applied for another position when she thought this company would be sold and the new position is a better fit for her. She also thanks me and says she values all the years she worked with Garrett. It ends with this notice and is effective today.

I have never hired anyone and started thinking of the process. Also, this is where my idea of cross-training comes in. Now if I can remember who I trained in the mail room to process all incoming and outgoing orders. Then I remembered I need Lori's file from HR to see what her birthdate is so I can keep up with the Rike way of hiring. I call Dustin for the file, there is a knock on my door and my cell phone rings simultaneously. Dustin had the file and said he had posted the note from Lori on my door that someone else had dropped it off. He stood there looking at me as my cell was ringing then asked if she was ok. I confirmed she was, not knowing if I should divulge the information of her fate then Dustin said Beau can help out in the mail room if Lori will not be in, says he will talk to him and turns to leave. I am still not convinced this company needs me, but it does give me something to do. I am fulfilling my duty to my family legacy. If I did wish to sell, I would want to leave it in a better state than when I took over and it provides a healthy paycheck. I opened the file and found the most important part; Lori was born in July. Not something I can advertise but surely it will be on the employment application. That is the next step, to provide online applications. Our turnover rate is extremely low, but I am positive people do leave for other opportunities occasionally.

I go to put Lori's file in the closet along with other past employees and call Dustin to make sure he knows to bring the files to me immediately of anyone who no longer works there.

Then I remember the call from before, I retrieve my voicemail. It is Detective Muncer asking for me to return his call. One of my pet peeves is when people ask for a return call but don't leave any indication of what they want. I feel it is best to be prepared when returning the call. I think I am just irritated that Muncer called me by name outside of Spinners when the shooting occurred. Of course, it could have been I had given my name as the witness and reporter of the crime but the way he looked at me I feel there was more to it than that.

I returned his call to the number he left which didn't look like an office number. He answers on the first ring with "Muncer." I state who I am and don't really have much prior interaction with the police, so I don't want to ask what he wants. He is still silent so I ask, "How can I help you?" He asks if I have thought of anything else about the incident at Spinners, doesn't wait long enough for me to respond, and says this is actually a personal call. Says his sister Jill is back in town, long story, may need a job, he will know soon and wonders if I have any positions open. Without thinking I respond with, "When is her birthday?" He tells me in July, being taken aback goes on to say that it is an odd question for hiring. Naturally, a detective would pick up on that. He thanks me and asks again if I have any openings. I immediately told him about the position that recently became available. Then he asks if it is ok to give Jill my contact information, the cell or office phone. I told him office so it can all be done properly even though she has the position if she can do the job since she was born in July.

Suddenly I feel as if I work here, as if I am in charge, original systems are falling in place. I open the administrative area of the website, add the application and post an open position. I know I will not be talking to anyone else about the mail room job but post it anyway. I quickly text Muncer the link to the application adding a note "if she decides. Thank you."

The day speeds by with all the activity and me surprisingly working as my job title suggests. This is the first day I have felt a solid connection with my suddenly acquired company. Not long after lunch, an application arrives from Jill Muncer. All information was filled out except for former employer contact. She has the skills to perform this job if she can do as she states on the application. I know there is more to this story and will ask Jill when I call her this afternoon to arrange for an interview tomorrow.

It is dark already and I am not familiar with the exact area of the Unicorn, so I leave a bit early smiling as I go, happy I am handling tasks as they arise. I saw Beau on the way out and thanked him for his efforts today by helping in the mail room.

I proceed north on I-90 and I-5 interchange to Olive Way and Pine, finding the Unicorn midblock with its brightly colored turquoise and black striped exterior. I find parking up the block aways and notice Willow walking towards the restaurant. We enter almost at the same time; it feels festive here to match my accomplished day. The multicolored walls and bizarre decorations fit the mood. I am so happy to see Willow and glad she recommended this place. We each ordered the Pine / Pike Burger, and she orders a Little Town

Lager, and I took a Horizon IPA. We sit and take in the décor then we see the photo booth and decide to get a picture before our order arrives. The arcade will be a fun activity after dinner. I haven't played pinball since I was in high school, the years rolling off me at the end of this productive day. Our dinner was fabulous, the arcade was such an unexpected surprise, and a bonus evening with Willow. This day is the best one I have had since moving here. I walk Willow to her car after we are done. We sit in her vehicle for an hour watching the foot traffic on the street and talking of the past and present. She yawns and I know it is time for this evening to be over. I think I am lucky not to have a dog or any other obligations I don't ever have to worry about getting home to. I desire more evenings like this in my future. I briefly kiss Willow and confirm our plans for Saturday. Mom will be at work, but she doesn't mind me showing Willow the house, she didn't ask me to who. I still need to talk to Mom on Sunday about her plans and have no idea why Willow wishes to see it, but we will make a day of it and go to the Locks afterward, if it is not too cold. I make it home at 9:00 pm, tired but too excited thinking of the day I just had to sleep. I open a beer that I had picked up at Metropolitan Market and watch something on TV, my mind not on the show but on the order my life is taking.

I get up the next morning ready to go, checking the website to see if there are any more applications for the open position. Luckily there is still only one from Jill. I am excited about our interview. This is the first one I have ever conducted. Jill arrives and is escorted up the stairs by Allison to my office. I think in retrospect that we could have conducted this interview in the lunchroom, a less formal location.

   Jill is tall, like Muncer, and has the same color hair but much finer features. I hadn't planned on any questions so just went with what came to me. This is a learning experience for me as much as it is for her. She sits stiffly across the monstrosity of a desk from me, I introduce myself and ask if she has had any work experience in Seattle. She says "No, I graduated from Franklin High School. Then I left town and recently arrived back here." She was evasive about her answers, I finally told her I would need some concrete answers. I informed her it was not my business what she was up to out of town, but I still needed to make sure she could do the job. Fear washes over her and she says she needs to get this job since I know Jeffery and she cannot give out contact to her last and only employer because she left without notice to come here and it was in Mexico. I can see her hope of acquiring this position fading and cannot stay in this office any longer with Jill and her unspoken secrets. We proceed to the breakroom and then the mail room where Beau is just starting to process the incoming mail. I ask if he can train Jill for the rest of the week since she will be taking over this position. Her head turns so fast I think she will break her neck, then she smiles. I can see the doubt roll off of her and know for some reason I am positive she will be a loyal asset to this company. Eventually, I will hear her story just not today.

August Island Rike Paper Company

Chapter 36

fkfk

February 2025
~~Detective Muncer~~
Jill

  Arriving home after the meeting of minds between
Agent Ford and me I almost forgot Jill will be there.
Today is the day of serious questions. I pulled into my
parking spot seeing her rust-colored Oldsmobile has not
been moved a few feet up on the parking strip on the
left. It comforts me that after all these years of not
being able to provide any help in the disappearance of
my family that at least one of them is here, under my
roof. Life is full of mysterious twists, if someone had not
murdered a person on this street or another detective
had called that night, I would not have seen the small
black and white for rent sign written in Sharpie on a
post driven into the flower bed if I had not been out
looking for evidence. I haphazardly wrote the phone
number and photographed the area. Later that evening
I drove by again then called the number from the sign.
Mrs. Johnson answered my call, and I have lived
upstairs here for over a decade then moved downstairs
after Mrs. Johnson's passing. She didn't know how
having the sanctuary of home to clear my head and rest

meant so much to me. Now I am able to perhaps give Jill the same haven to relax and rebuild her life.

Before going in I pull out my incident notebook and jot down some questions I need the answers to today or at least she can start thinking about. First, I need to know if she plans on staying, does she want to continue school, start a job, where she was for all those years, what was she doing, why had she been gone so long, where is the rest of my family, also where did the hideous car come from?

I gather my gear making sure everything is accounted for and enter not knowing what to expect. Jill is in the rocking chair again with the blanket over her. I checked the spare room and saw the bed had not been slept in again. She stirs and says she stayed up all night and just got to sleep. I am not used to being quiet when I return home. I generally turn on the music, have a meal, and prepare my mind for going upstairs and writing, placing words on the beats. I turn the radio on low, grab some lunch meat and chips, sit and watch her stir. She comes to the table and asks if she can have a sandwich and says she hasn't eaten today. She acts as if she is fearful of eating my food. I tell her please eat whatever you would like when you are hungry. She doesn't wish to overstep her boundaries, but my kitchen is surely open to her. She makes a sandwich counting her thin slices of turkey not wanting to take too much. I decided at that point we needed to go grocery shopping. Maybe if she helps pick some food out, she will be more comfortable eating it.

I ask if we can talk, and she looks scared and relieved simultaneously. I pull out my notebook with the list of bullet point questions. She looks it over and laughs saying, "You really are the police." This breaks the tension in the room as I place my badge on the table laughing with her as she picks it up to examine it and then hands it back to me.

I figured in her state of mind Jill may not be comfortable answering me, but she gave me precise responses to each question in the order I had written them.

Jill does plan to stay here with me for a short period of time, if that is ok with me. Truthfully in a city with all the incidents I see happening daily, I am relieved and would prefer her to stay here forever but realize that is not likely. She says she has not thought about school in many years but wanted to be a graphic designer after high school. She says, "You know we went to Mexico City for vacation but here are the parts you do not know. Two days after arriving there and the four of us having a fabulous vacation, a posh hotel with a swimming pool and sightseeing, I think it was the cartel that grabbed sixteen people while on a tour of the industrial district. Dad was interested in the industry of Mexico. He had gone on for days prior to leaving about the medical devices, electronics, and automotive industry. He may have been interested in investing in the stock market, so this was also a research trip for him, always looking for opportunities. It was supposed to be a four-hour tour entering the manufacturing plants then lunch and we were going to a salsa dance show that night with a special authentic Mexican dinner. We never made it out of the second plant. I was terrified being young and a female, my family all separated. I saw a person taking each of the sixteen people from the tour separately. The tour guides were involved. I was placed on the floor in the back of a cargo van with a wire partition between the rear and driver's seat. There was a heavy strap around the bar in the back that was connected around my waist so I could not move. Terrified, I rode for quite a distance maybe three hours or more. It felt like an eternity not knowing what would happen to me or if I would ever see my, our, family ever again. This story is as if it were yesterday and not more than twenty years ago. I have not told it to anyone before nor do I wish to repeat it, but I am aware I will need to if we wish to find Joshua, Mom, and Dad. After long uneven roads, I imagined the pavement had ended and we were going off into the desert or if we had been in Washington there would have been forests. We went over something maybe cattle grates that sounded metal, then I assumed it was a garage door closing. The darkness settled in, the men spoke in Spanish, a language I was not entirely familiar with but could make out a few words that had no meaning as to where I was or why I had been taken then the cargo door was opened. I was untied and led to a room in a shanty town three stories high with guards spotted around the area buildings made of corrugated sheets of metal, random pieces of plywood, and cardboard as if built from packaging scraps and discarded building materials. Some strips tied together others nailed all willy nilly. The alleyway, as I called it, had people sitting on the dusty ground and clotheslines strewn from shanty to shanty, doors wide open or non-existent. There weren't any children that I could see just forlorn-looking souls and I had no idea why I was there. I was shoved into a room at the end of this insane area that was more secure looking than the ones I had recently passed. Daily we were rounded up, taken to the garage, put into the van, and transported to a manufacturing plant located nearer than the one we had been kidnapped from. I was shown how to check schematics and compare them to the newly assembled circuit boards. Being given the job title of quality control, I didn't ever see a way out, there were guards at every step, and while at the plant times were okay even though I did not belong there. At first, I was terrified daily, moment by moment I did what they wanted. I was good at my job and didn't give the guards any reason to beat me as some of the other people did who rebelled with their actions. One day not long ago I saw a way out, I had become such a low-profile person they weren't watching me as much.

One day after getting into the van I noticed different people with me, they dropped us off inside of another garage and took us into a different plant. My room was long gone and now I had to start over with these unfortunate people. This one was a textile plant. I was in charge of quality control again for technical fabric used in the automotive industry. This plant was a bit laxer on security. I kept thinking about our family and Seattle, the only place I had ever known. After a couple more years I saw how the guards changed when the van took a different shift to another place. I wasn't sure where, but someone told me it was closer to Mexico City. I got on that van, didn't let the back door latch all the way, placing duct tape from the plant I had carefully hidden on my wrist over the hole where the latch rested, and held the door closed so the guard wasn't aware of my plan. At a stop I knew from previous trips along the way I slipped out with no one saying a word, pulling the tape off as I left. The van pulled away as I rolled toward the scrub brush next to the road. I could see the lights beginning to twinkle from the city still far away in the distance but nearer than I had been in many years. I wasn't sure how long but knew I was free. I had never received any money from my days of work in the plants so had to figure out a way to get home, finding our family was on my mind but I needed to get across the border and didn't even know where that was. I found a map and saw I was a great distance from the border and without money I could not acquire transportation. I rode a freight train the majority of the

way and stopped at the border guard station trying to
enter the USA. They wanted identification, something I
did not have. A Mexican guard who saw how dirty and
haggard I appeared, waved me through the footpath
with the turn style. The sign said Welcome to New
Mexico. At this point, I didn't want old or New Mexico
just Washington. I was stopped by the police station,
but they tried to press charges due to vagrancy laws; I
kept telling them my story they didn't believe me being
the case was so old and probably hear hundreds of
stories a day from people crossing the border legal or
illegal. They wrote me a ticket and gave me a criminal
trespass order for that area. My ticket still has an
outstanding balance, but I will not return to New
Mexico. I shall pay the ticket with my first paycheck,
whenever I get one. Oh ya, by the way, I got a job today
in the mail room at the paper company you said to
apply to. The interview with August went bad but then
he hired me and the car I took after witnessing a
murder not long after meeting with the police in New
Mexico. The keys were in the ignition, there was a pile
of cash in the console, and a full tank of gas. I drove to
Seattle without a license, a ticket in my pocket, and
watched my rearview mirror the entire way but never
broke a law except stealing the car."

I was glad Jill had opened up to her bubbly self. It was
kind of unusual to see since she had been little sister Jill
to me for all those years and now is back and
comfortable with me. I asked if she wanted to see my

studio. She follows me up the stairs and sits on the old, flowered couch like she is comfortable, and the years missed here have rolled off her back. I play some of my previously published music for her, she laughs saying, "I would have never guessed rap and you."

Chapter 37

February 2025
Detective Muncer

Through my day of sleep, I felt more turmoil than even rest. My motto is to keep every action above the board so as not to face any repercussions in the future. The story Jill told me and her part in the murder even if she only stole the car, it could have been caught on camera. She should have just gone to the local police after crossing the border and told them who she was and given my information. I also wonder how she found me, why didn't she get a motel, and where is the stack of money now?

I get up a couple of hours earlier than normal and knock on Jill's door, but she is gone. The suitcase lies open but empty. Fear washes over me that someone has found her. I know she was here this morning when I arrived home. I can't call her since she doesn't have a phone, of which I am aware. If this is going to work with her staying here, I will need better communication. Of course, she is free to go whenever she wishes I am merely shocked that she is gone. I do not feel right about rooting through her belongings to unearth the cash. She has brought too many secrets with her, and I need to unload them. I will close the door and ask questions later.

   As I am preparing for my night shift Jill knocks and walks in as if nothing has happened. I am irritated that I am the only one who finds discord in this situation. Jill smiles and sits down asking how my sleep was. She didn't want to wake me up when she left in the morning to take the bus to work. Says she figured the car shouldn't be driven since it is technically stolen. A cloud of relief settles on me as I ask which shift she works and if getting to work on the Metro system will suffice for now. We talk about the car, money, and any other details she is willing to part with. I let her know since the crime happened across state lines, I need to consult with an agent I know at the FBI. Her eyes become saucers; she wonders if she will need to turn herself in. I advise her to stay put and go about her business.

   The priority on my list tonight is to investigate the laundry services locally and get a list of companies that deliver green service coats in connection with the vigilante murders at Spinners Records and Bud's House. My mind keeps returning to Little Mel, Raven, and Meade. There have not been any more victims that I know of locally. I will contact Rubio tonight. The open cases and people associated with them are plentiful compared to just me, one detective in a large city.

   I start my night by contacting Rubio who wants to meet soon and after knowing him for so many years I know soon means now. About midnight I pack up all the current files that are cluttering my mind, taking James Street to E. Cherry seeing Rubio on the corner of 23rd pacing and on the phone in a deep conversation. Wondering if that is how I appear to the outside world when I am in my mind trying to solve a case. Suddenly he looked up as if he could feel me watching him. I parked easily at this time of night, got out, and entered the Dur Dur Café both of us deep in thought of the worlds we are called to penetrate, neither of us saying a word until seated. We chose a table for four and each sat diagonally so there was room to spread out the paperwork we had brought. I briefly tell him of Jill, knowing that it is not the subject of our meeting and my dilemma of the car, failing to mention the cash. He tells me there is a big operation happening at Little Mel's that he has been performing surveillance even during his off-duty hours. Nothing has happened that he can pinpoint. The clues lead in all directions. Everyone is busy at the site like an ant pile, his best guess is they are manufacturing a higher quantity than usual. We could never prove anything illegal was happening there before and there have been no leads on Meade's murder and Don has not surfaced either. The surveillance was mainly to spot him as he was the last person to be seen with Meade. We both suspected he was who we heard in the woods across the street from Nora Boyer's house where Meade's body had been disposed of. I am not entirely positive which other cases Metevior is working on, but this one is filling his mind.

We head back to headquarters for me to write up my requests for the extradition of Levi Maddox and for Rubio to work on making sense of his files. My request starts with the usual paperwork laying out the facts in order but there are many more forms when it involves crossing state lines. I have never done any work with North Dakota, but I suspect they would not wish for a murderer to live in their community either. I emailed the paperwork to the judge who is processing warrants this week then looked online for commercial laundries and uniform suppliers in the area. I would suspect the deliveries happen in proximity to downtown since that is where both crime scenes were located. There are far too many locations to list at first glance. My night is close to over, no new crime scenes to visit tonight. I email Agent Ford at 5:00 am asking if he will have some time in the near future for another case. My phone alerts me to an email from him almost immediately. He can meet but not at his office, I would need to travel to Seattle Sunshine Coffee on 35th Avenue NE at 6:00 am. I agree and take the time to narrow down the cleaners who supply most of the uniforms to the downtown corridor, wishing they would be open now to inquire about the businesses they supply green shop coats to.

I travel north on I-5 just as the traffic starts to pick up for the day but before it comes to a standstill. I arrived at the coffee shop located close to my other duplex. I laugh as I get out wondering if Everett ever visits here. Agent Ford gets out of his vehicle and asks what is so funny this early in the morning. I don't go in-depth but tell him my story of the duplex nearby and Everett Sunshine who resides there.

We enter, I see the bakery case and decide on a soda and some penguin cookies with a dozen to go. I know Jill will be impressed by these. Agent Ford orders a white-knuckle sandwich and water; we ascend upstairs for privacy. He doesn't ever appear rushed but even keeled when he only has a few minutes for me which I know is a lot to ask of him.

Instinctively we sit at a table where we can see whoever comes up the stairs. I think we have police written all over us since no one enters the upstairs the entire time we are here. As soon as we are seated, I thank him for his time again, the leads on Levi Maddox, and spill my story about Jill. He rubs his head, takes some notes, and asks where the vehicle is now. I let him know it is on Euturia Street, a few miles south of here. He makes a phone call asking for an agent to pick up what he is working on and follows me to my home which I have not revealed that information. We pulled up, the car is parked right where it has been for a few days. I am relieved to have handed my load over to Agent Ford, especially on this one. No matter what the outcome, it is off my conscience. The driver's door is unlocked, keys are under the seat, and I see nothing of Jill's in the vehicle. I checked the console and found it empty except for a gum wrapper and a gas receipt from Waterflow, NM. I know Jill is supposed to be at work and pray she doesn't come down the sidewalk at this moment. I wish to be the one to walk her through this. I know there will, at the very least, be questioning. The shiny light blue flatbed tow truck arrives with its lights and chains, carefully loads, and hauls the violating Oldsmobile away as well as a story that starts many miles from Seattle and is years long.

Chapter 38

February 2025
August

 I woke up unsettled this morning knowing there are many more underlying issues going on. This is something I am not used to. Before there were appointments and then the day was mine to enjoy. Anything else that popped up could be cleared at the end but now there are so many lives intertwined. In Milwaukee I was responsible for myself, Alice, the house, and vehicles. The dealership would call when it was time to service our cars. I feel the stack of issues piling up here is getting out of hand. Not in this order of importance but I jot the situations down on an envelope lying on the kitchen table. What is happening with mom? Why her sudden need to sell the house then wavering from that? Why did Willow wish to see it? What are the contents of the box that Hector was so protective of? What is Jill running from, if anything? Do her issues put my company and staff in danger? I feel Detective Muncer would not place the company in a precarious situation. As my newly appointed leadership role sets in, I realize just how large a part I play in making sure each and every one of my staff is safe, financially and physically. The largest issue I am having today is from the other day. I am not even entirely sure how long ago it was, but I keep mentally returning to that stop light and seeing the fire coming out of the barrel of his gun, the man in the green coat. Does being a witness to that crime put me in danger? He did run directly in front of my car but was focused in another direction. It was as if I was stuck there, held in place by an unknown force. The light turned red, I stopped and then heard the shots. Did he see me while firing off his weapon? I was the only witness that was alive at that intersection; he had taken care of the other two. My other question is, who is Remy? Why do we keep running into him in a city this large? It seems that would not be a possibility. Why was he exiting my warehouse when I was on my way to help Hector?

Suddenly, I have an idea: since I work in an industrial area, I could walk by all these businesses to look for others who wear similar green coats as the shooter. I leave out the back door without saying anything. Hector has the garage door open, letting all the crisp air into the warehouse, possibly awaiting a delivery or pick up. He would normally see me walk to my car, but not at this time of day, and this time, I walk in the opposite direction and up the road. It is not me watching Hector, but the story turns around. I didn't tell anyone here about the incident I witnessed. I could have told Hector three times that day on the way to his house, on the way back to work, and then during the return trip taking him home. He was so gracious in his asking; he even asked if he should walk home, but I truly didn't mind driving him, and the picture of him walking with his hand cart and precious box through the city did not feel right to me. When I dropped him off, he tried to hand me a tip of $20.00 for all my troubles. I declined, telling him to call me anytime he needed anything, and I would be happy to help.

I map out the area in my head going east on 6th Avenue, turning north on Airport Way. Passing Stacy Street, Walker Street, and arriving at Holgate Street. Being on foot, you see how many industrial buildings there are here. I map out this small area to scour for the green coat. I think about how each of these businesses in the strange mix of structures started with an idea, and every one of them has a leader like me. My world just became completely uniform, before I was in my office tower above the warehouse that looks like a ship and was solo. Now, I feel as if I am a part of this city, a contribution to the well-being of the people. As I stand on the corner of 4th Avenue and Holgate, I realize what a privilege it is to be here and to have been handed this business that makes products which introduce people to others and potentially creates more business. I recall the stories Dad passed on to me as a child with such depth to him as if I would need that information later in life. Now I wish I had paid more attention, but I know for sure that in 1870, August Island Rike the first stood right here on the mud-covered streets in this spot and created his dream.

I walked back, zigzagging a few streets. There is movement everywhere but no signs of the green coat, only many flannels, gray and blue overalls. I laugh imagining wearing those all day. Knowing I won't at any point in my life. I head back to the warehouse with the rain starting to pick up, a train whistle blows, the noise of traffic from waterfront and I – 5 collides in the industrial well of the city as a dumpster hits the ground and a garbage truck emerges from the alley. I feel right at home as I look up and see my name on the sign, but the questions on my list still remain.

I decided to eat in the lunchroom today. Jill and Hector are in one corner, sharing the comics section of the newspaper and laughing. It feels peaceful to see them happy. I realize I am just sitting here staring, I open my brown paper bag, feeling like I am in school. I think with all the nostalgia and the feeling of placement for myself in this city today, I have just completed a chapter in my life and now will know what direction to take in the future.

Chapter 39

February 2025
Detective Muncer
Detective Rubio

Rubio has been extremely distant in the past couple of weeks since Meade was murdered. In all the years I have worked on cases with him, he has always been present. Something more than this murder is on his mind.

It is 4:30 am, and the city is just starting to rise, at least for the blue-collar workers. Come to think of it, there are many out there still working last night's shift. I think of the bus and taxi drivers, an extended bus with one passenger in the far back either on their way to a job or up to no good, one driver in the front trying to decide which situation is his to deal with.

I can't take this anymore. I need to get to the bottom of what has Rubio in such distress. Making sure the garage door closes all the way as I exit the precinct, I head south to 509 and into Little Mel's neighborhood. There isn't a good vantage point to see the front without being spotted but the overgrown ivy along the chain link fence and the public land behind are my best angles. I drove through the neighborhood slowly, looking for Rubio. Not seeing him, I let out a breath I wasn't aware I was holding and parked behind a large commercial truck where I could see Little Mel's house from but not be noticed. Getting out of the cruiser, closing the door easily to keep noise at a minimum, I walk between the truck and my car. It doesn't look as if there is any activity at Little Mel's. All the lights are off, and the front door is cracked open. The garage door is completely open and doors on the side of the garage stand open. Suddenly, headlights come on, and a truck starts and rolls out. It is Donny's old truck, but it is not Little Mel driving; it is someone I have never seen before. With the gate open, the truck speeds out, turning right past me, but I have stepped to the side of the commercial truck and was not seen, I don't think. This place is vacant, everything is gone, I am not sure how Rubio missed the move or if he chose to keep this information hidden from me.

I text Rubio Little Mel's. He responds with OTW. In about two minutes, Rubio pulls in next to me, double parks, and blocks me in. He gets out, coming at me, almost stomping. He gets close and starts whisper yelling, "I have been working this case; it is mine. What are you doing getting into my business? Leave my case alone." His face is reddened, showing odd angles from the streetlights, and clouds of air are puffing from his nose and mouth on this winter morning. He is pacing between our two cars, exceedingly angry, maybe so mad he may not be able to talk.

I give him a couple of minutes to work some of the frustration out and then say, "Fortunately we are both here; the place is open and vacant." He turns around, looking at me in disbelief, places his hand over his face, and lets out a silent scream. I had never seen him rattled until the other night, and now it has escalated. He stated that it had been a couple of days since his surveillance being as it was off the books, and he needed a mental break.

He turns to me, still silent, but proceeds through the open large rolling gate. We walk around the house and garage, knowing they are all gone, but check to make sure anyway. Rubio, still silent, motions to enter the front door. The house is vacant except for a yellow 1950s-style Formica dining set in perfect condition. The house is clean; there is no smell, noise, or other items in the house except a packet of information on a prescription for Brixadi written to Melvin Scriptnor. This is the new drug we have been told about at a meeting being longer lasting than Narcan. Little Mel may have come to his senses after all these years, but where does that leave our investigation of the people killed from the tainted drugs? I call in the King County Hazardous Waste and Forensics. Metevior remains silent, I am not used to this new persona. He walks back off the property, stops at the fence, and leans with his head hanging in defeat. He looks at me with feral eyes, his emotions not tamed but being withheld in the silence he is maintaining.

His first words are, "As you know, Raven was my informant, and now, I have lost that connection, but she was more to me. Secrets always surface." He stops talking. I have no idea what his secret is, but I hope it does not incriminate us both once he spills it on this sidewalk. I do not want to be involved or hear the mess he has created. I can walk away, get in my car, and go home, or stand by my friend and listen. He paces for a while then says, "Raven was my son Albatar's girlfriend, she had his baby who my ex-wife raises. Raven was clean, had a job, and was planning on marrying Albatar. Then he joined the Navy, and she went off the rails and started using drugs and hooking up with this crew. I don't know what to tell Aleene. I have always helped her, but to raise this child all the way to adulthood is a lot since Albatar is overseas for two more years.

We wait while they process the scene, them taping it off with levels of manufacturing chemical that will need to be removed. I picture the garage being demolished and multi-story apartments built in this space as I return to my car parked on SW 119th ST with new knowledge of Rubio and compassion since I was handed Everett to take care of forever and now to unravel Jill and her mess she unknowingly created out of survival.

Chapter 40

March 2025
Detective Muncer

After my eye-opening meeting with Rubio, that trail being cold and Little Mel in the wind on the case we were working last year when the same thing happened, but the participants all remained in place except Don. He disappeared then and again now after coming onto the scene, leaving a few more victims on his trail. Something tells me he skipped town and not with Little Mel, but I should check the morgue and hospitals for him, leaving word in case he shows up.

I am up early again this time, needing answers from Jill about the cash and who may be trailing her. She enters, bundled up from being on the street after riding the bus across town, looking tired and then seeing me with a concerned look in her eyes. I know she has secrets, she says, "I have to get a car first thing, the bus is great, but it is cold out there and some guy was smoking pills in the back during my morning commute." I hate to see my sister out there walking on the streets where my cases are.

While fixing my lunch, Jill sits at the table and asks, "What's up?" I turned, asking about her safety and the cash. She says she used some of it to get here. "There was a stack. Ones, then fives, tens, twenties and hundreds, no fifties. There couldn't have been more than two or three thousand dollars there. That big old car used lots of gas. I ate and then stayed here in the basement but bought food." I also asked how she found me. Smiling, she turned to me, saying, "Public records. This one had the police car. I didn't want to bother you but felt safer here than in the open." I know for sure now that I will put this place and my other one in the name of a trust. It can't be that easy to locate me. I knew the assessor's office had records of all the properties, but in all my years, to the best of my knowledge, no one has tracked me down before. Luckily, this time, it was Jill and not someone unwanted from a case.

I take the stairs two at a time up to my studio, having not been there in a few days. Just wanting to sit and unwind, letting the music clear my mind before hitting the streets for another night. I still don't know if Jill has used up the money, but I know it was not in the console. I jot the words in my notebook: Seattle, place, lows, heartbeats, and leave, trying to bring those words into lyrics tonight.

I enter the bottom of the duplex; Jill is curled up in her blanket. I ask if she feels safe and if she thinks anyone is following her. She says, "I think it was like I was released on good behavior. I worked for twenty years, never gave them trouble, and then vanished. I don't believe they are looking for me because they know I will never whisper a word about where I was and what I was doing." I knew that with me leaving for the night, it was not a good time to push her for information. I did want her to be here when I returned in the morning. She had already given me some leads of where she was, I am not going to simply walk away from this story. We were a family of five, and I have been here missing the other four for over twenty years and do want to locate the rest of my family.

I hadn't been on shift for more than a couple of hours when there was a call that came across the radio about a robbery in progress, the shots fired almost simultaneously another, a hit and run with a pedestrian being run over by Pike and Boren. The description of the driver is what caught my attention amongst all the chatter that goes on 24/7. Forty to fifty years old, stocky, green coat, dark hair, wide jawline, driving a red Dodge truck. I hop in my cruiser, looking in all directions along the way for a red Dodge pickup, and drive by the hit and run before arriving at Alex's Tires on East Pike Street. Being the first on the scene, I already knew the shooter was in the wind from the last robberies that fit this MO. Back up is on the way being protocol, but we need forensics, the medical examiner, and tape to contain the scene. I think of Daniel and his tire shop, thinking I need to make contact for no particular reason except I miss him and the rest of the group. I also need to check on Everett, a responsibility I take seriously, and know that Micky will contact me immediately if she needs anything.

Back up pulls in, blaring their sirens. I remember the urgency in my early days of policing. This position does not require speed in most cases since the crime scene and victims are not going anywhere. I wish someone had gotten a better look at where that red Dodge had gone because now, we have stacks of low-profile tires and two more victims, actually three with the hit and run. I take my usual notes on the scene, stay to make certain the scene is processed correctly as if I am the only one who knows that but once they leave and it is handed over to me, I want to make sure the deaths of Haley Cummings, Lucia Barlow and Eric Gage the hit and run victim are investigated with every possible clue uncovered and the killer be brought to justice. This makes eight victims by this one man in the past couple of months.

I left and talked to the patrol officers who were first on the scene at the hit and run. They are making their report now. One looks up, recognizing me from various places no one wishes to be. The victim's last words were, "Right on Olive." I look up the road, not seeing anything, but know I am going that way also.

I waved as I left the scene. Seeing no extra tire tracks, he did not skid, attempt to stop, or peel out. Just simply sped away. There is no one on the road except me at this time. I enjoy the city at this time of the day, just not why I am out here. I follow Olive Way, thinking as I pass Melrose, Bellevue, and Belmont Avenues that he could have turned on any of them and then turned again and be stopped in front of anyone's house, his own or hidden in his garage. I slowly inch my way across Capitol Hill, pulling over on Broadway, texting Naomi to see if she will have a break soon. After pulling into Harbor View and getting through security, I think of my night not long ago here with Little Mel, who has added another adjective to his name: Long Gone Little Mel.

Naomi met me in the cafeteria and said I almost didn't catch her; this was her night off, but she got called in. At times like this, I wish I wasn't on duty; it is comforting to know Naomi and I are both working overnight, but when one of us is not on shift and the other working, it just feels like things are off. I asked if she wished to go somewhere else to eat, but she wanted to stay here, and then she would like a ride home if I am still available.

We talk about my life mainly, the green coat killer, our music, and when we are both off to go on a proper date. Next week, I will make time no matter which days she has off. I have accrued hundreds of hours of personal time and will use some. She says she knows of a few companies that wear green uniforms but can't think of their names now, but as they come in, she will let me know. I drive the short distance to her apartment, thinking of our first date on New Year's Eve and my leather pants from my days playing in Pioneer Square, which reminds me of Hector and the possibility of files. I walk Naomi to her door, knowing my lunch hour is over. I haven't eaten but will on the road from my carefully packed lunchbox. We hold each other for a bit, knowing a little while together can take the weight of our occupations off of us at least for a moment. I released her, realizing I didn't tell her about Jill, and this isn't the time. She leans up as I am in thought and kisses me, simply saying, "Next week for sure."

I go home, the words rattling in my head, making sense now: Seattle, place, lows, heartbeats, and leave.

Bare Winter Blues

Verse 1

Seattle overnight, the stars fade,

Cold winter hits, darkness invades

Ruthless streets, the shadows creep

Little M's in out of the cut, dreams buried deep.

Wind blowin' in alleys, whispers or pain

Random shootins, can't escape the rain,

cars rollin through store fronts, chaos reigns,

Big dreams down in a puddle on streets of blood stains.

Chorus

New year's resolution, life's a bitter pill,

Bare trees swayin', in the bitter chill,

Crimes gone wrong, got the detectives onto fate,

Morgue's fillin' up, in this Emerald state.

Verse 2

Dream big, but the path's full of sin,

Little M's lost, where do we begin?

Seattle Seahawks, where the highs meet the lows,

In a game of life, everybody knows.

Records keep spinnin', truth buried in grime,

Solving crime like a grind, losing track of time,

Wind howlin fierce, in these vacant streets,

Where dreams die young, and the cold heart beats.

Chorus

Bridge

They huslin' hard, but the luck runs thin,

Bare winter blues, where the streets wear sin,

Crime is a canvas, painting woes in black,

But the wild card's playin', aint no lookin' back.

Verse 3

Underneath the streetlight, shadows twist and turn,

A cycle of life, in the fire we burn,

Cars rolling through storefronts, hearts racing fast,

In this ruthless game, you either win or you're last.

Seattle's a beast, with the rain as a prize,

But behind every smile, is a thousand goodbyes,

So, we hustle, we grind, with that fire inside,

In the bare winter nights, it's a ruthless ride.

Chorus

Outro

Seattle's alive, but at what cost?

In the bare winter dreams, so much hope is lost,

But we ride with the storm, let the cold winds blow,

In this Emerald city, we reap what we sow.

August Island Rike Paper Company

#MunDet J #DJMuncer #Seattle Strong

Chapter 41

$\sim\!\!\!\!\sim\!\!\!\!\sim$

March 2025
August

Hector is smiling each day as I leave to take my walk. Venturing in different directions and further each journey without the success of locating the green coat. Today I went up 8th Avenue S, turning on S Stacy Street and walking towards Airport Way S. My walks are becoming more frantic in my search, peering into each warehouse. I have made sure I set a timer for thirty minutes so I can turn around at that point and make my way back. On the twelfth day of my journey, I saw a UPS driver leaving a warehouse, the roller door still open, packages being loaded from the dock, and I spotted the sleeve of a green coat. A shade of green that will forever be embedded in my brain. I stop and get behind a yellow box truck from a neighboring business. Through the windshield, I have access to the loading dock across the way. The person with the green coat is inside, so I can only see a piece of sleeve as they occasionally place another outgoing package on the cart, ready for transport. My heart is beating irregularly, not knowing if I am in danger. I am almost positive that whoever was in the warehouse not far from where I work did not see me. I walk around the front of the building to see the name of the company in small letters on the door with no indication of what they do in there. I found this ridiculous since my company says exactly what it does on the large sign that can be seen from the street.

I sprint back to my office, out of breath, with this new knowledge. Hector is looking at me strangely. Now, I wish I had shared the story with him when I gave him a ride so as not to have to carry this information by myself. I rush up to my office and realize all I saw was a partial green sleeve that could have belonged to anyone; there must be at least over one hundred companies who wear that exact color every day. I sit at my desk, fishing Detective Muncer's card out of my coat pocket from the day of the crime. His words remain in my ears, ones you hear on television, "if you can think of anything else." At the crime scene, I thought I would not have any other information and simply wished to be anywhere else other than there, and now I have started my own investigation. I don't know what is wrong with me since I have been back in Seattle. First, I follow Hector with obsession, and now that fixation has been turned onto locating the killer. This is not the type of person I am. Generally, I take people at face value, but life has become significantly deeper.

I get up, close my office door, dial Muncer, and leave a message, trying to act calm and like a normal person when, inside of my head, I am screaming. Then I remember it is 1:00 pm and he works the flipside of my days. I had barely sat down deciding what my next move would be when my cell rings. It is Muncer, who I regret calling. I know I woke him up for what, a partial view of a green sleeve. He doesn't sound asleep but amped up. Asked why I called to get to the point of this interruption. I could hear multiple sirens in the background, radios blaring codes and badge numbers, being glad that is not the profession I picked out to decipher that. He says the perpetrator I had witnessed on the scene a week or so back had struck again, only this time we have a description of his vehicle. "August, what was the purpose of your call?" I gave him the address and information I had seen, which may be nothing. I fail to tell him of my daily walks attempting to locate this man. He says, "Good information, good information. I need to roll. The vigilantes' truck related to these eight murders is on fire. "

I am relieved that they have leads on this case and have decided to return to the warehouse with green uniforms. Only this time, there is not any room for me to get close; the place is surrounded with police cars. I will drive by on my way home.

Chapter 42

March 2025
Detective Muncer

While at the scene with the burning red Dodge pickup, Officer Stanley approaches and asks, "What is this guy's MO? Could he possibly target elderly ladies in an alley?" I shake my head no, being tired but still up in the daylight and deep into solving this case. I can't believe this truck is right off the route I took yesterday on E Howell St. Why were there not any other vehicles parked along this curb? Then I see the do not park on this side of the street from 8:00 am to 3:00 pm sign up ahead, posted by Seattle Water for maintenance on this block, and look behind to see another. I know this truck was parked here intentionally; the vigilante could be anywhere. I radio patrol asking about their findings on S Stacy Street; he fits the description of an employee that suddenly left for the day. Now I need to call August and warn him the shooter probably did work there and may have possibly seen him. After phoning, I realize August isn't cut out for this type of situation and has helped us in solving this crime but may have put himself in danger. I could hear a thousand questions in his silence. Being polite, he thanked me and hung up.

We ran the plate and were given the information that James M. Lee owns the truck, and that is who is employed where we searched. The address on the registration from DOL is on E. Howell Street, several blocks away from the burned truck. He most likely recognized August while loading the packages, left work, saw the opportunity of a closed street to set his truck on fire, and ran home. His home is surrounded by now, his wife and or children will be questioned and will have had no idea he has committed these heinous crimes, or so they say. They have to know he is acting out of character. Life will become different for the entire family of this person who took these cases into his own hands and ruined many more lives, including his own.

I pull up to a two-story house wedged between apartment buildings. There isn't anywhere to park, so I block the road, being as I have to be here. I wish I was at home in bed, but here I am on Capitol Hill in a quiet neighborhood, making history. I enter the house without knocking, the front door already wide open, the screen door propped open, brutally cold air pouring in. An elderly lady who appears too old to be James Lee's wife sits in a mustard-colored velvet rocker in the corner, shivering, wearing a snap-up house dress, brown men's slippers, white bobby socks, and mumbling something about the cost of wasting energy.

Mrs. Olivia Lee claims she doesn't know where James is. He moved here a few months ago from Manhattan,

Kansas. His divorce just finalized, he was always in a foul mood, didn't stay to talk except to gripe about the traffic. He did shift work, so most of the time, traffic is not what set him off; it was his unhappiness. Mrs. Lee looks tired after her statement. After closing the door and clearing the sidewalk of onlookers, we kept asking her where James could be. She kept telling us he was at work. We had to search the house, knowing there was a high probability that he was not there. We have an officer with Mrs. Lee in case she sees James and tries to help. She doesn't even know what the severity of the charges would be. All she knows now is he is in trouble, and we have free reign of her house if she lets us search. If not, we will remain here and obtain a warrant. She wishes for us to leave, but that will not happen unless we take James into custody. We search upstairs to find a room that clearly belongs to James. There are multiple green coats, divorce papers with coffee-stained rings on them, and dirty clothes all over the floor like he didn't understand how the system of laundry works, letting his clothing drop in place but no James. We search the main floor, finding Mrs. Lee's bedroom. I feel bad pawing through her clothing but find the passage to the attic in her closet ceiling. We send in the smallest officer to wedge himself through the entry to the attic while I inform Mrs. Lee what we are doing. I feel she deserves respect; it is her house, and we are in her bedroom. The officer returns quickly with cobwebs in his hair and hanging from the basket weave gear on his belt. He shakes his head no, but in a whisper, so quietly

I had to almost put my ear to his mouth, he says, "through the vent I saw movement in an abandoned tree house in the back yard."

We position a couple officers on either side of the rear entry next to the window in the laundry room, unlock the rear door without opening it for a fast exit, and the remainder of us exit the front, asking Mrs. Lee to remain inside, leaving one officer with her for her safety and ours. She says, "I will never be able to show my face again after this fiasco." Two officers position themselves at either end of the alley, and the rest of us proceed to the tree house with the bull horn, asking for James Lee to come down peacefully.

He steps out onto a moss-covered platform, slips as the platform breaks, and nearly lands in front of us. He places his hands in the air and says, "ok, let's go." We escorted him to a patrol vehicle for transport and questioning, and to our relief, this went well. Another senseless killer off the street, cases solved. I knocked to inform Mrs. Lee we had him but realized she was most likely at the back window already watching her son being taken away. She had recently had him return to her, but now he will be gone forever. This is the day in her calendar of before and after with her son James.

I retrieved my cruiser from the middle of the road, feeling anguish for Mrs. Lee, all the other victims' families, business owners who had murders take place, and call August, then remember if August was in danger, so is Jill. August answers before the first ring is completed. I informed him that Mr. Lee was in custody and thanked him for his part in this investigation. He genuinely acts surprised and asks if he can meet with me on a couple of other matters. We set up a time for next week before I get off shift and earlier than his shift starts. It will be good to visit with August, a business owner in my city, our city.

Chapter 43

❧

March 2025
Detective Muncer

My shift started nearly eighteen hours ago; I am going home for a nap while they process James Lee. Depending on the extent of crime in the past few hours, it may take until my next shift begins for me to be able to question him. I am thinking about giving Jill a ride home, but her shift isn't over, so she will be taking the bus home.

I get home, go upstairs to write, my head full of music but with me being overly tired the sequence would be off. Without bothering to go downstairs and eat, I fall asleep on the old sofa that will be replaced once I build an indoor staircase.

Startled by the knock at the door, I look at my phone and realize sleep has only been my friend for just over three short hours that feel more like a moment. It is Jill letting me know she is home. I sit, not sure if I am steady enough to stand, but find my footing, head downstairs, and see Jill is making dinner. Thinking back to when I ate last, not being able to recall. When the cases, especially one as severe as this one, come to a close, I can finally rest, but the last few hours of waiting, chasing, gathering information, and pulling it all together is mentally and physically tiring. Some of the officers who respond don't have any other information besides the type of case it is. As in this one, August seeing the coat, the truck fire, and Mrs. Lee's house were all crime scenes being investigated suddenly, simultaneously, and with urgency. This was not a person for us to let slip through our fingers. His heinous crimes needed to be stopped prior to the ones that occurred today. I am not entirely sure if we would have known who he was if he hadn't hit Eric Gage, whose last words, "right on Olive," was helpful in every way.

I am not sure where Jill learned to cook, but this may be some of the best food I have had in quite a while. Complimenting Jill on our meal, I tell her she is hired as a cook; she laughs and goes on to say this is her go-to meal. I notice she has relaxed since she has been here; it still feels peculiar for her to be in my presence after all these years. I hope she is settling in ok, likes her job, and feels safe.

I look at the clock on the microwave and see it is time to get down to the jail to question Mr. Lee. Driving south on Westlake Avenue and winding my way over to I-5, which appears to take longer than normal this evening, I inch my way across town to headquarters, grab my files, and head through the building to the jail. Mr. Lee is sleeping; they say he has been asleep since he was processed. My first thought is that this is not a hotel. I instruct the guards to retrieve him and bring him to interrogation room number 4. I personally think this is the cleanest of all the interrogation rooms; most of the time, rooms one and two are occupied. I have never seen anyone else in room four, so I always opt for that one.

Mr. Lee enters in his orange jail suit that reminds me of scrubs; he sits across the government-issued table from me when instructed to do so. I usually stay silent for a couple of minutes just to get a feel of where the conversation will go. Mr. Lee pipes up after about ten seconds, saying he will be in full cooperation. He is not here to cause any more harm and is relieved to have been caught. The stress of being on the outside of his regular life in Kansas has been too much pressure since arriving in Seattle.

I have not had time to review his entire file, but I did not see the usual first page with a list of prior convictions. I open the file now; I cannot believe these murders would be his first crimes, but there are not any previous charges.

I looked at him and asked if he would write out his statement. He nods, saying, "Of course. I think once I got through processing, I realized how tired I was and just collapsed. This stay, no matter what the length is, will not be anywhere as stressful as the past few months have been on me. I am not generally an angry person."

I hand Mr. Lee the pen and paper, tell him I will be recording his statement, feeling no threat from this man who has killed eight people, seven in cold blood, one simply in the way of exit and sit back to listen. He doesn't write anything for quite a while but is eager to release his story to me or simply get it out of him.

He starts with his job, house, and wife, laughing while he says Mrs. Lee. "All gone. First the wife, then the judge made us sell the house since my wife had spent all our savings, ruined my credit and I couldn't refinance my own house to pay off her portion that she never paid in the first place. Then after that the company I had worked for, just think twenty-six years of my life in Manhattan, Kansas for my wife and my job and the wife wants something new. My employer informs me of the plant's closure in two weeks. I am divorced, have bad credit, am homeless, and my savings is all gone in her bank account now. My mother had moved to Seattle many years ago to help a friend. I know it was her boyfriend; she didn't fool me, not that it even mattered. My dad had been gone somewhere since I was a little tyke; she deserved happiness." He hangs his head, ashamed of the repercussions placed on his mother from his actions.

"I moved here to have a roof; my truck, rifle, and clothing were all I had. This job I found at the warehouse was shift work, more like whenever they would call you in. One day swing, the next graveyard. I am not even sure of what they were shipping. My area was small, cinderblocks making a room not even big enough for two people. The boxes came through a small door on a conveyor belt with an order number printed on it, and I added a label, making them ready for shipment. I was tired, fed up, and extremely unhappy. After a few weeks, I discovered the garage door next to me was connected to my area but cordoned off with a piece of thin paneling to resemble a wall, I listened carefully to the secret conversations. On some shifts, I could hear the men talking about when they would be breaking into somewhere and what was to be stolen."

"I was fed up with life before I arrived in Seattle, since the snowball events of Mrs. Lee. I would get off work and go home. Mom was always in the living room watching the news. I think she would memorize the stories to replay for me, like a sports recap channel. The second I would set foot in the house, she would be angry at the criminals, the police, the citizens, just angry at everyone. One day, it all hit me: I had never been violent before this. I would go hunting with my friends but only watch the beautiful animals. I never came home with anything; I was known as the unreliable hunter. I started listening to the neighboring warehouse and then would position myself prior to their heist and do away with them. I know I was in the wrong; not sure where my pathways became mixed up, but here I am. I feel mighty bad about the guy who I hit on Boren. That was never supposed to have happened. I suppose none of this should have happened, but now that it has. I am here; you don't have to fuss yourself over those criminals, and Mom doesn't have to gripe at me anymore. Good thing I had insurance on my truck."

Then he looks me in the eye, nods, puts the pen to paper, and is silent. I relax a bit, knowing he is locked up, and think of all the others who have been in his shoes and haven't chosen this route. I ask the guard to escort Mr. Lee back to his cell and go to the third-floor office I now call my own since the filming of the riots and place all the pieces of this puzzle into one case file. I text Rubio, but there is no reply. After an hour, I call, but it goes straight to voice mail as if the phone is off. I checked the schedule, and Rubio is on leave. It is abnormal that he didn't inform me he was going away. The last time we took a vacation it was together, to solve the crime ring involving Pearl Swanson and Ray Martin. This reminds me of Esmerelda and her uncalled-for death. I need to swing by and visit Bob Barton at City Square Cemetery. Life is all connected. Last week, I was reminded of Daniel and his tire company; this week, I was reminded of Bob.

Chapter 44

March 2025
August

Saturday night, Willow and I meet at Rhien Haus for dinner, then she wants to play bocce ball if I am okay with that. I have never played and have completely forgotten to look up the rules since the last time we talked about it with everything else happening in my life. I had not heard about this game before our meeting here last time.

We met at 4:30 pm to beat the dinner rush and ordered the Haus baked pretzel and a salad to share. We go into the bar area and order some on6 tap house beers and play a game of darts. We walk through the purple lit area; I see the clock hung in the center of the narrow walkway which says 6:05 pm then go back to the bocce ball courts. Time crawls slowly anywhere else, but when Willow is present it escapes me at a speed I have never experienced. Me wondering what she does in her time away from me. Surely there must be other people in her life.

Last time we were here, we didn't go back into this area, but Remy from the photography club came out and took over our conversation. Now I have seen him here twice, at the photography club, a place I expect him to turn up and my company the day I gave Hector a ride. He was not unfriendly except for ignoring me, maybe because his business didn't have anything to do with me, but he gives off a mix of vibes I have not experienced with anyone before. The photography club is a tight-knit community, they gather for one common interest that everyone appears to know a great deal about. Maybe my reluctance to fit in is simply because I do not have as much knowledge as they do about lens features, camera exposures and all the other terminology they have already acquired, and Willow instinctively knows from working at Kenmore Camera.

We enter the area, which is already full on a winter Saturday night. The conflicting noises echo off of each other in such a small space, music, voices, laughter, and bocce balls clinking. The wood framing and wall paneling absorb all of this and the aroma of beer. We find a seat not far from the courts; Willow asks if I am still up for a game or two. I explained that I have only read about it and watched a few YouTube videos. Just then, Remy comes up and sits at our table with a large beer in his hand. He genuinely annoys me with his surety, pompous nature and continually popping up where I am. Willow appears to actually like him and lets him join in on our time even though he does not appear to have anything to do with me and is only there to speak to Willow. Thinking back, I don't think I have been formally introduced to him. At that thought, I interrupt the conversation they were having and ask, "Isn't your name Remy?" he nods and goes back to continue the conversation with Willow, not seeming to want to know me. A man surer of himself than I have ever met. I hadn't thought about contributing to that conversation or anything after my question. Remy gets up to go, leaves his glass on the table, and pats me on the back so hard I almost fall out of my chair. If I were 100% honest, I was on the edge of my seat to begin with. I am just happy to have Willow back without her being distracted by him. He is the type of person who takes over an entire room when he enters. I am not sure if it is due to my feeling of having to watch him or if he just rubs me the wrong way. There is something not right about him, it could just be his way of comfort in all areas as if he is supposed to be fully present in each situation at any given moment.

We check out the people playing on the courts, I think they are approximately ninety feet long and four feet wide. Abruptly, I am taken from here to the continuous reel of my life. None of these activities have been in any of the slides, my mind runs through at a high rate of speed. I am not positive I belong here or with Willow. This is the place she is comfortable in; she flows with the movements of photography, has never revealed much about herself, and in return has not inquired about my past. We have briefly touched on a few subjects but have not gotten to know each other at all.

We are just existing day to day, having dinner now and then with no plan except to garden at Maple Leaf Park as our only commitment to each other. I set a reminder on my phone to call the parks department on Monday about a garden space if that will still be needed.

I look up, and Willow is studying me. She asks if I am having second thoughts about being here, playing bocce ball, or anything else. I smile, knowing my insecurities are coming from a sudden new life placed in front of me after such a long routine with each day calculated by Alice, Green Mechanical Engineering, and whatever route or function I was supposed to attend. Being a flexible person that all worked for me, and I was happy with my life. I loved our life just as it was all the way down to our weekly dinner out and movie at home, our home that I loved. It just hit me. I am not only in a period of transition but also grieving for the life I built and lost, but for my dad and mom as she is now, someone I am not positive I know anymore. I picture her as a hippie, wearing all the colorful clothing, floating through the city between home and work and wherever else she goes. She has always been such a private person, which is something I didn't catch on to being a child, but now thinking back, I never knew her preferences. My thoughts abruptly stop as I realize I have not answered Willow yet. A minute, maybe ten minutes, have gone by, and I am clearly not here. This is not fair to Willow; I get up from my seat next to the court without speaking, circle to the other side of the tall table, and sit on the stool next to Willow, placing my arm behind her. I tell her I am not up to learning a new game today but would prefer to watch from the same angle as her and play on our next visit. I can tell she knows something is wrong but does not pry. We watch a few games, have another beer, and agree to leave. I ask Willow if she meant what she said about the garden patch and if she wishes to see me any longer. She looks at me with hurt in her eyes, and now I feel like an idiot having possibly ruined the best part of being in Seattle and the connection to all of my new activities. I see the hurt on her whole being, she looks at me with different eyes. She turns and looks at me in disbelief. We were just having fun, and now these questions coming from me have nothing to do with her. She walks towards E. Marion St. I don't know where she parked since she was here prior to my arrival a few hours of fun ago, and now this may be shattered. She has not turned to look back to see if I am following her or asked for an explanation of my questions; she just keeps walking. I try to look in the windows of the business as I go by as a distraction to what I have just done. Willow turns west onto Marion, and I see her car. She gets her keys out of her pocket, and I know if this and the garden are what I want, I have a split second to make this right before Willow drives off for good. From what she has told me of her past, she is used to sudden goodbyes and not having attachments in her broken, unsettled life. She, finally as an adult, has control of where she is, what she does, and who she wishes to spend time with, and I should have considered her past before the unacceptable wording of my questions that never needed to be asked to begin with.

I ran to catch up with her before it is too late, knowing I for sure want Willow and the garden patch. Time will tell what else will happen between us, but right now, I need to let her know she is my first choice out of every option in my life and this city.

She turns to look at me as I take her hand holding her keys; the only expression I deserve is clearly on her face. She says, "I trusted you, and now I know my instincts are off." She pulls away from me. I don't know why I would ask questions in that way but know I may have destroyed this before it got started. Now, Willow is angry with herself because of my actions. I take her hand with the keys and ask for them; I hit the remote unlocking her door, tell her I am sorry that my words came out wrong, that she and her feelings are of the utmost importance to me and hope for the best. She looks at me and asks, "Why? What do you want? Do you want a garden patch? Is this the last time we will see each other?" I reach out to hold her near as the wind picks up carcasses of leaves left over from autumn that should have been long gone but are still swirling in the gusts as we stand heartbroken on a hill in the dark with temperatures below freezing.

I am freezing and positive Willow is too if she can feel anything after my stupid questions. I ask if we can sit in

her car and talk. I need to tell her the origin of my
questions. She says, "That depends on the answer to
one question then the rest. Do you want a garden
patch?" I feel relief that she is thinking of further than
this moment, where I was positive it would all end. I tell
her I do; I am relieved of the reminder I had put into my
calendar to show her there is proof I do want to.

We got into her car, the heater blowing cold air at us,
probably just as cold as outside, but I am relieved to be
in an enclosed space with Willow on our way to
smoothing out the speed bumps and roadblocks I
created.

The heat is finally kicking in, my words are flowing
naturally since my chest is not frozen, my limbs can
move, and my heart is attempting to reapply the pieces
back to a normal state. I am hoping I can explain this to
Willow, and we can go from here and forget about my
questions. She asks what indication she gave that would
show she didn't wish to see me again. I told her how it
was all observed by me entering her already existing
world and being in the way. We will leave it at this on
this early cold March night, a month that appears may
be the longest month of my life. Willow and I agree to
see each other a couple times a week instead of these
sporadic meetings. I know this is not realistic with our
schedules, but we will try.

As much as I want to sit here all night, that cannot
happen. Willow has work in a few hours, and I know she

will drive off with doubts filling her mind no matter what else I say. I kiss her slowly, place my now warm hand on her cheek, look her in the eye, and reassure her I still wish to participate in the garden with her. I have no idea where this came from, but I said, "I love you, Willow." She is stunned and exhausted from her roller coaster of emotions tonight but responds, echoing my proclamation. Then she put her car in gear, backed up to be relieved of her parking space that suddenly feels confined, and dropped me around the corner on 12th at my vehicle. We don't say another word, scared to jinx our last words. I place my hand on her cheek, run it down her arm to her hand and kiss it, and place it back on the shifter, knowing this will all work out, and we are over the first speed bump and have made it around the first curve.

I drove home, wishing Willow was with me, but she is not, and this is where I am and the place I need to start. I remember dinner with Mom tomorrow. There are questions I need to ask. I do want to know her. Thinking back, I didn't know my dad either, and if it wasn't for the paper company, I wouldn't be learning so much about him now.

Chapter 45

March 2025
Detective Muncer

The call came in I had been waiting patiently for from Slope County Sherriff. They boarded at Bowman Regional Airport with Levi Maddox in custody. They are requesting we meet with the officers in charge to sign the chain of custody and take Levi Maddox into our custody. The flight lands at Sea Tac International Airport at 3:07 am. When flying someone for extradition, they attempt late or early flights in case any ruckus evolves.

I drive into the airport, swirling my way to level three, meet Rubio who is still not himself, check into the airport at 2:30 am, being able to use my SPD badge at most check points. I finally meet the deputies and Levi Maddox, who had since cut his windblown beard with scissors. The deputy said Levi had been hiding in boats on the river where he generally resides, but I can see from his boots he must have been in town walking the dirt roads with the clods still stuck to his soles, even after the flight.

We sign all the custody forms and change handcuffs, something I never understood. Why can't we simply keep the original pair on the one in custody and hand over the cuff? Levi Maddox has a belligerent look in his eyes and a defiant way about him like one of those people who don't obtain a social security number for employment, a side job guy. He is a renegade who lives on the riverbank. Then why was he in Seattle at least twice? Once to kill Randell Rinwell and then a couple months ago to celebrate New Year's Eve at the Space Needle. Who were the other two males with him? After viewing the footage multiple times, I do not see any resemblance in him to his accomplices.

After an extensive investigation, I am ready to take the elevator, get him in the back of my cruiser, and return to the station for processing. Which I will wait for since I need to question him. He has declined to say a word so far. Even after reading his rights, he just grunted when asked if he understood. We get in the cruiser, take the round maze of roads out of the airport, and go north on I-5, exiting at Dearborn Street and heading to the back to check him in. He has been silent for the duration of the ride. Rubio will meet us at headquarters in an hour. I am not sure why he wishes to be there since it is not his case, but I work in unison with him whenever needed. Me wishing I could follow him to see what he is up to instead of taking Levi in, and suddenly, that seems more important than this. I know this is what I have been working on for months, bringing justice for Randell Rinwell. I haven't spoken to him, but after questioning Levi Maddox if he chooses to speak, I will notify Amos and Vada, Randell's younger siblings. I wonder if Vada is still the manager of the pot shop. Then I will stop in the morning, making a point to stay up until at least 9:00 am to walk over to Toe Tip Production to deliver the news of this capture to Fleur Fensby, Randell's girlfriend of more than two decades. I feel this news should be delivered in person; she is not the type of person to make a phone call to, although I am considering it, so I don't have to sit on those dainty velvet and metal chairs again.

I requested priority processing, but with Levi Maddox being cooperative, if someone else comes in that causes trouble, that would have to be taken care of ahead of Levi for the safety of everyone locked in this jail.

At 6:12 am, after pouring over every note I have on this case and rewatching all footage involved for the hundredth time, Officer Stanley informs me that Maddox is waiting in Room 1 for me. I cringe at the thought of Room 1 being the one used the most, but grab my notes and proceed, wondering about Rubio's absence.

Levi Maddox sits sideways in the chair, wearing his orange jumpsuit and newly issued socks with flip flops. He is relaxed and appears as if he has stopped over to watch a football game. I sit across from him, trying not to touch the table, just one of my quirks, imagining all the people who have been here before me. Levi glances at me sideways, then looks back at his newly acquired footwear. I ask why he made visits to Seattle. He responds, saying, "I was just staying in touch with my brother, well the closest I have to a brother anyway, who got out of the system and suddenly moved away from North Dakota. It wasn't fair that he left me there at the home, the group home for delinquent boys. All I ever did was unroll several sections of a farmer's fence. It was just a joke that I was pulled right after Daddy passed on. Mom sat around with the bottle. Of course, she did that before daddy's passing, but the last time I saw her, she was in her faded floral housecoat drinking from a pint of cheap vodka. I stayed at the home with Jeff, who I visit here a time or two a year. He usually buys my plane ticket. He fled town the second he got his degree in diesel mechanics. Someone he knew offered a job working on the boats, bigger than our riverboats, but boats all the same. Jeff never looked back. I don't know why I didn't move here. Every time I was in Seattle, I knew it was where I belonged. With Jeff, my only family, but instead, I went back home and stayed in the huts built on the river, selling fish and whatever else I could get my hands on. Why am I here?"

I was surprised Levi had opened up to me like that, but it still didn't tell me why he killed Randell. I told him he was under arrest for the murder of Randell Rinwell. He swivels his head around so fast I thought it would break off, me picturing the beard that is no longer there jutting out. He says, "What is a Rinwell?" I read from the notes on the timeline taken from the footage of the night of Randell's death. He shakes his head; I am hoping nothing jumps out of his uncombed mop of hair. He appears genuinely confused. Yes, he went to the football game, then to the airport with the round garage to return home. "The Seahawks won that game, I think. Maybe I had too much to drink; my water bottle was filled with vodka. Oh my, I have turned into my mother. I drank only a couple, maybe four, beers along with my 26 oz. bottle of water. I was surprised how quickly it emptied, but with all our cheering, I was thirsty. That is why I bought the beers to celebrate my time here. What a big event in my life to attend an actual NFL game. You say I did what?"

I show him the footage of Randell Rinwell, aka Stu, and Levi Maddox, Jeff, and another unidentified male leaving the game. Levi heckling Randell on the south side of the stadium, and Jeff and the other male prompting him to leave the guy alone. They proceed towards the Diamond Parking Service to retrieve their vehicle. Randell moves away from Maddox, further behind Lumen Field. Maddox charges him and pushes Randell after demanding to know his true identity. Randell falls, hitting his head on the anchor bolt of the stadium. Maddox leaves to catch up with his friends, who, I think after watching this again, probably are not aware of Maddox's actions.

Maddox looks at me with genuine shock in his eyes. I have seen this before: people who have committed crimes and all the way to sentencing swear they didn't do it. This appears different, as if he had no idea he committed a murder. He wants to see the footage again and again; he swears he has no recollection of his actions. He starts to cry, saying he would never hurt another living being. Even with all the bugs by the river, he captures them and sets them free.

I ask for Jeff's phone number, which is in Maddox's cell in evidence. At approximately 7:30 am, I placed a call to Jeff Simmons to request he come into the station for questioning regarding the murder of Randell Rinwell. Jeff states he doesn't know Randell and is going to work, maybe later. I explained to him the extradition of Levi Maddox, we have him in custody, and you are involved. He says he hasn't been back to North Dakota since relocating here. I am not sure what part of Seattle Police and showing up here he didn't understand but I will send someone to pick him up if he doesn't agree to come in now.

Jeff Simmons arrives in fifteen minutes, being as he resides in a flea bag motel downtown, one upstairs from a convenience store that you can rent by the week. I remember being called there for a homicide a few years back and putting on disposable shoe covers after leaving so as not to transfer whatever was in that rat trap hotel in my cruiser. I wish I had put them on prior to entering since now I had to throw my shoes away. My stomach recoils after thinking of the stairs with something resembling vomit and the smell of urine ever present throughout the upstairs floor.

Jeff Simmons is escorted into Room 2; I can smell his residence on him if only from memory. I ask him the usual questions. How long he has been here, three years or so, maybe ten, he doesn't know for sure. He asks, "What is this really about, and where is Levi? I thought he was here." I inquired about the night of the football game and what happened after they left. He states, "Levi was super drunk, and we were scared he wouldn't be allowed on his plane, so we rushed him out of the game, took him to the drive-through at Jack in the Box on Pacific Highway by 509 and fed him almost everything on the menu. We were ready for him to go home. Please don't tell him that I said that. I don't want to hurt his feelings. He did get a bit rambunctious, leaving the stadium, but caught up with us right away." I showed him the footage, and he was shocked at Levi's actions. He thought it was just a little teasing, not physical contact. "Can I see Levi?" I shake my head no, feeling defeated as Maddox possibly does not remember this unjustified murder and wonders where this will end.

My night has turned into the next day, and the morning rush is in full swing. Levi Maddox's fate is in the hands of the judicial system, and Jeff Simmons may have sadly lost a friend. I am walking up towards Spring Street on 5th Avenue, then back down 4th, hoping my stroll through town will clear my head with the urgency to meet with Fleur Fensby about the break in this case. I go to her dance studio before the doors are open, but I can see her in the back room through the enormous windows. I know knocking will bring back memories of her discoveries and open old wounds as she looks up and sees me, taking my need to knock away.

Fleur opens the door with reluctance, not expecting my visit, and says, "Morning." I responded by saying "We got him in custody." I am not at liberty to discuss the newly filed case and do not wish to deliver the unfortunate facts to her. This case is not dissimilar to any other, just more personal to Fleur, and I wish to let her rest easy in the fact that I did my job.

Chapter 46

March 2025
Remy

  The bakery is officially listed for sale on the Commercial Real Estate Brokers Board. Any interested parties will meet with me at my convenience when Elora is not present. However, I would not be aware if an interested party popped in and posed as a customer prior to making any further inquiry.

  Elora has been acting differently even though I have not made this previous fact known to her. She is onto something I have done, has secrets to hide, and that makes working here more grueling. I just wish to sign the contract and be done. My files are in order and ready to transport. A small carry-on bag is packed and stored in the trunk of my Subaru. My food storage has nearly been depleted, only necessities will be purchased. There is one photo I shall keep of me, Mom, Everett, and Logan from somewhere on the waterfront many years ago. Traveling light will be the key to a hasty escape from this wheel I turn daily. The longer I am here, the more each minute becomes prolonged. It wears on me retrieving each scoop of flour, then sugar, wet ingredients, and then add the dry. It is getting monotonous, minute by minute is all I can imagine.

Then there is Elora to watch. I make no phone calls except for orders, and there is nothing for her to witness, but she still scrutinizes my every move as I do hers. My original thoughts were to ask her about purchasing the bakery, but with whatever knowledge she has of my actions, I do not seek to make her privy to my departure. I owe her nothing, zip, nada. She has made my carefully planned departure an uneasy event so she can be left in the dark. Either stay on with a new owner or clear out, both her and Niko. I am not sure how he fits into this picture, but I am just content he has not wandered into my establishment.

With the unfortunate circumstances of Mrs. Peterson's body left in the alley, who they think was attacked after the signing of our contract, or maybe they figured she had come back. With circumstances as they are, signed contract at her residence along with my final check that has not been deposited it seems as if it would come to light that there is a hole in that story but that is all they have from the investigation and witness I know was undoubtedly right at my back door. Squealing stories, bringing Officer Stanley to my doorstep, my parking space, questioning me as if I was guilty. This may be good for the sale of my business, but it makes me operate with uneasiness having SPD use my bakery as their hangout. I am fortunate they were not here on the day Mrs. Peterson arrived with accusations. I am not entirely sure of what her claims may have been, but she took them to the grave.

I go over my every move, think about Remi and his pet gorilla, wishing I had never met that little dog. It hit me with great concern that the sun was in my eyes, and I will never know who waved at me the day I exited the bus at the corner of 36th and Aurora, on my way to gain answers about the car and the contract. Then, the meeting of the dog, I am not a barbaric individual, keeping the dog overnight proves my point. I just wish circumstances did not line up that way. Maybe all Elora knows is about Remi, but I assume there is more to her story.

Chapter 47

March 2025

Hector

Jill

August

Detective Muncer

I didn't know a message was left, the phone never rang, and I had no idea where Jill was. I was frantic; this has not been like her since arriving in Seattle. She has become routine with the addition of her job. I can only imagine what could have happened to her. I should have followed through more thoroughly and with urgency. Did the cartel or whoever it was she escaped from in Mexico track her here? I don't even know who they are. I need to stop trying to protect her and turn the investigation over to Agent Ford.

I call August on his cell, who has no idea what friend Jill is meeting for dinner. "Since she takes mass transit, she leaves out the front, and I park around back. She appeared fine when I saw her about 2:00 pm."

It was nearly 7:00 pm when the voice mail came through, alerting me that a message had been left at 4:06 pm: "Hi Jeffery it's Jill. I will be late tonight as I am having dinner with a friend. Will take a cab home later. Love you." Relief and anger flood my entire being. She is hopefully safe, but why the delay in message delivery? Now I wonder who Jill is having dinner with, but she is an adult and fully capable of making sound decisions. I am confident she will talk to me about this later. She could have even run into someone from high school. Putting this aside and learning to be a brother who is not overprotective has brought a flood of emotion in my being. All those years with her gone and now that she has returned, it still feels unbelievable, and where is the rest of my family?

Hector and Jill hop on the 124 across town, exiting near Pioneer Square. Hector has never brought a lady home to his grandpa's place before. He is not sure why he cannot mentally claim the residence as his own yet. They walk leisurely under the Pergola, selecting a bench to sit and discuss dinner options, the decision made for Hatback Bar and Grill. We both get a to-go order of a Crispy Chicken Sandwich with Washington Apple Coleslaw and head up to my place. I don't know why I feel so self-conscious about bringing someone home. Grandpa has been gone for quite some time. I feel as if I am a teenager, and there will be introductions made. My plans when I left this morning were not to bring anyone home, but the day progressed, and it felt like we should have dinner, so we are. Why didn't we eat at the restaurant? I open the enormous wooden, glass, and brass door, but today it is different. Jill is with me, observing actions. I am not sure why this makes me anxious, but it does. This may not have been a good idea at all. We take the stairs to the second floor, making our way to the third door on the right. Upon entry, I realize Jill and I have not conversed at all since picking up our dinner order. I turn and smile, breaking the tension that has obviously set in, and say, "Welcome. It is just dinner; we can do this." Jill smiles, sets her backpack in Grandpa's recliner, peers out the window to the crowd below, comes over to the small wooden dining table, and takes a seat. We eat, play backgammon, realize it is going on 9:00 pm, and discuss a taxi since neither of us drives.

Our first date was a success. The relief floods over me just as suddenly as I am handing my cell phone to Jill and needing 911. I don't think it is the food with such a sudden onset, but something is physically wrong with me all of a sudden. My stomach cannot be acting like this on our first date. I need medical attention now. The ambulance carts me away, Jill says she will wait until I return as she cannot ride in the ambulance, which has a "no extra passenger rule." I left her my cell phone since there is not a landline, and she will need communication to get home. Instantly, I feel guilty about her having to catch a cab alone at this hour. It wasn't as if I had planned this.

Arriving at Harborview ER, my testing is high priority, all the while I am thinking of Jill in my home or out in the neighborhood by herself. Almost immediately, they informed me that emergency surgery will be needed. My appendix is ready to rupture. I don't remember much after that, with the medical staff being diligent with my care.

Jill

It feels strange to be in a home that isn't mine. I go back to the table and pick some more at my dinner that is ever so good. I feel like an adult for the first time in my life tonight. Here I am above the city, acting as if I am in my own apartment and not Jeffrey's, who has only tried to protect me all along but is still my big brother. I am extremely worried about Hector; I hope someone calls to let me know how he is doing. I will call Jeffery and let him know I will stay here tonight since it is already so late.

The voices travel up the brick wall and lull me to sleep as I comfortably sit in the recliner by the double set of windows looking down on the busy antics of the ever-increasing noisy crowd milling about. This night, except for the tragedy of Hector, has brought me direction and peace. I fall asleep watching the lights twinkle and dream of Mexico, waking with a start. I am unable to rest now, being in this new environment and out of my element at Jeffrey's.

I am standing at the window when Hector's phone rings. It is him informing me of his appendix and surgery, me realizing he is not returning tonight, picturing him not being able to navigate the stairs. I am fearful to be here alone, but it is nearly 2:00 am, and I will not chance leaving here tonight.

I check the refrigerator and find carrot juice. Who drinks that? There are parmesan pita chips in the cupboard tucked into a container for future use, but not any real food, just a few other snacks that had to have been purchased from a specialty store. They don't sell these products at Safeway.

I pour a tiny amount of carrot juice in a 1970's orange coffee cup, place a few pita chips on a napkin, and begin dipping them into the cup. There is something addictive about this flavor, one I will forever remember and now wonder if Hector has tried this combination. I wander around the apartment that seems like it has been lived in for centuries, peering into areas that are not my business, but look as if they have not been touched in decades.

An ancient cardboard file box sits just behind the recliner where I had slept. It is not my business, but knowing I will be alone here tonight, I place the box in the second chair by the small wooden table and pull the contents out, one file at a time. I sequence them by date, they all have one common thread, a death had occurred. The first one on record was in 2018, Eugene Montgomery suddenly passed away after a company picnic. Well-loved father, a machine operator, and loyal friend. The enormity of this box became obsessive, so much so I knew I was calling into work tomorrow but also was aware I didn't belong here, shouldn't still be here, this is not my home nor is this my box to have opened. Each file held the passing of someone, but I couldn't connect the commonality in the trail of injustice, but someone was onto something.

Now wishing I had a cell phone to take photos of this evidence, I vow to purchase one today, but that will be too late for me to decipher this mess. I find a sheet of paper in the heavy oak desk by the front door and grab my pen from my backpack that now looks out of place as I feel I have deceived Hector by invading his privacy but am unable to stop now.

As I place each meticulous file back in the box which appears as if it may burst at the seams, I worry the box will disintegrate. Gingerly, I place the box back behind the recliner in the exact indentation left in the old area rug and speedily jot down the names, dates, and any other pertinent information as the sun rises in a city that has new meaning to me. Carrying each file back to its original home behind the recliner, there is one left, and I hear the outer door open. I return the last one, fold my sheet of paper, and sit back in the recliner just as Hector opens the door.

Elated that he is home, but now I have placed a damaged layer to our relationship that hasn't even started. He is surprised to see me still here, and I tell him of my insecurity to leave after dark, then open up about dipping the parmesan pita chip in carrot juice. He says he needs a few days off for recovery, but I can stay as long as I wish. We both call in for a personal day after the night we had. I need to call Jeffery for a ride since he is probably just getting off shift. I will go home and get a couple of changes of clothing and stay here for at least tonight to help Hector and go to work from here tomorrow. That is as far as I can see in my future, but I will need time to do more investigation on my sheet of paper.

Chapter 48

March 2025
~~August~~

Six months into this new life, I am settling in. Company profits are up from the website, and we were on a strict rule of having each order ready two weeks early. However, with the expansion due to word of mouth and the website, we have cut that back to a one-week window. Our production rate and the expanded workload of current employees has become more labor intense, but I feel no one has made any forward motion in this company in many years. If we need to hire employees to pick up the slack, we will or bring in temporary workers.

Blake leaves to meet with a new customer in Portland, Oregon at 9:00 am. We have these short trips down, and he has rustled up quite a few accounts. The sample brochure packets, free sample set of business cards, some cupcakes, and finesse have brought this company through the passing of my dad.

I am downstairs in the lunchroom, checking spreadsheets when Remy walks in carrying four black and white striped boxes, each containing a dozen cupcakes. Abruptly, it hits me why he has been seen here before; I can't believe it has taken me six months to connect Remy to Burgett's Bakery, which we used for all our events. Today, there is lightness to his step and a sparkle in his eye radiating from his entire being. This is a version of him I have not seen previously; now I am questioning myself from our other encounters. Maybe he is a nice guy after all, and it was my interpretation of his surety. He asks if this is where we want them and says, "Hi, August." I am in shock that he is even speaking to me directly, using my name.

 I offer him a cup of coffee, but he declines. He has never been this personable before, just arrogant, standoffish, and haughty, in my opinion. I will ask Willow what she actually thinks of him.

 Blake is loaded and on the road by before 9:00 am. He truly enjoys these journeys. Probably mini vacations for him. Today, he will meet with a window screen manufacturer, a pet supply company, a local veterinary chain, and two animal shelters that we will discount their product due to the nature of their business.

 By the end of the day, I check the website and see there are orders being made from Blake's trip, knowing my employees will get a year-end bonus.

Chapter 49

March 2025
Remy

 A generous offer came in on the bakery, my bakery as I
had thought of it for all these years. It is time to leave
before anyone else discovers my actions. I am free and
clear. 9:00 pm, backpack packed with two new sets of
beach attire, shorts, flipflops, and a couple of tank tops
and the picture of my family protected in a zip lock bag.
All of the worldly possessions I will need except maybe
the spatula Mrs. Peterson left for me, but on second
thought, I want no reminders of this life. A fresh start
lies in front of me. I lay the backpack next to the front
door in preparation for the beach life I have been
feeling in my bones. I am working as usual in the
morning, coming home to make dinner over the fire of
roasted hotdogs, potato salad, and baked beans. All
files will be burned by night's end, marshmallows are
included as a celebration on the list from the 7-11
located on 3rd Avenue. I add a toothbrush, toothpaste,
and anything else can be obtained on the way.
Tomorrow morning, I will get in the car and drive away
like any other day. Only the buyer and I know of the
sale. I leave as usual for my employment, except I will

no longer own the bakery nor head there but to Sea Tac International Airport for my flight, my freedom. This mess will be someone else's trouble. 9:00 am, cupcakes are baked, orders fulfilled, I have never been in this mind frame before. I do not need to order anything, check inventory, or check tomorrow's orders because I will be on a flight to Montego Bay, Jamaica. My mind is having trouble adjusting to this blank slate. The check-in time is forty-two hours from now, the flight is nearly seven hours long.

Jill

I have left Hector's wishing to stay and help him after his surgery, but I cannot remain here with the paper in my pocket, needing to know more about the investigation his grandfather was in the middle of compiling. I leave feeling guilty for my deceit, and I remember my vow to obtain a cell phone. My nervous energy takes me through downtown to Metro to purchase a phone. Do I need a plan? I have ID. This need to be an adult has suddenly hit me. I am alone in the city, buying a phone, and need to check out the paper in my pocket. Phone purchased, I have no idea about the technical terms and features offered but picked up a pay-by-the-month plan for now. I just need to call, text, and use the internet for bus schedules.

The library, a place I loved to hide away in during high school, is up ahead on the right. Finding a table with a computer in the back, realizing I may be the only person in this section who is awake, not wishing to alert anyone of my level of discomfort, I stay in place, being glad I took a table that allowed me to keep my back to the wall. I pull out my pen and paper and start researching each of the scribbled notes I took a few hours ago.

  The list is extensive, all relating to deaths but not murders. Why would the articles be at Hectors? There doesn't appear to be any connection, except they are all Seattle businesspeople. Maybe they are coincidently individuals Detective Martinez knew. Then I see the name Garrett Rike in another article written by a Seattle Times blogger in connection with Officer Samuel Dufort and the funeral which collided with Mr. Rike. Finding the obituary of Garrett Rike, I see he is August's dad. The connection of all the names on my list hits me. I call Jeffery, my first call. I am shaking as if I may have solved something enormous. Was anyone else working on this? How can I face Hector? I really do like him.

  I realize Jeffery does not know my new number, and it is the middle of the day. He is sleeping, but my words spill out. It is impossible for me to steady my voice. Jeffery is on his way, and after one night away from his shelter, I have ended up in a state where he needs to retrieve me. I don't have the address of my location but am able to get ahold of myself enough to let him know I am safe.

Elora

Niko has been hounding me to blackmail Remy every time I see him. He pops in at odd hours as if to torment me, catch me at my weak point like when he barged in while I was in the shower last week. Today is Monday. I took the weekend and thought long and hard about how to get out of this mess even though I only work here. It is not me that has a problem with Remy's personal life. I simply wish to work, but Niko, with his newly found information, will not allow that to happen. Today is the day I call the detectives and relay all the information Niko has told me in his drunken, drugged-out state. I am unable to tell them of my part with breaking and entering or anything else I know. With all the tables cleared and customers gone, I take my break, having only tea with my entire being on edge. Never before have I considered calling the police; my usual response is to avoid them.

The bell rings, and in walks Niko. He has spilled something down the front of his ill-fitting trousers. He is loud, demanding, which instantly brings Remy from the back. I see upon his entrance into my territory the recognition of Niko. Niko swears he has never set foot in this place prior to this, but Niko is a liar. Remy knows him, yells about the time he tried to rob him and only got food. I reached for my phone, knowing it was the moment of decision to call 911, but then Niko blurts out about the purse in the alley. Remy looks on in question.

I study him, but he doesn't waver from his questioning look and says, "Get him out of here. He's drunk, trash." I take Niko to the sidewalk and give him twenty dollars to get another cheap bottle, hoping he is in a blackout stage, but know I can never return to my position just inside the door with the bell that has rang so many times before.

August

Blake calls at 11:00 am, talking so fast I can hardly understand where the conversation is going. Something about Portland Oregon Medical Examiner and recognizing the signs from a case before. He had taken someone from a meeting to the hospital, but on the way, they passed away in his car. He says he will never drive it again. They were dead, in my car. As a boss, I have no idea what to say but ask if Blake would mind having a conference call with Detective Muncer. I am not sure that is the route to take, but Muncer has been there for me though the most horrific scene in my life.

Detective Muncer

The call from Jill was upsetting, to say the least, after her first night away from me, and then she was on edge enough not to have her wits about her. Relief floods over me as I see her leaning against the Pay Parking pole located on 4th Avenue. I come to the reality that it is the middle of the night for me after knowing Jill is safe, or so I think. Jill runs to my cruiser and hops in just as my cell rings with August's name appearing on the screen. I answer, not knowing it is a conference call, needing to find out why Jill needs me and why she is not at work. I am not sure why, since I am not the one who provides information, but I tell August I have Jill with me. He tells me of Hector, and he called in for a personal day, then about Blake and his dilemma in Portland. Jill is pulling at my sleeve, and August and Blake are relaying a story I am not positive, I need to know. Horns honk to push me on my way even though I am obviously SPD. I turn right on Spring Street and enter the first parking garage I see to have a place to sort out Jill, Blake, whoever he is, and August.

Remy

This morning, I baked and packed up four dozen mixed cupcakes in our classic black and white signature boxes and delivered them to August Island Rike Paper Company. August always appeared unsure of himself, but today, I was in a spectacular mood and wanted him to remember me with a cheerful thought. I addressed him by name. I know he is good for Willow and the city of Seattle, so I will make him feel comfortable and call him by name. If I wasn't a loner, a solo man, I would have tried to spend more time with Willow, but she deserves to be happy, and August is the one who gives her that.

I returned to the bakery one last time, the nonsense with Niko is averted and with him so inebriated no one would believe his story but now I know I would need to fire Elora, pay her off, be rid of Niko or some other drastic measure but if I can go just thirteen more hours I will be gone.

Elora returns to retrieve her belongings. I tell her of the night when Niko tried to rob me and return to my den, kitchen, office. I am in here by myself, leaving Elora in the dining room with the questions of whether she should leave, stay at her position, or what to do. In fact, I don't care what she does, she could walk out or stay, her choice now. I have waited countless hours to stand in my kitchen and enjoy my final cupcake one last time. All these years, I only had one each Monday. It always sat in the cupboard to the right of the sink, in the special container only for me, chocolate cake with chocolate frosting. That is why I picked today to be the last one owning this establishment because Monday is always chocolate, and if baked any other day, it could throw my destination off.

I lean against the spotless stainless-steel sink, savoring the flavors, knowing the cost of the vanilla bean paste has made all the difference in my products. I feel a twinge in my chest, thinking it is remorse for selling and the turns my life will be taking, but I know from the need to sit, sit immediately at my desk I now know instantly there is no turning back. I see my files, the marshmallows still at the store, and my farewell party to myself is not happening. I have made a tragic mistake with all the commotion, and I have become a victim of myself, another statistic. I slump at my desk, sitting in the red vinyl roller chair that holds flour in the wheels. What a way to die. A disastrous inaccuracy on my part, one simple slip up, knowing there is no antidote for my error. I am embarrassed and ashamed; my eyes and mind roil with the Seattle business groups I associate with. They will all know I have made many mistakes and now this ultimate one. My upstanding citizenship has never been above the law, starting with Phillip, but ran just under the surface. The gridded calendar sits under plastic on my desk, unused from 2014. I grab my Sharpie before succumbing to my death and write one simple word "justice".

Muncer

We arrived at Burgett's Bakery. I am not comfortable with Jill attending this occasion and may get her a car home, but she has broken this case, one I wasn't working on, but once it was brought to my attention, I had to act on it immediately. Once Jill sees we are at an actual crime scene, she takes the bus home, but not until I give her my word about not telling Hector of her connection to this crime. I assure her everything she brought me was all public knowledge and her secret is safe with me. Knowing I will need a back story, but I am relieved Jill trusted me today.

With a warrant issued, we surround the place. The alley door is locked, suspecting Remy Morilli would escape from this direction. Elora puts her hands up as we enter through the front and says Niko went that way, her suspecting Remy called the intrusion in. She recognizes a few of the officers and greets them as if this is an ordinary visit, but it is not. We show her the warrant, ask her to be seated, and proceed to the kitchen, where we locate Remy slumped over his desk. There isn't a pulse; he is gone. A sudden flash in my mind of the night I saw Remy at the corner of 36th Avenue NE by the bus stop, and I somehow by instinct know he has killed Mrs. Peterson.

Elora is shocked by our finding and wishes to leave, but she is part of this crime scene and not leaving without a lengthy statement. She is the only witness to this crime, if indeed there was one today. She cooperates, telling of Niko, her entry to Remy's houseboat, and swears all she knew was of a stuffed gorilla dog toy but not the severity of the connection.

Forensics, the Medical Examiner, rotation tow company, and other investigators cordoned off the scene, which is inside the bakery. Elora gladly handed over her set of keys, leaving through the front door with a weight lifted.

We travelled north to Remy Morilli's houseboat on Fairview Ave E, not knowing what we would find, but with the warrant and keys we found sitting on the desk next to the Sharpie, we enter. There is a backpack, airline tickets, a burner phone, and one picture of a family now dissolved. One who had been fractured from the start. As the waves lap at the pilings on the boat and the sway keeps us on our toes since we live on land, we see this was a calculated exit. The refrigerator and cabinets are empty, and the drawers all open as if to say I gave it all up. A single camera is on the shelf next to the bed, and thirty-six files are all neatly organized next to a bundle of kindling and a small stack of firewood. A single box of wooden matches lies on top, never being able to fulfill their purpose.

The End

Summary of Characters

1. Andre -maintenance – January
2. Paul – graphic designer – January
3. Tara – maintenance – February
4. Greg – graphic designer – February
5. Heidi- ink tech – March
6. Patrick -shipping- March
7. Sven – custodian- April
8. Carlton -delivery – April
9. Ian – sales rep- May
10. Patricia- office manager – May
11. Cory – customer service vendor- June
12. Allison office manager – June
13. Lloyd – printer -July
14. Lori– mail room – July left company for another job
15. Jill – mail room replaced Lori-July
16. Beau -quality control – August
17. Dustin- human resources – August
18. Clem – pressman – September
19. Blake- outside sales rep – September
20. August – Owner- October
21. Rene- order sequencer- October

22. Alana – folding- November

23. George – warehouse- November

24. Hector Martinez- warehouse – December

25. Erin- part time quality control – December

Chocolate Angel Food Cake

¾ cup sifted cake flour

¼ cocoa

¾ cup sugar

1 ½ cup egg whites (about 12)

1 ½ tsp cream of tartar

¼ tsp salt

1 ½ tsp vanilla

¾ cup sugar

Sift flour and cocoa with ¾ cup sugar, beat egg whites with cream of tartar, salt and vanilla until glossy. Add remaining sugar a little at a time until egg whites are stiff. Add ¼ cup flour mixture at a time and fold into egg whites.

Bake in a 10-inch Angel Food Cake Pan @ 375° for 35 to 40 minutes. Invert to cool.

Contributed by Nancy Lane

Also by Josephine Plummer

Cemetery Sitting Series

Book 1: Cemetery Sitting

Book 2: Passing Through